Stranger on the Point

Emma Batten

Emma Batten 2018

First published in Great Britain by Emma Batten

ISBN 978 1 9995820 3 6

Printed and bound in the UK

A catalogue record of this book can be found in the British Library

Edited by Maud Matley

Proofread by Rosemary Bartholomew

Cover painting by Zoe Beardsley

www.emmabattenauthor.com

About the Book

I return to Dungeness with my sequel to *Secrets of the Shingle*. This novel, *Stranger on the Point*, can be read as a stand-alone, but best read after the first book.

As in the previous novel, all places mentioned are real and as accurate as my knowledge enables them to be. But one location has changed its name – the first copies of *Secrets of the Shingle* featured a fictional place called Stoneness; in later editions, and in this book, Stoneness takes a real place name: Denge.

Many of the buildings mentioned did exist such as the lighthouses, Dungeness School, the cottages within an old Napoleonic fort, railway carriage homes and the tearooms; the exterior of these are described as accurately as possible but the interiors are entirely imaginary. Some of these buildings, or their remains, can still be seen today.

Moving away from Dungeness, the story also takes us to Lydd and Ashford. Again, every effort is made to be historically accurate. For the first time, I have turned to social media groups to ask for historical help and got a fantastic response.

My thanks to Maud Matley for her on-going enthusiasm for my writing and for the hours she spends checking through my pages as I write them, making suggestions, pointing out any words which are too modern, and making so many nice comments!

Also, thanks to members from both Marsh Ink and All Harrowed writing groups, for their support and advice.

With thanks to Liz Grant, Louise Pyke and the team at the Romney Marsh Visitor Centre for their on-going support with selling my paperback books.

And a special mention for Mary and her staff at Mary's Tearooms, Dymchurch, for being so supportive in offering me my first author talk and selling my books. I must say that the fictional Mary bears no resemblance!

This 2020 edition features cover art by Zoe Beardsley, and I am delighted that all books in the series now feature Greatstone Art.

This book is dedicated to all my new friends who have supported me through Facebook in the last year. I really appreciate every positive comment and all your enthusiasm for my work. I can't mention everyone, but a special thank you to Caroline and Alec Hobbs for being my first social media supporters!

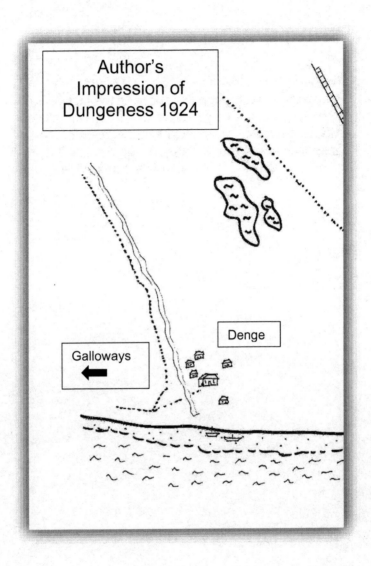

Author's Impression of Dungeness 1924

Denge

Galloways

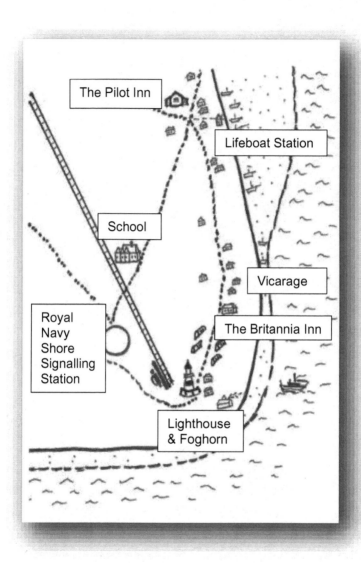

The Pilot Inn

Lifeboat Station

School

Vicarage

Royal
Navy
Shore
Signalling
Station

The Britannia Inn

Lighthouse
& Foghorn

Chapter One
1924 – Ashford, Kent

"Oh, blast!" Lily muttered, as the flame blew out. A gust bowled spring blossom through Victoria Park and whipped at the hem of her skirt. Turning her back to the wind, she hunched up a little, cradling the matchbox in her hand and keeping the slim cigarette holder between perfectly formed lips. Slender fingers dragged the match over the striking surface again and a flame took light; Lily held it to the tip of the cigarette and pulled air through the holder.

Dropping the matchbox into her bag, Lily cupped both hands around the smouldering end until she felt the tobacco was truly burning. She inhaled deeply and walked on briskly through the park, passing the Harper Fountain but barely glancing at its ornate figures balancing shell-like basins. As she walked, Lily's hand moved, almost mechanically, from her side to her mouth. It paused for a moment as she pulled the smoke into her lungs and then lowered again. Short auburn waves bobbed and, a couple of times, grey eyes looked up to acknowledge a passer-by, while her mouth gave a half smile.

On nearing the park gates, Lily flicked the cigarette to the ground and nudged it to the side of the path with the toe of her shoe. She slipped the holder into her bag. Pausing at the road, she watched with some interest a

9

motorcar pass by before crossing. Then her heeled shoes tapped on the hard surface as she crossed Jemmett Road and turned towards her family home.

The house was red brick with square bay windows, and some inset coloured glass at the door. It was a smart, semi-detached house bought by her father at the time of his marriage. Lily walked up the front path, past small but neatly manicured lawns. The tulips and daffodils were in full bloom and not a weed dared to poke through the crumbling earth.

The front door wasn't locked, and Lily walked straight into the hallway with its decorative tiled floor and ornamental cornicing. She placed her coat and hat on the heavy wooden hall stand and tossed her bag onto the floor. Her mother would be in the kitchen, she always was at this time of day, and Lily moved through to the back of the house.

Wearing a starched white apron over her dress, Alice was taking a tray of biscuits from the modern gas oven. She turned and smiled as her daughter entered the room, but Lily sensed her mother's eyes were searching for a reassurance they wouldn't find.

"Good day, darling?" Alice smoothed her apron.

"Dull as ever." Lily dragged a chair away from the table and slumped, elbows on the old pine top and her chin propped up in her hands. "At least it was half-day though; six of us met for a slap-up tea in Ye Old Cottage and I'm full to bursting. Oh, and Sarah decided not to marry Tommy; did I tell you he had asked?"

"You did, and what a shame; I thought he was a lovely young man and with prospects, too." Alice hauled the heavy kettle from the hob and poured boiling water over tea leaves in the everyday teapot before continuing, "I felt sure he'd be manager before he was thirty."

"Thirty? Mother, that is forever away and, yes, he is decent enough but Sarah's not ready for nappies and housekeeping yet."

"Lily, I don't think..."

"It's not as if we're going to go off on marches and all sorts, complaining that we've not got the vote until we're thirty – although it's darned unfair – but we've all agreed that we don't want to marry quite yet."

"We were all rather fond of Robert." Lily heard the familiar wistful tone in her mother's voice whenever she spoke of the young man who was destined to take her father's place as headmaster at Beaver Road School when he retired. "And we thought you were, too."

"Mother, you married the headmaster and settled into suburban bliss." Lily rolled her eyes. "Three children – boy, girl, boy. Neat pattern. We have darling Winnie coming in daily to tidy up after us and the highlight of your life is displaying your watercolours in town exhibitions." She poured herself a cup of tea and placed it, without a saucer, in front of her. "I'm not complaining, but this is the 20th century. We've lived through that dreadful war and buried Uncle Harry, God bless him, and young people want to have fun."

"But Lily, darling, I worry that you are *not* having fun," Alice replied, handing her a saucer. "If you were, then I wouldn't fret so."

"It's dreadfully dull working as a bank clerk," Lily admitted. "I'd rather be in a department store like Helen and Polly."

"You were always so good at arithmetic."

"I write numbers in a ledger, Mother. It requires a neat hand and an orderly mind, not an aptitude for calculations." Lily reached for a biscuit from the cooling rack and Alice watched crumbs fall on the clean linoleum. "I wish I'd trained as a nurse or at least something useful, but it didn't seem right, not after the war. Not to train when the need was over. Well, not over but there wasn't the desperate need."

"I did enjoy my years as a teacher." Alice's eyes seem to glaze over as she recalled those memorable years.

"I just feel I'd like to do something, not marry a bank manager and settle in a new house in Willesborough or Kennington. I don't expect you to understand, Mother." Lily tipped the cup up and gulped at the last of her tea. "And you did well to teach for several years and not to marry until you were twenty-three; I admire you for that. But you've never been anywhere. Not really – you can't say a day trip to Canterbury or Hythe is experiencing... experiencing life."

She paused and looked at her mother, who stood with her hand resting on the dresser. Her mid-brown hair, now streaked with grey, was pulled back in a loose knot at the nape of her neck. Lily had never seen it any different, although if she stared hard enough at her parents' wedding photograph it appeared that Alice had once had a carefully curled fringe. Admittedly, Alice's hemlines now fell to just above her ankles and her blouse was low enough to show a delicate necklace at her throat. Lily hadn't meant to be harsh; she was just so bored at the bank and it seemed that the highlight of her week was a half-day when she met with her friends at the teashop and enjoyed a good gossip.

"Will you be out courting with Edwin at the weekend?" Alice changed the subject.

"I don't think so. No point in him having expectations."

"If that's how you feel then best not to encourage him," Alice agreed. She looked out of the window into the garden and then back at her daughter. "You're wrong, Lily. I *have* been beyond Hythe and Canterbury. I lived away from Ashford for over a year, when I was a lot younger than you in fact."

"You lived away? But I thought Grandpa was always the vicar of St Mary's?"

"Oh, he was. I went alone. All the way to a place called Dungeness and it was so different, not somewhere you could possibly imagine. You've never seen anywhere like it and neither had I."

Dungeness: the word rolled around in Lily's head and she frowned, not knowing of the place but sensing already that it was somewhere rather unpleasant. Dunge – visions of a bleak, boggy place came to mind. Hunched figures with hooded robes who trudged around exchanging grunts and nods, as they scavenged for food. Dunge Ness, a miserable, wetland area from where the stench of rank ditchwater pervaded everything.

What role could her mother have in a place such as this? Lily shook her head, trying to shift the image. "Dunge Ness, where is it, Mother? What made it so different?"

"Dungeness, with an 'e', all one word." Alice looked out of the window, as if seeing beyond the flowering cherry. "Oh, it's not so far away; just a train ride really, but it seemed further."

"Because you were leaving Grandpa and Grandmother?"

"Not really," she considered the question. "It was just that when I got there, it was so remote, although I had gone by train, all the way. It was – well, it still is of course – it was a place by the coast, a shingle headland, but not just a stony beach, the shingle stretched back almost... almost as if it went on forever, with just a few scruffy bushes and rough grass, all bent over from the wind. And the wind, gosh, it blew straight off the sea, thick with salt and sometimes a mist hung over the place for days.

"And the people who lived there, the fishermen, they lived in wooden huts just put wherever they wanted. There were no roads, you see."

"No roads?" Lily frowned as she tried to picture the place sounding as foreign as India or Africa. "How did they get about? How did the deliveries arrive?"

"There was the train, of course," Alice continued. "Or carts, but not the type you'd see here. These had wide wheels to take them smoothly over the shingle; a narrow wheel would just get stuck or bump along erratically."

"It sounds like a shocking place!" Lily gave a short laugh. "What on earth took you there? Did you run off with a fisherman?"

"Of course not."

Had her mother just snapped at her? Lily studied Alice's back as she remained looking out of the window. She tried again. "What made you live there – for a whole year, you said?"

"A year and a month or so," Alice reflected. "I arrived in October and left the following December. I went to teach, didn't I say?"

"Oh, so there was a school. It wasn't quite as bad as I was imagining!"

"A school, a lighthouse and the keepers' cottages and the fishermen's shacks."

"And a church of course, some shops and the other houses, the ones where the other people lived."

"No, no, the school was used as a church. I lived there in the school and it was quite apart from the other buildings. All alone at first and then Hazel joined me;

14

what a difference that made, having some company."

"And did you ever go back?" Lily asked.

"No, I returned to Willesborough and never made the time. Although I did exchange letters with Hazel and Bess, the lighthouse keeper's wife, for many years." Alice turned around and sat at the table with Lily. "Nothing much changes there, at Dungeness, just the people getting older; it's not like here with our cars and modern houses and the town growing so fast my grandparents would hardly know it."

"Well, I don't know why we've never been there for a trip out." Lily drained the last of her tea. "There's sure to be a nice café. When Father buys a motorcar, he can take us all there and we can see this place."

"I told you, Lily, there are no roads. Not roads that a motorcar could use; it would be no use at all."

"Oh, it won't be like that now, Mother. Not in the twentieth century!"

Lily couldn't see into her mother's mind although, with the arrogance of youth, she believed she could. She couldn't imagine the desolate wastelands where the mist rolled in from the sea and sometimes hung over the peninsula for days, or the light rain which penetrated your clothing in minutes, or the wind pushing all plants into stunted versions of their true selves. Lily had no notion of the type of people who lived by the tides and the weather in low wooden shacks, who moved across the shingle with flat boards under their shoes.

Knowing only the town and the countryside, Lily knew nothing of this other place without the ordered streets, shops and modern transport of the town, nor the narrow lanes, hedgerows, woods and fields of the countryside. Trust Mother, with all her fussy ways, to make out as if it were somewhere that was almost, well... sinister, dangerous even. As if Grandpa and Grandmother would have sent their nineteen-year-old daughter, their only child, somewhere that wasn't quite suitable for her to be.

She was curious, nonetheless. Having previously wondered if she could possibly begin a new life in London, or at least Canterbury, Lily was now drawn to see this hapless place. It wouldn't be a bit like Mother said, of course. But something had stirred her interest and she had felt rather irritable and uninspired by life for a while now.

Perhaps it was something to do with the war, Lily having been just a little too young to do anything useful, yet old enough to see the harm done. She felt helpless to do anything for the blind ex-serviceman who begged on the town centre streets, or the one with a wooden leg who shuffled around looking through people's rubbish. So, she smoked cigarettes, went to see silent movies with young men, drank tea with her friends and shocked her parents by wearing skirts that ended at mid-calf.

Over the next few days Lily's curiosity grew, fired by her mother's unwillingness to speak any more of her year spent away from Ashford. Did she sense a wistful look in Alice's eyes or a resolution to keep the stories of her youth tucked away beneath her light corset? There was no more to say, Alice told her; it was a miserable place and nothing much ever happened there. Nothing to interest a modern young woman.

"Mother has been telling me about her time as a teacher, in a place called Dungeness." Lily curled up in the armchair beside the coal fire in her grandmother's front room.

"I don't know what Alice was thinking of." The old

16

lady eyed the slim calves gleaming in nylon stockings. "When she started showing her ankles, I was so ashamed. She'd dishonoured us so much already with her foolish behaviour."

"It's the modern way, Grandma." Lily tugged at her dress, pulling it down a little in respect for her staunchly Victorian grandmother. "Now I can't imagine Mother ever causing you the slightest worry, but it must have been strange when she worked away."

"She went as a teacher, of course. Respectable, just as her father and I had raised her to be. It was all arranged between the vicar at the place by the seaside and your grandfather. She was to spend nine months there and come home with money saved for the future."

"But she stayed longer?"

"Oh yes – and it wasn't quite the place we imagined it to be." Grandmother's lips tightened. "All shingle, no roads and wooden huts."

Lily's eyebrows raised, expressing her disbelief.

"So she said." There was something about Grandmother's tone that made Lily believe that she had an ally in her. "As if any place in the south of England could be as uncivilised as that. We didn't hear from her for weeks and when we did..."

"When you did?"

"It was all very foolish; it seemed as if the place made her a little… a little wild." Grandmother gazed into the fire and Lily waited. "She wasn't our Alice anymore," she finished lamely.

"But she came back," Lily reminded the old lady.

"Yes, but she took her time about it." Grandmother shook herself, just a little, and shifted her position in the chair. "She settled in the end and married your father, but she took her time. It was going to that Dungeness place that changed her; I rue the day she left."

17

Grandmother stood and busied herself with the tea tray. Lily, hoping for more confidences, tried to encourage them, but it seemed as if there was no more to be said, or no more her grandmother was prepared to say.

Lily carried her weekend suitcase down the stairs, trying not to bump it against the paintwork, and placed it by the coat stand.

"I've decided to take a trip," Lily informed her parents, as her father sat in his armchair beside the fire with his morning paper and her mother fluttered about with a duster. It was almost Easter weekend and her father, George, was on a break from his headteacher duties.

"A trip?" Alice's voice was high, objecting to an arrangement that had clearly already been put in place. She had noted the awkward movement of Lily bringing the case downstairs.

"It's all the same in Ashford." Lily waved her hand as if dismissing the whole town in one gesture. "I've a fancy to see a new place."

"With Helen or Polly?" George asked.

"No, I'm going alone. I've taken leave from work on Tuesday, so I'm going today and will be back in time for work next Wednesday. There is sure to be a place with rooms to let."

"But Lily, you do have a plan, I hope?" Alice stood, duster hanging limp at her side. "If only you had said, we could have..."

"A plan? Of course, Mother. I'm catching the 11:03 to a place called Lydd and then travelling on as I have a fancy to see this place, Dungeness."

Chapter Two

"Lydd, Lydd. All alight for Lydd! Next stop New Romney." The stationmaster stood tall. This may not be St Pancras or Victoria, but he took his role seriously. "The next train for Dungeness will leave at twelve minutes past two. This train goes to New Romney only."

"Damned annoying," Lily muttered to herself. The woman sitting opposite, with a capacious bag on her lap, raised her eyebrows but said nothing.

With her handbag hanging at her elbow, Lily pulled her suitcase from the overhead rack. As she wobbled a little, struggling to maintain her balance, the coach door was opened by a Southern Railways porter. Soot-laden steam seeped into the coach, riding on the cool breeze, assaulting Lily's taste buds. Dismissing any assistance from the porter, she stepped down onto the platform.

The station building was built of a soft orange brick with a scalloped canopy under a slate roof. Window boxes displayed hyacinth and narcissus, vibrant splashes of colour in a place where everything was soon encased in soot. It was typical of a branch-line station, Lily concluded.

"The train for New Romney is now departing. Stand clear, stand clear!" the stationmaster called, his voice ringing out across the platform. The train eased its way forward, gradually building up momentum as its coupling rods pushed huge wheels and steam belched from the chimney.

Porters stood poised to carry luggage, give directions or escort passengers to the waiting Allen's Horse Bus. Lily approached one of the porters, a young lad of no more than fifteen years. "I was planning to go to Dungeness. Is there a tearoom? Somewhere to wait?"

"Best go into the town, madam," he replied, careful to enunciate each word in his best English, as decreed by his employers at Southern Railways. "If you care to walk to the road, you can't miss the church, madam, and beyond that is the Beehive. Nice tearoom there for a lady such as yourself."

How grown-up his words were for a lad barely out of school. Lily smiled and replied, "Thank you, I'll do that."

Leaving the station buildings, she opened her handbag and fingers probed for her enamelled cigarette case. With the lit cigarette smouldering in its holder, Lily continued. From the main road it was clear that it was no distance to the town. A slim church tower presided over a cluster of rooftops and she used it as her guide. The entire town was on the flat landscape which Lily had become accustomed to on her short train journey from Ashford, across the Romney Marsh. Walking at a brisk pace, pausing a little to draw some comfort from the cigarette, she was soon passing short terraces of Victorian and Edwardian houses before reaching the older cottages which flanked the churchyard. Lily left the road to pass through the church grounds, stopping only to stub out her cigarette before passing through the gates in the low stone walls.

The teashop was rather fussy, harking back to the pre-war years, Lily noted. Lace tablecloths were tatty, yet clean, and paintings in heavy gilded frames jostled for position on the walls. The dark wooden counter stretched across the back of the shop and behind it a woman was placing fresh teacakes onto a plate.

"Take a seat and Mary will be with you," the woman said, glancing in the direction of a girl who was swathed in a crisp white apron.

The girl turned and gazed wide-eyed at Lily, noting her auburn curls under her cloche hat and the good woollen coat which she had conceded to wear when her mother advised her that the wind would be unseasonably chilly at Dungeness. As Lily turned to choose a table, she felt Mary's eyes on the straight seams of her stockings and neat T-bar shoes. The poor girl wore the uniform of a waitress, yet in Ashford their hems had risen to above their ankles. Here Mary's dress was almost sweeping along the floor and she wore black lace-up boots. The place was terribly old-fashioned. Had her mother come here and sat at one of these tables and, if she were to return, would it be just the same as she recalled?

Settling for a small table by the window, Lily looked out on the square and the slim church tower. She could watch the people from Lydd go by while she passed the time.

"There's teacakes and crumpets, with butter an' jam. Or a bit o' Victoria sponge cake," Mary said, standing beside Lily. "Or would you like some dinner? We've shepherd's pie, nice and fresh.

"A *slice*, Mary. A slice of Victoria sponge." The older woman's voice rang out.

"A slice." Mary's figure slumped.

"Crumpets, please, two of them and a pot of tea." Lily smiled her encouragement. "Thank you, Mary, that would be lovely."

It was quiet in the tearooms. A young couple sat in

one corner. In his Sunday best suit and polished shoes, the man looked anxious to please. The woman kept crossing and uncrossing her legs, clad in woollen stockings, and smoothing her dress, which had clearly had the hem raised as a nod to current fashions, yet retaining the detailing of an older era. There was a group of three much older women and another woman who sat on her own, a shawl clutched tight around her.

When the door opened and a man of about thirty strode in, everyone turned to watch his progress across the shop. He was tall with broad shoulders, dark hair trimmed short to the back and sides, then slicked neatly on top. His suit fitted him well and his shoes were pointed two-tone black and white. Lily held back a smirk as she imagined her mother's horror if she ever introduced a young man who wore shoes as outrageous as these.

"Hello, Ann, my love, have you seen my sister? Said I'd treat her to a warm dinner. Nice and cosy it is in here, the bleeding wind's getting up out there."

"She called in an hour ago, Charlie. She had to go to work and asked me to tell you. You'll stay for a bun though, won't you?"

"One more won't hurt!" He looked down at his widening girth. "Lots of butter and a splash of cold water in the tea. I'll not stop if Susie's not here."

Lily watched, no longer occupied with the view through the window. She saw a spiv or two about Ashford town centre, wheeling and dealing under the counter or at the back doors of the High Street stores. But already she had assessed Lydd as being rather old-fashioned, and she hadn't expected to see such a flamboyant character in these dated tearooms. He drank his tea in a flash, still standing at the counter and left with half the teacake still in his hand. A smile and a wink were sent in Lily's direction as he stepped out onto the street.

Having finished her crumpets, Lily contemplated what she could do until the train departed for Dungeness. It must be no distance at all and there was a fresh breeze, but she had her woollen coat and, in her suitcase, some stout boots – something else her mother insisted on. She would walk there, along the road, for there was sure to be one. At least she would be doing something, and she had no wish to search out entertainment in the town.

"Mary, would you mind?" Lily beckoned the awkward girl to the table. "I've come by train from Ashford and am looking to find a room at Dungeness for the weekend."

"A room?" Mary repeated, eyes round with wonder. "A room, like for a little holiday?"

"That's just what I want," Lily nodded. "But it's a lovely day and no need to wait for the train. I thought I'd walk there if you could tell me which direction to go."

"Walk there? Well..." the girl came closer as if to confide. "There's some who walk down the tracks, it's the quickest way. But... but not in the day, not with all them trains."

"No, not the way to go at all," Lily agreed. "But a road...?"

"There's no such thing as a road," Mary began, "But there's a good track, good enough for walking and horses and carts. And if it's a room you're wanting then my aunt always has a bed at Galloways."

"Is that the name of her cottage?" Lily asked.

Mary pondered for a moment before replying, "Oh, yes. Easily found and a nice view out to sea. Very nice. I'd say if I were going on holiday a view would be lovely."

"And how do I get there?"

"You turn out of here and cross the Rype. That's what we call it, the green. Straight across and take the road on the other side, then follow it to the west. Now keep going straight ahead, and as you reach the end of the green, take the path to the right straight ahead again and you're on the track to Galloways. It's a fair walk mind, in them fancy shoes."

"Oh, I've boots in my suitcase and I like a walk," Lily replied. "Now let me pay and I'll be on my way."

"Perhaps take a teacake for a bit o' nourishment on the way?"

"Excellent."

It was an odd place, this green called the Rype. Not a bit like a village green, although it did have houses around its perimeter. It was just too big and the grass sparse as if poorly nourished by thin soil. There were some stunted trees, some type of pine perhaps, certainly unable to grow tall and straight. Children played with hoops and carts and balls in small groups, making little impact on the vast space.

Crossing the green, Lily turned to the right as instructed and went past a tithe barn whose thatched roof hung like long skirts almost to the ground. At the end of the Rype, the road offered various choices and Lily was relieved that Mary's instructions had been so clear. Noting that the track was rough, she opened her suitcase and retrieved her boots. Then, leaning on a tree-stump, Lily removed her slim shoes and replaced them with socks and sturdy black boots. Looking down, she almost wished that her skirt did come low enough to hide the incongruous image of her nylon stocking-clad calves with woollen socks at her ankles. She was tying her laces when a familiar voice rang out:

"'Ello darlin', if you're setting off down the Galloways

Road, it's no place for a young woman like yourself."

Lily bristled, in a manner not unlike her mother's, and scowling she turned to the man who was standing just a couple of yards away from her. She recognised him as the spiv from the tearooms.

"I'm perfectly capable of walking down a track to the sea."

"It's a long way to the sea and there's more pleasant beaches hereabouts." He grinned as if it were all a big joke, looking down at her boots and socks.

"But this is the one I choose to go to."

"Look darlin', you're a big girl and I'm sure you know what you're doing, but I can't let you head off down there without saying that maybe you've got it wrong."

"The girl from the tearooms gave me directions." Lily leaned down to take the handle of her case.

"And you're going to Galloways?" He looked at the suitcase, "Planning to stay?"

"I'm going to Dungeness. My mother lived there for a time, so it's perfectly fine."

"Right." Looking down at her, with that irritating grin on his face, he shook his head slightly. "So, you want Dungeness. You need to go by train. It will be a fair wait, but it's the only way for a young woman."

"The only way?" Lily tossed her head in annoyance. "I'll walk, just as planned. It's a lovely day and I'll enjoy it."

"The wind's getting up and there's a bank of cloud over Fairlight." His eyes became more serious, but Lily didn't notice; she was looking out along the rough track. "Take the train, love, it will only be an hour's wait by the time you get back to the station, and it will have you at Dungeness Station within minutes. If you don't like what you see, then you can just stay sitting on the same train and be back here in Lydd in no time. There's rooms at

The George if you want a little holiday; tell Jenny that Charlie sent you."

"Thank you, Charlie, but I'll do very well on my own and if Dungeness doesn't suit then I'll walk back to The George as you kindly suggested."

The track, for she could hardly call it a road, skirted an army camp. A sharp reminder of the war, it was not something Lily had considered she might come across during her seaside break. She had noted a military presence in the town and this was clearly their base. Numerous tin-topped huts were scattered about the place, not far from the menacing wire fence built to keep civilians away from the training ground. If she had cared to look, Lily would have seen the young soldiers going about their duties, but she chose to turn her snub nose to the left and disengage from the reminders of war.

Moving at a good pace, Lily was soon able to look both ways and take in the scenery, as army camp buildings were left behind and only the wire fencing reminded her the land to her right was under the control of the military. The landscape was bleak and barren, not like the flat pasture she had travelled through by train. The grass had become sparse, growing in ragged tufts through thin soil. At first it seemed that the land was flat, but it undulated very slightly, as if it were petrified waves.

What a very odd sort of place this was; Lily began to believe her mother's ominous warnings about Dungeness were not entirely unfounded.

"Well, it can't be that bad or she could never have stayed there for a whole year, not Mother!" Lily spoke aloud. A slight smirk played on her face; she was unable to imagine Alice living away from the comforts of Grandfather's vicarage.

26

What reason could there be for a village to be at the end of the road? It would be a place of fair size in order for it to have its own railway station. There must be a pretty bay, fishing boats, tearooms and a promenade. Perhaps a hall for dances and some beach huts. It was not a fashionable spot, Lily was sure of it, for she had never heard of anyone who had ever been there. It had never been spoken about when her friends discussed Whitstable or Broadstairs. How exciting to be visiting somewhere new and to have tales to tell when she returned home.

Glad of her stout boots, Lily found it was easiest to walk in one of the parallel ruts forged by whatever traffic used this road. The track, more shingle than earth, seemed to be used on a regular basis, most likely by horse and cart. Now, as she fumbled in her handbag for a cigarette, Lily moved away from the track and placed her suitcase down amongst the stones, perching on it for a moment.

It took a few minutes for the flame to stay strong and steady enough to light the cigarette. Inhaling, Lily felt herself relax and she rubbed her calves that were stiffening from the unaccustomed exercise. The road had been so uneven, causing all Lily's attention to be on where she was stepping but now she looked into the distance, hoping to get a glimpse of Dungeness. To the left she saw a lighthouse, which was reassuring, although it was still some distance away and the road would have to take a sharp turn soon. To the right, the hills were now obscured. Lily didn't know where Fairlight was, but the bank of cloud, mentioned by the irritating Charlie, was thickening and closing in. The air was beginning to chill. Lily knew she must keep going if she was to reach the coast before the mist completely descended upon her.

27

An hour later, Lily stood, case in hand, with feelings of uncertainty beginning to taunt her. She had been told there was no road to Dungeness, yet she had taken a road. A stony pitted track, but a road of sorts. Now as she was standing on the edge of a cluster of makeshift buildings, the first doubts crept through the approaching mist and clawed at her usual feelings of belief in herself.

The sea could not be seen, yet its scent carried on the damp air, leaving her skin sticky and a taste of salt on her lips. Concealed by a pale blanket, the cliffs at Hastings were gone, as was Lydd and its slim church tower which had been her reference, allowing her to gauge how far she had walked from the town. With distant landmarks fading away, Lily no longer had a sense of place in this barren land.

It was just Lily, some ramshackle buildings, the sea-mist and the gulls. But no, even the gulls had gone. Where their screeches had mocked and taunted, there was near silence, punctuated by the distant boom of a foghorn.

This was it, Dungeness, and every bit as miserable as her mother had said. No, it was worse. The school was clearly long gone; there was no substantial building here. And, as for the lighthouse, she had seen it from a distance and assumed the road would turn towards it. There was no sign of it now, no comforting beam of light.

On the brink of retreating to Lydd, Lily faltered. It was an awfully long way to walk back. One of these places must be Galloways Cottage, offering a bed to visitors. It would be a humble place but perhaps warm with a nourishing meal on the table.

It was as Lily took a few steps forward a door opened, rubbing and pushing at the shingle, revealing the dimly-lit interior of a cottage. A woman, bundled up

28

in a thick shawl, stepped out and, having taken a few steps, became aware of the stranger's presence.

"Oh, my Lord, what's this young miss doing wandering about like she's going to the vicar's tea party?" This was accompanied by a short cackle.

"I'm..." Lily looked down at her sturdy boots, "not really dressed for tea. I've come visiting to Dungeness, but I wonder...?"

"Dungeness, you say? You've come a funny way about it and wi' the mist closing in I'd not like to venture there meself." The old woman shuffled towards Lily and peered up at her. "Galloways this be. Close enough but not Dungeness proper."

"Galloways! Galloways Cottage?" Lily felt the tension release from her body. "That's exactly where I wanted to be."

"You did?"

"Mary sent me. Mary from the teashop in Lydd."

"Oh, she did, did she?" A wide toothless grin spread across and creased the leathery face. "She's a good girl is our Mary. A good girl."

Chapter Three

"Come away in, then." The woman placed her weathered hand on Lily's forearm. "You don't want to be wandering about in the mist, not now you've found us here at Galloways."

"You weren't...?" It had seemed as if the old woman was going out somewhere, but what could she be doing out in the mists?

"I was just gathering the goats in, but they can wait a while longer. We'll get you settled first."

The cottage was low with a pitched roof, not of slate or tiles, but corrugated iron. There was a window on each side of the front door, but both already had shutters fixed across them, even though it should not be dark for hours. Lily looked straight at the dim ball of pale yellow light hanging in the sky and realised that it wasn't going to cast much light on Dungeness for the rest of the day. Dusk had come early. The walls of the cottage were tarred planks and it seemed as if they sat directly on the shingle; there was no obvious plinth of brick or stone. And this is why the door was barely raised in its frame causing it to push upon any loose stones which fell into its path. Apart from the brick-built chimney stack at one end, this home was not much more than the garden shed her father was so proud of.

For a moment, Lily faltered, words shouting in her mind: *Turn back; follow the tracks back to Lydd.*

But the door was pulled open and the hand on Lily's

30

arm was tugging at her. "It's lovely and warm inside, my love. Come on in, away from them mists that will soon chill a young lady like yourself."

Inside Galloways Cottage heat engulfed the visitor as she stood in the doorway, eyes smarting from the wood-smoke and struggling to adjust to the dim light. The room was long and rectangular, stretching out on either side of Lily. The source of the heat was clearly from the range encased in a chimney breast on the end wall to the left. There were no gas lamps on the walls, just an oil lamp on the central table and another on the dresser set in the alcove beside the chimney breast.

On the far side of the room, sitting in an easy chair, with his legs stretched out towards the warmth from the range, was a man. It wasn't until he spoke that Lily could make a guess as to his age and it wasn't until he stood that she saw he was very tall.

"Hello there, I wasn't expecting... not in this mist," his voice was gentle. He pushed down on the arms of the chair, lifting himself up until he stood with his head not far from the low ceiling. He was not much older than she was, perhaps in his late twenties. As he took a step towards her, Lily noted that he was a little stooped, as tall men often are, and perhaps this was a necessity as he had to manoeuvre himself through the low doorways of the cottage.

"Mary sent the girl here, to see us," the old woman announced, with a hint of triumph in her voice.

"Oh, she did, did she?" He was standing just a few feet from Lily now, looking down at her. His height could have been threatening, but it wasn't.

"She's a good girl, our Mary is. I said she'd do us proud one day." The old woman kept her hand on Lily's arm as the two of them stood at the doorway.

"You did; you seemed sure of it, Ma." He looked as

31

if he were about to turn away but then asked, "What's her name?"

"I didn't ask; you'll be wanting to know of course." Turning to Lily, she asked, "He was asking what your name is, my dear?"

"Lily, it's Lily. I've come about the room, but of course you must know that if Mary has been sending people." She couldn't just stand there, holding her case. It was getting heavy and the looks they gave were rather disconcerting. But they seemed so pleased to have her there, especially the old woman. They must need the money from summer visitors.

"Well, just leave your case there for a moment, Lily, and sit yourself down in the other chair, next to Joe." The old woman nodded towards the second armchair.

Lily removed her jacket and placed it on top of her case then moved around the large table to reach the chair. It was placed beside its partner on the far side of the room with a low box, or crate, between them, draped with a piece of lace. Easing herself into the chair, she realised how long the walk from Lydd had been and how thankful she was finally to sink into the cushioned comfort. Looking down at her dress, which was nipped in neatly at the waist and fell to mid-calf, Lily felt strangely uncomfortable about her skirt length. A change from her usual defiance about the latest fashions and her mother's disapproval. She had noted the woman's brown skirt hem brushed on her boots and sensed Joe's eyes looking in wonder at her slender legs. Tugging at one of the blankets draped over the chair, Lily tried to cover a little of the smart dress. The neat T-bar shoes were safely in her suitcase, somehow her boots seemed more appropriate for Dungeness. Her mother had been right, Lily realised.

The woman – Lily still didn't know her name – was

pushing the kettle onto the hotplate. "Nice cup of tea is what you need," she said. "What a way to come, but we're thankful that you did."

"That would be lovely, Mrs... I'm sorry, I don't know your name?"

"Oh, we don't stand for being all formal around here." The old woman looked back and gave a crooked smile, her lips sucked in where her teeth had once been. "Evie, you can call me Evie, my dear."

"Thank you, Evie. A cup of tea would be lovely." Lily returned the smile.

She looked once more around the room. The walls were made of wood and it seemed clear they were no more than one plank thick. They were painted in a cream colour, or was it a grey? With the only light coming from two lamps it was hard to tell. A hotchpotch of materials hung at the window frames, the two to the front and one to the rear. The curtains appeared to be rather limp, perhaps lacking in a decent header tape, Lily mused, or was it that their hems weren't straight? Again, it would be easier to judge when the shutters were thrown open in the daylight. But the greatest amount of material, and this seemed to be a bold flowered velvet, was stretched across the whole width of the room at the opposite end from the chimney breast. What was behind this? It could only be a bedroom area; she could think of no other reason for separating the living space.

Placing the huge brown teapot on the table, Evie went to the dresser and took a collection of cups and saucers from the shelves and placed them beside the pot. Then, from a cupboard with a cooling slate base, there came a metal jug of milk. Finally, again from the dresser, she brought a cake tin, a knife and some plates. Lily watched her progress from the comfort of the armchair draped in knitted blankets.

"Now then, Joe, you can shift yourself and make a start on tidying up that room of yours. You could sleep here in front of the range, but it might be more proper if you go to your uncle's."

"Oh, I didn't mean… I thought you took in guests." Lily felt the colour rising in her cheeks. "That's what Mary said."

"She did, and a good girl is our Mary." Evie lifted the lid on the teapot and stirred slowly, looking towards Lily, but as if she gazed into another place. "You're very welcome, isn't she, Joe? We've been waiting for a nice young woman like yourself to come visiting here at Galloways."

"We'll treat you well," Joe replied, looking down at his large hands and picking at a fingernail.

"It's goat's milk," Evie said, as she poured some in the cups. "You'll be used to cow's milk of course, but here we find the goats settle better on the Ness."

"I've not tried it before, but it must be difficult to keep a cow, or any animal here really." Lily thought of the sparse grass; there wasn't much to nibble on.

"You'll get used to it and think it better than cow's in no time at all," Evie smiled, as if she held secrets about this place, Dungeness or the Ness as she had just called it. Then, facing her son, she raised her voice just a little and it became sharper, "Now then Joe, stop that dallying and get to it. Put your clothes in a carpet bag and tidy up anything that isn't proper in a bedroom for a young woman."

"All right Ma, I was just wanting the tea first." He got out of the chair, again filling the corner of the room with his height.

"It's too hot for now and will be all the better for five minutes cooling." Evie busied herself with the cake and a huge knife for cutting it.

Joe eased his way between the central table and Lily in her armchair; his boots scuffed against hers and she tucked her legs in. He took a few steps and placed his hand on a door at the rear of the building, near the floral velvet hanging. Then he returned and, taking a candle from a side table, he lit it from the oil lamp on the table. Turning back to the door, he pressed on the latch and it swung open into a back room.

"She's rather smart, Lily is," Joe muttered as he left the room, stooping as he moved through the doorway. "A bit too smart for the likes of us."

"She'll soon settle to our ways," his mother replied. "She'll have no choice."

"Thank you, Joe... for the room," Lily raised her voice a little as he moved away. "I didn't realise... didn't want to make a fuss. It will only be for a night or two."

"No fuss at all, my dear." Evie placed a slice of cake on a plate. "He was going to have to tidy it up at some time and there is no reason better than your coming to be with us here at Galloways. Now here's your tea and a nice bit of fruit cake."

The tea was a little grey under the light of the oil lamp, Lily thought. She would have liked a little less milk. Taking a tentative sip, she frowned a little. What was it that was different? Surely it had a salty taste about it and... what else was it that made the tea not quite as she was used to? Her mother liked to put a clove in an apple pie and it wasn't a taste that Lily was fond of. It seemed as if the tea had a similar taste about it. She took another sip; there was no improvement in the taste.

"Do you draw your water from a well?" Lily asked, noting a jug by the sink and no tap. Perhaps that would account for the salty taste when they were so close to the sea?

"We do, there's one for all the cottages and another for the coastguards," Evie replied, as she settled at the table with her tea and cake.

"All the cottages?" Lily's eyes widened. "My goodness, what if it were to run dry? And you must be queueing up for a turn?"

"It's a bit of bother sometimes," Evie agreed. "But there's only the six cottages."

"Only six?"

"Six and the coastguards and them at The British Sailor."

"The pub?" Lily queried.

"Not for the likes of you," Evie replied.

"I hadn't said that my mother visited here; she worked at the school." Lily took another sip of the rather odd tea. "It's gone now, has it? I saw nothing substantial enough and she said she lived in rooms there too."

"It's still here, lass. Quite a walk though, over the shingle. No road leading to it, but our Joe could show you sometime if you were wanting to walk that distance."

"Oh, of course," Lily felt her body relax. "I couldn't make sense of it all, but Mother said that the school was apart from everything else. I remember now."

The cake was good, moist with plump raisins and a sugary crust. Lily ate with enjoyment, while taking small sips of tea. She would have to drink the warm liquid, it would be rude not to, although the odd taste lingered on her tongue. She found herself relaxing in the comfy chair and reflected that it had been quite a trudge along the path to the coast, so no wonder she was weary despite its only being late afternoon.

Joe reappeared carrying a roll of bedding and a

drawstring sack. He placed them on the floor beside Lily's suitcase. His mother looked over and nodded her approval. She opened a chest and pulled out a bundle of sheets along with a blanket, then moved towards the open doorway leading to the bedroom.

"Sit yourself down, then," Evie said to Joe, who had taken a long slurp of his tea. "You're making the place look untidy. I'll just make the bed and then you can get away to tell your uncle that you'll be stopping there overnight."

In the chair next to Lily, with only the lace-topped crate between them, Joe kept his eyes firmly on his tea and cake. It was left to the guest to try to make some conversation.

"Thank you for letting me have your room. I wouldn't have liked to walk all the way back to Lydd, not with the mists drawing in and, besides, it was quite a walk."

"I don't mind," was the reply, as Joe pulled at the cake and placed a chunk in his mouth.

Lily took another sip of her tea and allowed her eyelids to close a little. It seemed normal etiquette didn't apply here at Galloways Cottage.

When Lily opened her eyes, Joe was gone, and Evie was sitting at the table rolling out some pastry. Still in a drowsy state, Lily watched the rolling pin move to and fro, finding the movement quite mesmerising. There were three shallow pie dishes, each one topped with a circle of pastry. Then, with her thumb, Evie pressed around the edges before making a slit in the top of each pie with a knife. The pies were placed on the dresser with a piece of linen draped over them.

With a glance towards her guest, Evie gave a brief nod, lifted the brown teapot and poured more tea. Lily tried to put up her hand, as if to say that she didn't need or want any more, but it all seemed like too much effort and rather rude. So she smiled and accepted the warm grey-brown liquid. Her eyelids rested for a moment longer.

Evie was certainly industrious. No sooner were the pies lined up on the dresser than a large mixing bowl was taken from the cupboard and placed on the table. Packets were opened and varying amounts of flour, sugar, fat and dried fruit were added with gusto and without having been weighed. Eggs were cracked open and flowed in, then a wooden spoon began to mix, first slowly and then, as the ingredients began to bind together, the spoon moved at a greater pace.

Sipping cautiously at the tea, Lily was trying to form some thoughts in her head. Such as suggesting she might take a short walk or asking if Evie minded if she smoked. The nicotine would surely clear her head a little. It was just that she was still so terribly tired. Her mother always said that a short sleep in the afternoon could leave you feeling drowsier than ever. It seemed that Evie was comfortable with the silence as she busied herself with her baking, muttering to herself at times or breaking into a few words of a song.

A gust of wind came with Joe when he returned to the cottage. His mother had her eye on him as he took a few steps towards his bedroom door. "Not done yet, Joe? The girl will want to see her room, to settle in."

"I just..." Joe lifted his hand, which had been concealed behind his back, and showed a small collection of grasses, delicate flowers and seed heads. "It was for her room." He looked towards Lily. "Nothing much, not like a young woman should have, but it was all I could find."

Lily's heart warmed towards the man who stood there, so tall, yet wanting to shrink away from them both. "That's so kind of you. I'm sure my brothers would never think of such a gesture."

"Put 'em in a little pot, then." Evie took a jar from the dresser and handed it to her son. "I didn't think you were born soppy, Joe." Her tone was soft and it seemed that Joe's mother approved.

Leaving her baking for a moment, Evie opened the chest and lifted out a piece of lace. Then, taking a broom and dustpan from the corner of the room, she followed her son into the back bedroom. There was a murmur of voices and the gentle swoosh of bristles on the plank floor. Joe appeared with a rug rolled under his arm, and again a gush of salt air refreshed the room as he left the cottage. The fresh air helped to lift Lily's weariness and so, when Joe returned, presumably having beaten the dust from the rug, she stood and supported herself on the kitchen table

"There, there, love, you've had a tiresome day." Evie was back at the table, wooden spoon in hand. When had she returned to the main room? It must have been while Lily had been looking down at the tea or perhaps resting her eyelids again for a short time.

"I am terribly tired," Lily said. "You must think me very rude. Some people say the sea air relaxes those who are unused to it. Or perhaps the warmth of the room?"

"That will be it," Evie smiled her agreement. "It's warm in here with the range. It weren't as hot when I cooked on an open fire."

"You're very busy." Lily looked at the mixing bowl. "Is there anything I can do to help?"

"Oh no, love." Evie reached out and patted Lily's hand. "You enjoy your little break. Our Joe has gone now, off to stay with his uncle and no doubt the pair of them will spend the evening at The British Sailor. It's only right that the men spend the evening together and us women will do the same."

"The women?" Lily frowned, her snub nose wrinkling. "I don't know why, I thought it was just you and Joe living here."

"Oh, it is." Evie began to ease the cake mixture into a large bowl. "But my sister and her daughters, and the cousins, they'll be coming along later, after supper."

"Is that why you are baking?"

"I'm baking for tomorrow. They'll all be wanting to fill their bellies; you can be sure of that." The cake mixture was now smoothed within the tin and, with a thick cloth in her hand, Evie turned to open the door of the range. "We've a family celebration. Our Joe is getting married."

Chapter Four

Lily woke on the day of Joe's wedding. It was the first thought which came into her head. No, it was the second: *Of course, I'm here at Galloways Cottage; it is the day of Joe's wedding.* With shutters at the window of the room – Joe's room – it was still in partial darkness but the dim light spreading through the cracks and at the edges gave the clue that morning had arrived.

She had slept through the whole night, not surprising given that Lily had been remarkably tired by the time she went to bed. How many times had she apologised for her drowsiness throughout the evening? It seemed there had been moments she could barely form half a dozen words into a short sentence. The wine must have been more potent than she realised, although she had only had the one glass, or was it two?

The small room with its plank walls and floor had a certain charm to it. The bed was comfortable, and a piece of lace had been thrown over a side table, then topped with the glass jar of grasses and seed heads. There was a small chair over which Lily's dress and cardigan were draped and some hooks on the wall. The chest of drawers and trunk would hold Joe's clothes and belongings, but any signs this was a man's room had been removed. It must be used for holiday guests on a regular basis, Lily decided.

Stretching out on the small double bed, Lily wondered what the day would bring. It was to be Joe's wedding. But who was he marrying? Some girl from the village, no doubt, but she hadn't been present during the previous evening. There was talk of Joe's bride and a great satisfaction that he was to be married, but no mention of a name. Evie had spoken of the food she had prepared: the cake and three rabbit pies. The female relatives had spoken of their contributions to the food and there had been something about the family veil and hagstones.

Hagstones. Lily had meant to ask what they were. But the chatter flowed so quickly between the women that there never seemed to be a chance and, when there was, the questions didn't form in time before the moment passed.

Swinging her legs out of the bed, it seemed to take a moment for Lily's head to steady after the sudden movement; it was as if it had to catch up with her body. She needed the lavatory, and no surprise after the wine and that dreadful tea which had been pressed upon her throughout the previous evening. Evie had provided a chamber pot; there it was tucked away under the bed. But Lily preferred to brave the outside privy, so she put her coat and boots on, and opened the door to the main living area. There was no-one in sight and so she pressed the latch on the front door and stepped outside.

The sun was still low in the sky to the east, showing itself as a comforting glow through the swathes of early morning mist. Dampness hung in the air, settling on Lily's coat and hair, giving a refreshing tingle to the skin on her face. There was no wind; her mother had said it was almost always windy at Dungeness. Gulls swooped and screamed above and, closer, a couple of nanny goats pulled at tufts of grass and broom. The sea was nearby and, although it couldn't be seen, it could

42

be heard as a rhythmic showering of shingle on the beach, followed by the pull of the tide dragging the stones back. And amidst the sounds of nature, a foghorn persistently blared its warning.

The other cottages loomed nearby, their chimney stacks standing proud and with roofs of various heights, but none of them high. They didn't appear to be lined up alongside a track, but merely placed upon the shingle as if scattered on a whim. These must be the homes Evie had spoken of, the six who shared a pump. There would be the pub too, and the coastguards' cottages, somewhere within the swirling mist.

With her hand upon the rough plank wall of Galloways Cottage, Lily stepped over the lightly undulating stones, using the wall to keep her balance. It seemed an age since she had walked out with confidence along the stony track from Lydd. Now, despite a sound night's sleep, she felt disorientated and her steps were tentative. At the back of the cottage, she calculated that it must be ten to twelve steps to the privy. It seemed as if it were a near impossible task, to move from the security of the cottage wall to the slim upright building housing the wooden seat over a pit. For the first time, Lily questioned that she might be suffering from some ailment such as the flu. What else could cause such unsteadiness in her body and her head to struggle to fit her thoughts into any semblance of order?

Just ten steps, maybe twelve. Count them one by one. A booted foot moved forward and then another, steadily, keeping up the rhythm. The privy was reached and Lily clutched at the corner before pressing on the latch. She gave a sigh of relief, never having welcomed the damp wooden seat of an outside lavatory. Back in Ashford, in Jemmett Road, they had an inside bathroom and separate WC, with porcelain furnishings.

43

Evie was there, in the living area, when Lily opened the cottage door and stood in her coat and boots.

"I've just been..." Lily started and then paused, no need to offer so much.

"To the privy," Evie finished. "There's nowhere else to go with the mist so thick. They've missed the tide, the men have. Can't go out in a mist like this."

"I'll just get dressed now." Lily moved towards the bedroom door. "I wondered if I could have some..."

"Hot water," Evie completed her words. "It's already there for you, love. I knew you'd be wanting some and I scented it for you, knowing you'd want something special today."

"Thank you," Lily smiled her appreciation. "You are kind."

"The kettle is on the boil and I've porridge with raisins." Evie nodded towards the range. "It'll be ready when you're dressed."

"Do you have..." Lily didn't want to sound ungrateful, but her head had a terrible pressing sensation over it and a cup of tea was as good as anything to put her right in the morning. "Do you have any brown tea, normal tea such as, well, anything really? Tea leaves from a shop is what I was meaning."

"Of course, we can't be without a nice pot of tea."

When the tea came, it was the same grey liquid with that slightly salty tang, which Lily could only assume was from the water drawn from the well. Evie seemed so pleased to be placing the pot before her, and it would be churlish to ask again for a more traditional brew. While spooning porridge, Lily tried to recall the last time she had smoked a cigarette. She had thought of it the evening before, but it had always seemed like too much effort to go to her bag and extract one. Only one of last

44

night's party had smoked; Evie's sister had chewed upon the end of a pipe, while the bowl of the pipe smouldered, letting off strong fumes.

"What time will the wedding be?" Lily wondered as she devoured the last of the porridge.

"We don't follow time in the usual way." Evie came closer and poured more tea into Lily's cup. "But at noon or thereabouts, when the sun is at its peak and casts no shadows on the stones. That is the moment when the exchanges will be made."

Unsure of how to respond, Lily took another sip of her tea. She had meant to apologise about her arrival at this time, to say she would return to Lydd the following day. She had meant to say this was a family occasion and she had no expectation to be a part of it. But the words had remained trapped inside her, which was odd. Usually she said exactly what she wanted to say and made her thoughts perfectly clear. But now, suffering from something which made her mind weary, the words were left unsaid. It seemed Evie and the other women wanted her here to celebrate alongside them. It hadn't been said, but perhaps they remembered the time her mother spent here and didn't see her as a stranger to them.

"You'll be wanting to go along to the shore and choose a stone," Evie said, as she cleared away the dishes and placed them in a huge earthenware bowl. There was no running water and she poured water from the kettle into the bowl before adding soap flakes.

"Choose a stone?"

"Of course, it's not the fairest of days and no shadows to speak of, unless the mist clears, but you'll need a stone nonetheless."

"From here, just outside the cottage?" Lily asked.

"No, from the beach." Evie turned to look at Lily, a

wet dish in her hand. "Just follow the track to the beach and take your time to find the right one."

"How will I know it's the right one?"

"You'll start looking and at first you'll think you could never spot a hagstone among so many, but it won't take long and you'll pick it up, and then another and when you pick the right one, you'll know it." Evie nodded and turned back to the dishes.

Sensing that no amount of questioning would solve the mystery of exactly what a hagstone was, Lily stood and turned towards the bedroom. "I'll just get my coat; I imagine it's chilly out there."

Leaning against the tarred plank wall, Lily put the cigarette holder to her lips and drew in the familiar taste, letting it lick around her mouth before pulling it into her lungs. Just what she needed; she would be on top form again in no time. She inhaled for the second time before stepping out along the track to the sea. Damn and blast, the stones made her rather unsteady, but she hadn't come to Dungeness to sit drinking the local tea with an old woman. She had come to the seaside and so a visit to the beach was in order.

Then there was the wedding and surely a chance to meet some of the people who had known her mother. Perhaps some of her former pupils. Lily grinned to herself; imagine Mother as a teacher stuck here without her comforts! How old would her pupils be now? At least thirty, some as old as forty! There was no church here; Mother said the school became a church on a Sunday, so no doubt that was where the wedding would be held. Unless Dungeness had become civilised and built itself a church in the past twenty-five years.

Pausing to crush the end of the cigarette into the shingle, Lily watched her boot grind away at it. The

46

sound of the sea was almost upon her now and she realised she was on the top of the beach and there, not more than twenty yards away, was the tide lapping at its highest point. It was lazy today, rolling in without breaking or frothing. There was a boat to her left and several more to the right, their details obscured by the mist. She could see the droplets in the air and taste its damp saltiness. For a moment, the young woman stood watching the sea, allowing her body to sway a little, almost mesmerised by the rhythm.

After a few minutes, Lily shook herself a little. Almost like a dog shaking off a flea. It wasn't like her to be so dreamy, to be lacking in action. Now, what was a hagstone? She wouldn't find out if she didn't look and then surely there would be a stone different from the others and she would know. Kicking at the shingle, Lily occasionally reached down to pick up a stone which attracted her interest. Pocketing a pure white stone, she felt its smooth coolness, but knew such beauty could not bear a name such as hagstone.

Then she saw it: a small almost-black stone, long and narrow with a hole through its length, and wondered if it could be the one? Others with holes came to her, some smooth and regular, many rough and distorted. She pocketed the smooth ones and discarded those not as pleasing to her eye. She must have collected six good specimens when a noise of displaced shingle caused her to look towards the fishing boats.

A tall figure emerged, his stride long and back rounded as if he too was searching the stones. Lily recognised it as Joe before he saw her.

"Oh, it's you." He stopped just a few yards from her. "I mean, I didn't see… you took me by surprise."

"It was Evie, your mother, she sent me here." Lily

put her hand deep in the pocket of her coat, pulled out the stones, then held them in the palm of her hand. "She sent me for stones, but I wasn't sure."

"Of course she did," Joe nodded knowingly. "You'll be needing one."

"And are they? These ones with the holes, are they hagstones?"

He stepped closer so they were at arm's length from one another. "You've got a nice collection there. Not the white one, although it's a lovely, just no hole you see."

"I was drawn to it," Lily replied.

"And which is your favourite?"

"Oh, the dark one: look at how the hole goes straight through the middle." Lily slid the others back into her pocket and offered the black bullet of a stone.

"Then you keep that one and the others can go back on the beach."

"I thought I'd take them home, back to Mother, to remind her..."

"Back home?" He frowned. "Well, if you think so."

Turning away, Lily was about to walk back to the cottage. She wasn't sure what else to say to this tall stranger who stood before her. But remembering her manners, she felt her step falter and looking up she said, "I hope you enjoy your wedding." It didn't sound quite right, but for once Lily was unsure of exactly how to phrase her thoughts.

"I'll see you there," he replied. "Don't forget the stone."

The search for hagstones had led Lily almost to the high tide mark, and so she had to trudge up the shingle bank as she left the beach. Not that there was much to differentiate between what was beach and what was not. Whereas the beach was strewn with seaweed and bits of driftwood, the land was dotted with wiry broom bushes and sea kale.

Passing a long, low, timber building with a lookout tower, Lily noted the windows facing the sea were shuttered, but the tower was open to the weather. This must be for the coastguards, she thought. And there they were, at the open back door, two of them smoking pipes. She gave them a short nod as they stared openly at her and, although determined not to look back, Lily was certain their gaze followed her progress across the stones.

A little further inland and the cottages began to take shape. The mist was lifting a little and now the lines of their weatherboarding, the uprights of their chimney pots and angles of additional extensions became clearer. Other features became distinct, such as ladders at their ends leading to small loft doors, the shutters at windows, and small pens for animals. There were raised timber-framed boxes holding earth, a place to grow vegetables which couldn't hope to thrive in this infertile ground. And all of it scattered in no particular order. Not set out in rows, as one would expect. It was as if no one claimed any one area of land and fenced it off as their own. Instead they took a little of whatever suited them, and no one presumed to take any more.

Feeling refreshed by the exercise and quite certain the cigarette had been beneficial in clearing the rather fuzzy feeling in her head, Lily decided against returning to Galloways Cottage quite yet. She would circle the group of cottages and see if there was any sign of a schoolhouse. It would be some way from the wooden homes, but the sun was becoming stronger by the minute; the colours and textures of the landscape were now more defined. She could now see further across this place, which was like none she had ever witnessed before.

Some laughter and a cry of joy punctuated the air, previously only carrying the sounds of nature. Curious, Lily picked up her pace, although she wondered if it made much difference; the faster she stepped on the shingle, the faster the stones moved and hindered her progress. It came again, more gleeful than the screech of a gull and surely coming from the other side of the cottages.

Then, through a gap between the wooden plank walls, she saw them. Two girls: they must be girls for their voices were high and youthful. Their arms were outstretched, and heads thrown back as they gazed at the sky. They whirled round and round, and it was a wonder they could keep their balance, Lily mused. As they turned, there was something in their hands twirling with them. Something long and slender, perhaps a knotted rope or a scarf. Their skirts were long, flaring out as they moved, and they wore no jackets or shawls over their blouses. Hair was an unrestrained tumble of golden and brown curls – another clue these were girls, or at least unmarried.

As she moved between the cottages, a final cry came from the girls as they tumbled laughing onto the ground. One of them looked towards Lily and gave a wave, the other turned and they exchanged a few words before lying on their backs, hands behind their heads and facing the sun. Scrambling over the stones, it took a few moments for her to reach them.

Chapter Five

"I'm Lily." Lily went to offer her hand, but hastily withdrew it. These girls were still sprawling on the ground; the rules of polite society were lost on them.

"Oh, we know that, not many new people come here to Galloways." The one with the dark curls raised herself so she was now sitting upright. "I'm Jennie and she's Martha."

"You're having a look about the place then?" Martha rolled onto her stomach and propped her chin in cupped hands.

They were both very pretty, in a wild, ragged sort of way. On the cusp of being young women, they were about sixteen or seventeen years old. Seemingly untouched by current fashions, their skirts were long, falling to just above their ankles. Yet unlike Mary from the tearooms, whose dress clearly harked back to Victorian times, these young women wore panelled skirts of floral material. In fact, they were possibly made from old curtains or some other reused material. Their blouses were again unique to them, a hotchpotch of styles, and Martha's was secured with ribbon rather than buttons. Of course, they wore boots on their feet; already Lily had realised this was necessary here at Dungeness.

"Yes, I arrived yesterday, but it became so misty I couldn't see a thing." Lily glanced toward the sun, which although still low in the sky was now free from its shroud of mist. "But I've just been to the beach and I was wondering where the school is. My mother used to work there."

"The school?" Jennie frowned. "That's a fair way away. Would take an hour or more to reach it. We didn't go much, hardly worth the effort."

Martha grinned and nodded in agreement. "There was no one going to make us, was there, Jennie?"

It was while Lily pondered on this lack of commitment to education, she noticed lengths of stones on string beside the girls and recalled they had been swinging something through the air. Bending down, she pointed at the stones. "Are they hagstones? I have some of my own." Reaching into her pocket she pulled out her stones and held them on the palm of her hand.

"You got them from the beach," Martha stated. "For the wedding."

"And which did you choose? Which is your favourite?" Jennie asked.

"Oh, it was this one. The dark one." Lily slid the others back into her pocket. "But how did you know?"

"Evie would have sent you, if you didn't know to do it for yourself," Jennie replied.

"How *would* she know?" Martha pushed herself up so she was now sitting cross-legged on the stones. "She's never been here in her life and that teacher mother of hers wouldn't know of these things."

"I didn't know," Lily agreed. In fact, she still didn't know. She didn't have a clue as to why a hagstone must be chosen, other than it had something to do with the wedding. "What were you doing, swinging them around? Was it a dance?"

"A dance?" Martha's tone was scornful.

"She wouldn't know..." Jennie reminded. "No, we were chasing away the mist."

52

"And it worked." Martha pointed towards the sun. "It needs to be clear in the sky at noon, for the wedding. We needed to chase this mist away from Galloways."

"Galloways?" Lily queried. "You've said that before, but isn't Galloways just the one cottage, Joe's home? He's the one marrying today, but why talk of Galloways and not Dungeness?"

"It's all Galloways here," Jennie replied.

"And Dungeness around the point, where your ma was a teacher," Martha added.

"But I came to Dungeness; I came on a train from Ashford to Dungeness. I'd never heard of Galloways, not until I was told I could get a bed at the cottage. Galloways Cottage."

"You came by train to Galloways?" Jennie shook her head.

"Well, no, I came by train to Lydd and, rather than wait, I walked down the road to Dungeness."

"But you're not in Dungeness. You took the road to Galloways." The girls looked at Lily as if she was simple and then at each other, silently communicating their amusement.

"Yes, to Galloways Cottage at Dungeness."

"It's all Galloways," Jennie said. "There's not one called Galloways Cottage above any of the others."

"It's all Dungeness really," Martha added.

"Well, it's either one or the other," Lily snapped.

"The whole point, sticking out to sea, it's all Dungeness," Martha explained. "But to the east, round the point, there's Dungeness proper, where that ma of yours did her teaching. And closer still there's Denge and then here we are at Galloways. It's all the Ness and it's all Romney Marsh, although that hardly makes sense."

"There's no marsh hereabouts," Jennie added.

53

A memory came back to Lily. A memory of the man – Charlie was his name. It all seemed like so long ago, but it was only yesterday when he had told her she was on the wrong road for Dungeness. She had taken no notice, thinking she was in the right and he was treating her like some delicate young lady who couldn't walk a mile or two. If only he hadn't stood there, looking down at her, as if it was all so amusing. If he hadn't given the impression that it was all a joke and at her expense, she might have taken more notice of him.

Even her mother, Alice, had said there was no road to Dungeness. Lily had mocked the very thought of it. A seaside village with no road going to it! But now she saw that if Dungeness was anything like Galloways, then the twentieth century hadn't quite reached it yet.

Another memory came to Lily, that of the girl from the tearooms and the directions given. "But I was in the tearooms and I asked the way to Dungeness, and Mary told me..."

"Oh, it were Mary, she sent you this way, did she?"

Back in Galloways Cottage, or Evie's Cottage as Lily now tried to think of it, she was once again having tea pressed upon her.

"...And I hadn't realised I wasn't in Dungeness, well not the part of Dungeness I meant to be in," Lily tried to explain. But it seemed that Evie wasn't really listening, or not quite understanding Lily's distress.

"But you're here at Galloways and liking it," Evie stated. "You've been down to the beach and seen we've some fine boats there. And Joe's is one of the best, I'm telling you that."

"I have." Lily thought of the steep stony bank, the grey sea rolling in and the landscape which lacked bathing huts, a promenade, an ice-cream booth or a

54

tearoom.

"And you met Joe's cousins, Jennie and Martha, and thought them very nice."

"I did," Lily admitted. She had found them interesting, their ways seeming so different from those of other young women their age.

"You've a comfortable bed here; you slept well, so you said."

"It was very comfortable." Lily took another sip of the drink Evie called tea.

This was all very well, sitting here trying to be polite, but it was time to walk around the Point to Dungeness. She had arrived on Friday and was due to leave on Sunday; no more time should be wasted at Galloways now she realised her impetuous nature had led to her reaching the wrong settlement.

"So, you see, I really need to go to Dungeness if I am to see the school where Mother taught and meet some of the people she knew," Lily began to explain again.

"I've said our Joe will take you, but it's a fair trek." Evie topped up the teacup.

"You did, and it was very kind, but if I'm to return home on Sunday then I had best set off today." Lily paused before hastily adding, "I'm very happy here; you've been so welcoming. But it's not where I meant to be."

"Not where you're meant to be?" Evie murmured. "I don't know about that. There's a Galloways wedding and you don't know how pleased we are with a young woman like yourself coming along at just the right moment."

The wedding was so important for those who were keen she was to be a part of the celebration. Knowing it would appear so rude and she couldn't just walk off,

Lily cradled her warm teacup in her hands and allowed her eyelids to drop. She was feeling terribly tired again. If the wedding was at noon, she would stay for a little food afterwards, and if she set off within a couple of hours that would give her plenty of time to reach Dungeness by mid-afternoon.

"I've been thinking about what's to be done about your wedding costume." Evie came from behind the curtained area with a bundle of material in her arms. "It's not seemly to have your legs showing like this, not here in Galloways. Whatever they are doing in Ashford or these fashionable places, we stay with the old ways here. Women keep their legs mostly covered and the men respect that. At least my Joe will, him being brought up to treat a woman nicely."

Lily looked down at her smooth calves and tugged a little at the hem of her dress. "I've only got this dress, and a skirt and blouse in my case. The skirt is no longer." As she straightened herself, Lily's head began to spin, and she reached out to place her hand on the central table.

"I thought as much," Evie nodded, her eyes narrowing as she surveyed the youthful legs. "There's no point in thinking you'd fit into a skirt of mine, but my sister is not much bigger than you and so I've got one of her skirts. Good of her to lend it, but none of us want to see you not doing your best for this special day."

A skirt? A borrowed skirt. Lily tried to focus on Evie's words; surely there was no need... But the bundle was being pressed into her hands and Lily was forced to take it, and as she removed her hand from the stability of the table, she felt her world sway. The material fell loose before her and Lily saw a long skirt of a coarse woollen material. It was a dark grey in colour, with some

56

bands of black lace trailing down the stitched panels.

"She's been sewing away all morning, making it fancy." Evie's small brown hand reached out to the lace. "You'll look fine in that. Finer than most at a Galloways wedding."

"With my own blouse?" Lily tried to picture herself in her own blue blouse and this long skirt. And her boots, would she still wear boots at a wedding, or should she try to manage in her smart T-bar shoes? It all seemed so hard, so difficult to understand why they were making such a fuss of her. Why couldn't she just walk out and across the shingle ridges to Dungeness? But now it seemed as if whatever ailed her that morning had returned and Lily hardly felt fit to walk across the room, and certainly not able leave Galloways.

"And my own wedding shawl." Evie held up a creamy bundle; letting it fall open, she showed the delicate lacework, a little discoloured over the decades, but free from damage. "I wore this myself when I was not much older than Jennie and Martha."

"Your wedding shawl?" Lily began to sway as the lace moved before her eyes.

"Sit yourself down, my love, we've an hour before the sun is at its highest point." Evie took Lily's elbow to support her and pulled a chair out from the table. "You need a bit of Evie's fruit cake and a nice cup of tea. Set you up nicely that will."

It must have been an hour later when Lily left the cottage, supported on each side by Evie and her sister, Grace. She had been bundled into the skirt and blouse by the two women, who had fussed over her, tugging and tucking her blouse and borrowed skirt into place. Lifting her arms like a small child, she seemed unable to do anything but meekly follow their orders. They had dithered over her neat auburn waves, fretting at her hair not being long enough to be feminine, before covering it with the wedding shawl. This now seemed like more of a veil as it shielded the sun from Lily's eyes.

Why they hadn't just left her to sleep on the bed was unclear; Lily was desperately tired, and her body seemed to have no strength at all. Thoughts swam about and as she tried to put them into some order in her mind, they shifted again leaving her lost. She had a feeling that some fresh air and a cigarette would help restore normality, but Evie and Grace had not thought to place her bag in her hand. It was still on the chair in Joe's bedroom.

Wanting to ask for her bag, Lily tried to form a sentence in her mind before expressing the words, but it seemed to be impossible. She looked down at her boots and remembered her shoes; surely she should at least be wearing shoes. Again, she despaired of being able to say the words that were needed. Swept along by Evie's intention to have her at the wedding, Lily's feet moved mechanically over the gently undulating shingle, brushing past clumps of rough grass and low-lying plants. It appeared so important she was a part of Joe's wedding. The hospitality from Evie and Ivy was faultless as they immersed the visitor in Galloways life.

A stout pole was embedded in the shingle, standing upright, its tip reaching towards the sun. Unadorned and free from bends or blemishes, it was partially supported by additional stones at its base. Circling it from a distance of several yards were the people of Galloways: the females forming half the circle and the males the remainder.

An elderly man stood beside the pole. His beard was long and stained a yellow-brown about his mouth, the rest of it being made of coarse grey-black hair. He was thin to the point of being gaunt and, although his joints were crooked, he stood as tall as possible, supported by a walking stick. Dressed in black, the man was adorned with a string of hagstones, hanging low to the gentle mound of his stomach.

As they approached the small gathering of about thirty men, women and children, Lily saw the women part and a space was made for the three of them. For a moment all eyes were on Lily; it was as if they appraised her, silently absorbing her long skirt, the good blue blouse and Evie's own special shawl.

Jennie and Martha were there, trails of mismatched beads draped around their necks, adding further texture and colour to their outfits. The female relations who had been at Evie's the evening before turned towards her. Unsure of their names or positions within the family, Lily gave a weak smile. There was another familiar face and Lily frowned before she recalled who it belonged to; of course, it was Mary from the teashop.

The long black dress was gone, replaced with a neat grey skirt and high-necked blouse in a pale grey. The skirt fell to midway on Mary's slim calves and her buttoned boots shone from polishing. Although this was far from the height of fashion, it was now Lily's turn to feel out-dated in her ankle-skimming skirt borrowed from Joe's Aunt Ivy.

Of course, it was Mary who was to marry Joe. They all seemed so fond of her, pleased to hear Lily speak of their meeting and to report it was Mary who had led her to Galloways. Was this the reason the waitress had misled Lily: she wanted another witness to the wedding, for more people to be a part of it. Mary seemed a little young to be marrying, Lily mused. And what of the job in Lydd? She would miss it, no doubt. Or was she to walk there and back daily?

While these thoughts flitted about, Mary's gaze remained fixed on Lily. In fact, everyone seemed to be looking towards her. It must be because she was a stranger in this desolate place. No one really spoke, they just stood and waited, and whispered to each other occasionally. Lily swayed gently, still partially propped up between Evie and Ivy, her head feeling as if it had water circling within it.

No words were uttered as the central figure lifted his hand. All eyes were on him and everyone stood still, alert to his next move. With no wind, even the spiky broom and wispy grasses stood still and waited. Only a lone gull passed overhead and let its mocking cackle rip through the sky.

Chapter Six

"The sun has reached its peak." His voice was low yet reached everyone who circled him. "May the man, Joe, come forward."

With his head hung a little, eyes on the grey-brown stones at his feet, Joe moved to the centre at a steady pace. Just six steps and he stood with one hand resting on the pole.

"While the sun is at its peak, bring the woman forward."

Lily glanced at Mary, but Mary merely looked back, her expression vacuous. She looked towards Jennie and Martha; they too looked back at her, the merest hint of a smile on their faces. Then she felt it, the gentle push of a hand on her back. No, two hands, for both Evie and Ivy were pressing as if urging her forward.

With her head feeling as if all the earlier mist had descended upon it, Lily turned towards Evie, needing to ask what they wanted of her, but as her lips moved no words came.

"Step to the centre, my love," Evie urged. "All will be well."

"My legs are weak," Lily whispered.

"They will find the strength and my Joe will keep you steady; lean on his arm and you'll find him strong enough."

Looking towards Joe, Lily saw him tall and sturdy. Dressed in a suit, his muscular limbs were defined within the dark cloth. Brown hair was in neat waves and he looked to be freshly shaved. Joe's expression was empty, displaying nothing to offer the onlookers a hint of his thoughts. He looked at the pole or maybe beyond it, but not to any one person in the surrounding circle.

"While the sun is at its peak, the woman must step forward."

The pressure on Lily's back increased. "But why?" she whispered.

"Why not?" the low murmur came from Evie.

One step, then another. Now Lily was free from the comforting support of the older women. Two more steps and she stood vulnerable, pushed from the outer circle. Another step and she looked at Joe; he returned her gaze. Recalling his gentle manner on the beach and his kindness in preparing his room for her, Lily felt he represented a safe harbour following her expulsion from the circle. Unable to stand unsupported, she took the final steps, almost lurching into Joe's arms.

"Sorry," she muttered.

"Does this man support you in life?" the old man asked.

Lily straightened herself a little, removing some of the need for Joe to hold her. She reached for the pole; it held straight. "He does."

"And you'll care for this woman?"

Joe's voice was low, barely more than a whisper: "I'll care for her."

"Show me the stone you chose for this woman."

Reaching into his pocket, Joe withdrew a pure white stone with a hole worn straight through the centre. It was perfectly round, with a leather lace threaded through it. Lily was drawn to the pure beauty of the stone and reached to touch it with her fingertips.

"And the stone you chose for this man."

Lily recalled something Evie had thrust into her hand as they left the cottage and opened her clenched palm to reveal the long bullet of a black stone, now also threaded with a leather lace. Joe reached to touch the stone and nodded, recognising it from the time they met on the beach.

"With this holy hagstone, I bind this man to this woman. They chose the stones and chose each other and in Galloways tradition the stone will be worn about the neck." The old man's words flowed without pausing, gradually rising in volume and, as he spoke, the threaded stones were placed at first around Lily's neck and then Joe's. "And the union is now blessed by the circle of family who live here, at one and understanding the ways of the sea and shingle landscape of the Point. May the coming of Galloways young bring new life to us and keep our ways alive." Now he raised his arms to the sun and his voice became elated as the final words were uttered: "Celebrate this glorious day!"

Mesmerised by the words and feeling the cool of the stone pressing on her neck, Lily felt brave and free and elated. She thought nothing of the meaning of the words, only understanding that she was a part of something tremendous. Facing her, Joe now had both hands supporting her at the elbows. She knew without his solid form before her, she would crumple and fall upon the stones. Her world was hazy and body weak.

"The sun has passed its midway point and we are done," the old man cried out.

Then the circle of Galloways family began to hum and the hum turned into a wail, which in turn began to form into a chant. The words were unclear, but it didn't seem to matter. It was as if a lightning charge ran through them; they were all-powerful. Gradually they closed in on Joe, Lily and the old man, and the chant

63

ricocheted in Lily's head. The feeling of joy turned to fear, for they were so close and so loud; then it stopped. Without warning, there was silence.

Lily looked up at Joe; now his arms were wrapped around her. "We're done now," he said, and then, for some curious reason, he bent down and kissed her gently on the forehead.

Joe carried her back across the stones. Lily wasn't entirely sure why; he clearly recognised she was ill although exactly what ailed her was a mystery. And then he was gone, and she was left feeling strangely bereft. She was ushered into a chair in Evie's cottage and a cup of grey tea was pressed into her hands. The tea was no better than before, but Lily found herself almost grateful, suddenly aware her mouth was dry.

With the mists gone, Lily saw the cottage in daylight for the first time. Not only were the shutters open, but the front door was pushed back against the outer plank wall and secured in place with a pile of pebbles. Shafts of light showed the wear in the textiles and wooden furniture, but also that the room was clean and in a good state of repair despite its being a humble home.

The older women were filling the table with the dishes of Evie's rabbit pie, stacks of sliced bread and butter and a variety of cakes. Somehow a second smaller table had been squeezed alongside and the women brought in plates, cutlery, glasses and mugs. As fast as the kettle boiled on the range, teapots were filled. Bottles of wine and other alcoholic drinks in unlabelled bottles jostled for position.

While the wedding feast was being prepared, Jennie and Martha fussed around Lily asking her any number of questions about her life in Ashford. Lily replied as best she could, not really thinking about her responses and often reaching to feel the unfamiliar weight of the cool white hagstone at her neck. How kind of Joe to find one of pure white, knowing that it would be a favourite.

"Where is Joe?" Lily wondered out loud. "Where are the men? Have they gone fishing now the mist has gone?"

"Fishing!" Martha laughed.

"They're at The Sailor," Jennie informed. "The British Sailor. It's tradition of course."

"Galloways tradition," Lily murmured, thinking of the sun high in the sky, the old man who stood by the pole, and the feeling that something momentous had happened.

The men returned not long afterwards, every one of them smelling of ale and tobacco. They queued up, piled plates with rabbit pie, and sprawled on the land outside the cottage. Then the women took their turn and Lily, her stomach gnawing with hunger, placed gravy-rich pie on her plate.

The sun blessed the stones with a comforting warmth; cushions and blankets were strewn upon the ground. And so the area between the six Galloways cottages became the place for the people to eat and drink, talk and sing, and later dance until the chill in the air drove the men back to The British Sailor and the women to their homes.

It wasn't until after the dishes had been washed up and the living space tidied that Lily recalled her intention to leave for Dungeness by mid-afternoon. Galloways-brewed wine had flowed throughout the afternoon and Lily's brain struggled to send the messages needed to enable her limbs to move in any rational order. Of course she still suffered from whatever illness had descended upon her and Evie was kindly plying her with more tea, which was comforting. Time had passed by in rather a blur and now, with the sun departing beyond the distant Sussex hills, it was too late to consider a trek across the shingle. There was always tomorrow…

After a sleep of indeterminate time, it seemed that it must be bedtime. The lamps were now low, and Evie had gone perhaps out to the privy or to see a neighbour. Or perhaps she was just settled behind her curtained-off area. Joe kindly lifted Lily to the bedroom and turned his back while she unfastened her clothes and slipped her nightdress on. Then she lay facing the plank wall while Joe changed into his nightshirt. It was all a bit odd; there must be some reason why he could no longer stay with his uncle. But what of his bride? Lily tried to ask about that, but somehow the words stayed muddled in her head and she knew they could never leave her lips in any sensible order.

"It doesn't seem right, not with you like this," Joe murmured, as he slipped under the covers beside her and cradled Lily's head to his broad chest.

Lily woke to find herself pressed against the slightly damp wall; something warm and solid was preventing her from turning and stretching out in the bed. She lay perfectly still, apart from her heart which thudded at an alarming pace within her slim body.

She was at Galloways and had been terribly ill the day before. Confusing images emerged, undefined and incomplete fragments of memories. But her thoughts became disturbed by a new realisation: it was not silent in the room; there was the sound of someone else sleeping and it was the bulk of that person's body keeping Lily confined within this small space. Of course, it was Joe who had supported her during her times of extreme weakness the day before.

But this was all wrong; he shouldn't be here. Yesterday had been his wedding day. Who had he married? It had been her, Lily, who had stood beside him while words were said in the Galloways tradition? And here he was, beside her in the bed... But there had been no vicar and she hadn't consented. At least she didn't recall...

Then came another sensation: she needed to use the privy and soon. Inch by inch Lily shuffled to the base of the bed; Joe snored and threw his arm out but continued to sleep. As the last of her body slithered onto the floor, Lily crouched for a moment, her heart still pounding. Then she stood, reached for her woollen coat, and slipped it over her nightdress. Her boots were on the floor and she picked them up, tucking them under one arm.

Outside the sky was lightening to the east; there was a misty rain driving in from the sea and already settling on Lily's coat. She was poised to press the latch and step back into the cottage when a vision of Joe's sleeping bulk came to her. How could she return to the bed in which, for whatever reason, Joe was now sleeping? Her mind was still sluggish but, as she breathed in the salty-sweet night air, it became less befuddled.

What was she doing here in Galloways, in the bed of a strange man? Had she been part of some strange ritual the afternoon before, or was it that some illness had caused her mind to become confused? Whatever had brought her to Galloways, and led her to remain here, it now seemed clear there was something very odd going on. She had been invited into Evie's home,

67

fussed over and made comfortable, but now Lily felt it was almost as if she had been held against her will. She had said she was meant to be at Dungeness and yet they had insisted on her staying. It had all been very polite and nothing was too much bother as they cared for her, but it seemed almost sinister.

What had been wrong with Lily to stop her mind from placing all its thoughts in some kind of order? Why had her body seemed so weak and unable to stride off across the shingle in the direction of Dungeness? Whatever had ailed her, the mists in her mind were now clearing and her body was gaining strength.

Suddenly it all became clear and Lily turned away from the cottage door. She must leave immediately, without hesitation. By returning to take her bag, Evie or Joe were bound to be disturbed and Lily now understood that they wanted to hold her here. For what reason, she was still unclear, but they meant to keep her here. Galloways bride – where had those words come from? She was unsure but it felt as if she were to be tethered to this strange place and, unless she moved on before dawn, it may well be too late.

Lily walked towards the coast, for it was hardly suitable to return to Lydd in her nightdress, and neither could she set off aimlessly across the shingle. Unhindered by her case, she scurried along the best she could, wanting to put a fair distance between herself and the cottages before sunrise. Within minutes Lily was passing the coastguards' cottages and felt a little of the tension ease from her body as they merged into the misty rain behind her. Now she was on the bank where the fishing boats lay beached, awaiting their next trip out. She turned towards the east, planning to follow the shingle beach-top ridge until she reached Dungeness. How to explain her arrival there was as yet undecided, but Lily could only hope to find someone who would understand her need to leave Evie and Joe.

As the sun rose it was merely a glow behind a veil of misty rain. To Lily, watching its progress upwards, it was a sign of time passing. Would they have discovered her missing by now? She felt sure of it. And would they accept her departure or set off to search for her, perhaps with the intention of forcing a return to Galloways? She must press on, despite the way her boots slipped on the stones and her body feeling as if all energy had been wrung out of it.

It was the type of rain which did not invigorate a person and, although seemingly lacking in quantity, it steadily soaked. With her head down and sodden nightdress pressed against damp calves, Lily's mind stayed clear of thoughts as she concentrated on the physical act of walking. Her head was not yet able to think beyond this moment. The distance increased between Lily and Galloways, and another set of timber cottages began to materialise from the gloom.

"Dungeness?" Lily murmured. "No, they said it was further; there was somewhere else first."

Lily couldn't remember the name of the place and it hardly mattered. If possible, it looked to be even smaller than Galloways. Her instincts said to shy away, to avoid the people of this settlement. Lily began to negotiate the steep bank with the intention of walking, out of sight, along the shoreline. But something alerted her to it being different here. Where were the fishing boats? The Galloways boats had been on the beach, and so it seemed unlikely that these would be out. And with the sun now making steady progress on its upward path, surely the people would be starting their day? Yet no smoke poured from the chimney stacks. Could this place be deserted? Could it be a place to rest her exhausted body?

On nearing it, even through the veil of rain, it became clear this was an abandoned settlement. The cottages at Galloways were simple, yet well maintained. Here windows were empty eye-sockets, black and sightless, with shutters hanging lopsided or slumped on the ground. Chimney stacks ended with ragged tops, some rising no higher than rooflines on which the thin timbers showed, their coverings whipped away by the wind.

With her legs aching from battling across the stones, and head still unable to focus on any one thought and reason with it, Lily took her first steps towards the tumbledown shacks. She had reached the place called Denge. Once a small fishing village, not unlike Galloways, it had been deserted since the time of her mother's visit to the area, back in the 1890s. Knowing nothing of the history of the place, only sensing a need to hide away until some of her energy was regained, Lily pressed on the latch of one of the smaller cottages; one that seemed to have its roof still intact.

Standing on the threshold, Lily viewed the one-room shack. Nearly all its contents had either been removed by the previous occupants or taken by scavengers when they left. The fireplace was a lifeless void; floorboards were cracked and rotting. A couple of broken chairs, skeletons of their former selves, were slumped in the corner and ragged curtains of indeterminate colour or pattern hung without grace at the windows. A rusty pan and some broken crockery were strewn upon the floor alongside a tangle of netting. The room smelt of salt and seaweed. To the exhausted and bewildered newcomer, it was a haven.

70

Lily removed her thick woollen coat, which although sodden on the outside was barely damp against her skin, and laid it on the cleanest patch of floorboards, against a wall with no window or doorway. She fumbled with her boot laces and removed her boots. Her nightdress from above her knees to her ankles was wringing wet, but all she could do was suffer this discomfort. Lily's need for sleep was great; the grey Galloways tea still flowed in her veins and dulled her senses, although its effects were lessening as every hour passed.

It was two hours later when the door to the shack opened and a woman gave a stifled scream on seeing the body of a young woman lying there on the floorboards.

Chapter Seven

"Oh, my God, I thought you were dead, lyin' there like that!" The words poured from the woman standing at the doorway. She held her shawl tight about her slim body, pale hands clutching at the folds. "Oh, Lord above," she continued, "this ain't no place to be sleepin'. Are you ill or something?"

"I'm not sure," Lily replied, raising herself to a sitting position. "I've not been well; I know that much."

"Well, if you're not, you'll soon get yourself a chill lying in the damp with your clothes all wet." The woman took a step closer and reached down to touch the wet cotton of the nightdress which hung about Lily's ankles. "Sheltering from the rain were you?"

"I… I had to stop," Lily faltered, unsure of what to say. "And I came across this… this hut."

"But this ain't no place to be out havin' a walk, not for a young woman like yourself." Now the woman knelt on the floor, grey eyes wide in her gaunt face. "Not for someone who talks quite posh, if you don't mind me sayin'."

"Do I?" Lily mused. "I didn't realise."

"Not posh like real posh, but like a teacher or something."

Frowning to herself, Lily tried to collect her thoughts, having been roused from a deep sleep. Her body felt chilled and stiff. She needed dry clothes and the heat from a fire, that was clear enough. She pulled her arms back into her coat, but it gave little comfort, and ran her hands through her thick hair.

The woman knelt within arm's reach, a shaft of light from the doorway highlighting the threadbare patches on her coat and the pattern in the knitted shawl. "Can you get up? Are you strong enough?" She placed her hand on Lily's arm and as she did so, her shawl slipped from her head revealing thick red hair, flecked with grey and tied back in a loose bun. She was about the same age as Lily's own mother, yet life had been harder for her, Lily reflected.

"I think so. I walked all this way, so I am sure I can stand now." Lily raised herself until she stood, supported a little by the stranger. "I ache, in fact I thought I was ill, influenza maybe. But now I'm not too sure; I really don't know what was wrong." She bent to rub her cold legs and stared in dismay at her nightdress. "What must you think of me? I forgot I hadn't dressed. I just had to get away."

"This is no place to run to," the woman replied. "You need some warm clothes and I've a daughter about your size. She's got nothing posh, but you must have something dry to wear, and the sooner the better."

"I was going to Dungeness," Lily offered.

"I'm going back there myself, so you'd best come along. What's your name? You can trust me with it. I know what it's like to be scared and away from home. I won't do you no harm."

"I'm Lily."

"Lily. That's a lovely name. I'm Emily." The woman smiled and it softened the lines in her pale skin. "Emily Brooks, but you must call me Emily; we don't do Mister and Missus around here. We'll take a slow walk back to Dungeness and you can tell me about what brought you here."

They walked in silence for some time. Emily led the way, walking inland, following no obvious track yet clearly knowing exactly where she was going. The misty rain was still carried on a light wind; it was as if the headland was covered in a fine gauze. The sun remained a pale-yellow ball of soft light and everywhere else was varying shades of grey, with the occasional patches of dull green looming before them on the ground. The mournful wails of gulls and scrunch on the shingle were punctuated by another sound: the rhythmic blast of a foghorn.

"Where have you walked from, Lily?"

"Galloways," Lily replied. "I meant to go to Dungeness, but…"

"And how long have you been at Galloways?"

"How long?" Lily thought of the hours sitting drinking the grey tea, the blur of other people coming and going as they celebrated Joe's wedding, the man standing and calling for the woman to come forward, the strings of hagstones being whirled through the air. "How long? I am sure it was just a day or two, yet it seems like longer. I felt so ill, so tired, and everything became such a muddle."

"And now, is your head clearing?"

"It's like a sea-mist inside." Lily looked towards Emily. Somehow she knew the older woman would lead her to safety.

"And they looked after you nicely at Galloways, did they?"

"They gave a me a decent bed, food and plenty of tea..."

"But you took ill when you were there, did you?" Emily's tone became a little sharp. "You were all right before and then you had a turn for the worse?"

"I was absolutely fine." Lily couldn't be sure. It was

all so muddled, but she must have been, or she wouldn't have set out on such an adventure.

"And they gave you tea, did they?"

"Grey tea," Lily confirmed, picturing the cup of liquid held in her hands. "I think I asked for brown tea, normal tea, but it seemed to be all they had."

"They gave you their special tea." Emily shook her head. "An' they kept you there, against your wishes."

"I don't know." Lily's heart slumped. "I just don't know."

"We won't talk about it no more." Emily laid her thin hand on Lily's coat sleeve. "Look, there's the lighthouse, and the station. You're at Dungeness now and we'll soon have you safe and warm."

Raising her head, Lily saw the black bands of a lighthouse through the rain and gradually the whole tall and gently tapering shape came into focus. Having looked no further than the stones at her feet, a natural curiosity now spurred Lily to concentrate on the other shapes which materialised. Huts or cottages, some looking to be solid buildings of brick or stone and others reminding her of the wooden shed-style homes seen before at Galloways. A building with a curved top sat high on a shingle bank – could this be the railway station?

They were now walking close to the lighthouse and passed an odd circular building. "The old lighthouse were there, with its ring of keepers' cottages below," Emily informed on noting Lily's interest. "This one here," she said, looking upwards, "this one was new just twenty years ago, back in 1904. You should have seen it being built, it were ever so interesting and my Ed, he got some work there, which gave us a bit of extra money and we used it wisely, building onto the cottage."

"It's very tall," Lily said. Her thoughts were not quite

75

in order yet. Any more was too hard.

"Look at me, chattering away. Your head will be all of a muddle if they've been pressing that grey tea on you." Emily reached out and patted Lily on the shoulder. "We'll have plenty of time to talk when you're warm and dry with some food in your belly. Now we've a bit further to go. Ed and me, we live down by The Pilot, at the far end."

As they moved away from the lighthouse, the buildings became sparse. Now Lily became aware of a rhythmic slapping of the sea on the beach and roar of stones being pulled back with the tide. They were walking not far from the shoreline and at times the sound of the sea seemed all invasive within the young woman's fragile mind. On and on they trudged, seeming to move further from Dungeness until finally she asked, "I thought we were going to Dungeness, with the lighthouse and..."

"Oh, we are, it's just a bit spread out. There's the lighthouse and keepers' cottages and a few of the newcomers in their railway carriage homes, then along here it's the fishermen. See the boats up on the ridge? They'll be going out later. The men are probably at church now, praying for a good catch."

"Is it Sunday?" Lily frowned; would her family be at church? Would they be thinking of her and wondering how she was enjoying her little holiday by the sea? Mother was right, it suddenly dawned on her that there was no road here. At least she hadn't seen one yet.

They reached a ragged row of wooden-plank homes, much the same as those at Galloways. The main buildings had various extensions and there were smaller buildings too: no doubt water closets, store rooms and some of rather odd shapes giving Lily no clue as to what their use was. Emily led them towards

76

a cottage with planks stained black from tar; grey window frames were evenly spaced either side of a matching front door. The roof came low, with the eaves covering a narrow veranda at the front. It was an attractive home, with an extension on the side, possibly built from the money earned by Ed Brooks during his time working on the lighthouse.

"Don't you worry about meeting anyone. Ed has gone to help young Edward with his new home; he's married with a daughter of his own. And Allie, well, she's courting a nice young man from Lydd." Emily pressed on the latch and the door opened outwards, allowing them to step into a long rectangular living area.

Pausing in the doorway, Lily let her eyes become accustomed to the dim light. To the left was a traditional black range sitting within a wide brick fireplace; the recesses either side were filled with deep cupboards and shelving. Crockery was lined up in an orderly fashion; earthenware jars and colourful tins stood in neat rows. Emily went to the range and moved the kettle onto a hot plate.

"Now, love, you just sit on one of them chairs for a moment and I'll fetch you one of Allie's outfits. It won't be special, mind, and she keeps taking up her hems, but it will be better than a wet nightdress." Emily nodded towards the central table surrounded by mismatched wooden chairs, then disappeared through a doorway to the rear of the room, opposite the front door.

Lily slumped at the table and reached down to unlace her boots. Emily returned with a grey skirt and a white blouse, then placed them on the table before going through another doorway. "I'll give you one of my shawls." She returned with a dark blue bundle and Lily smiled her thanks.

"Now, with young Edward gone, you can settle in

his bed for a nice sleep after you've put something warm in your belly. I'll pop a brick in the range to warm through and that will air the bed while you have a nice bowl of this soup I made yesterday." Emily placed a pan on the range and a brick in the oven, seeming to do it in one fluid movement. Then she was pouring hot water in a jug and bustling back across the room. "Follow me and you can have a nice wash, then put them clean clothes on."

Stepping through into a small square of an inner hallway, Lily followed Emily to the right and into a narrow bedroom, one of two running along the seaward length of the cottage. The room was sparse but had a narrow bed, with thick blankets inviting the occupant to have a comfortable sleep. There was a pine chest of drawers, a row of hooks on the wall and a washstand where the jug was placed. Lily's toes sank into a colourful rag rug and some amateur seascapes adorned the walls.

"Oh Lord, you're in a nightdress with no underwear to speak of!" Emily's words gushed out. "I'll get you some and nightwear too, and you can choose what's best. Thank goodness I have my Allie still at home." Then she was gone, and Lily removed her coat, placing it on one of the hooks.

When she awoke, many hours later, Lily had lost all sense of how much time had passed. For a few minutes she lay savouring the warmth and comfort of the bed. Gazing at the seascapes, she wondered if they had been painted by the previous occupant, Edward, now a young man and a father. She could hear the sea crashing on the nearby beach, withdrawing and plunging forwards again. Another sound caught her attention: low voices could be heard in the living room.

78

Someone had returned, probably Emily's husband, Ed. What would he think of her arrival?

Cautiously, Lily pulled herself up into a sitting position. Her head no longer felt full of the mist. She had good soup and brown tea in her stomach; tealeaves bought from the shop in Lydd, Emily had assured her! She couldn't lie about here all day and so Lily eased herself out of the bed until she stood, toes buried in the rag rug. Her body felt a little weary, but so much better than when the Galloways tea swam about her veins.

Having dressed in clothes belonging to Allie, whom she might meet later, Lily pulled the shawl about her body for comfort as well as warmth and moved towards the voices in the living room.

"Oh, there she is." Emily's slim face filled with a smile as she looked towards the open door. "Come along in, love. It's only my Ed here and he might look fierce but he's as gentle as they come."

The man rose to his feet; his hair was salt-and-pepper coloured, coarse and unruly. Eyebrows met over dark eyes, which crinkled at the edges when he smiled. His beard was thick but trimmed neatly into shape. "Good to meet you, Lily. I hear you've been drinking the Galloways Grey and it has you in a muddle."

"I'm feeling a lot better now," Lily replied, a little shy of this tall man. "I didn't know..."

"Of course, you didn't." Emily reached for the teapot. "Now sit yourself down in a comfy chair by the range; I'll come and sit beside you and you can tell us exactly how you came to be at Galloways."

"It was my mother..." Lily began the tale which led to her impetuous journey to Lydd, the meeting of Mary in the café and the walk to Galloways. "Even some man I met tried to tell me to catch the train, but I thought I

79

knew better than Mother, who hadn't been here in over twenty-five years."

"We all do foolish things from time to time," Emily smiled. "Even us old folk who seem so set in our ways now."

"But your mother..." Ed leaned forward in his chair, as if to study Lily's features. "We knew her, if she were the young teacher here, Alice, back at the end of the last century."

"I was wondering if you might have done." Lily's eyes widened at the thought of meeting people her mother knew from the days before she was born. "I guess everyone knew who the teacher was in a small place like this."

"Oh, it was more than that, your mother and Tom, well they helped us no end." Emily continued the story, "If it hadn't been for them, I don't know what would have happened to me and Ed. We was in a bad way."

"Tell the girl later."

"Of course, it's too much," Emily agreed. "But our Allie, whose clothes you're wearing, she was named after your mother and of course she wrote and told us about you and your brothers. But when I heard the name Lily, I never suspected. I wouldn't, would I? Not with you being at Galloways and in a right old state."

"You named your daughter after my mother? I had no idea!" Already Lily had seen how different life here in Dungeness would have been for her mother. With Alice not offering any stories of her own, it would be down to Lily to learn more of the year spent here. "I'd like to see the school. I know it's by the railway tracks."

"You'll stay tonight, won't you? Mrs Stubbs who worked with your ma, she is retired now. A Miss Coombes is headteacher now. Hazel Barton teaches there a couple of times a week and a young woman assists them, just like when Alice was there." Emily gazed into the distance, as if seeing it all. "We were younger than you, me and Alice. What a time we had, but it all worked out for the best in the end. I thought she'd stay, become one of us, but it wasn't to be." Then Emily was up, tipping the leaves from the pot and rinsing cups and plates at the sink. "We'll go along to the school tomorrow. If we're lucky then the rain will clear, and you'll see a bit of the place."

"She's best off on the train to Ashford soon as possible." Ed's voice was low but commanded the women's attention. "We don't know what they wanted from her at Galloways and she's better out of Dungeness altogether. In fact, I'll take her to Lydd myself in the morning. I want to see the girl on that train and off Romney Marsh."

"It seems a shame if Lily can't see the place after all she's been through to get here." Emily's face fell. "But he's got a point. You're not safe here."

"Thank you." Lily no longer felt as brave as she had done when she set out from Ashford only two days beforehand. "I think you're right, but I would have loved to meet some people who knew Mother and see the places she knew. It's best to go home though. I'll package Allie's clothes up and send them back. Mine are left at Galloways; I won't see them again."

It was warm sitting by the range; Ed had turned to his newspaper and Emily was busy in the kitchen area. Lily began to unwrap the shawl from her shoulders and pulled herself upright in the chair; she really must offer to help Emily with something. Her movement caused Ed to glance in her direction and she noted his eyebrows knit together as he spotted the hagstone at her neckline.

"God above, what's that around the girl's neck?" His

81

voice was low, yet it caused fear to clutch at Lily's heart and his wife turned, her face paling as she knew there was trouble to come.

Rising from his chair and taking a step towards Lily, Ed Brooks leaned forward, towering over her. His huge hand reached out and, as he took the pure white hagstone between his fingers, his face was a picture of horror. Lily's heart raced and her body threatened to tremble. He only held the stone for a second before stepping back as if it had scalded him. Then he turned to his wife and spat out the words:

"My God, Emily, did you not know she was a Galloways bride?"

Chapter Eight

"I couldn't take it off," Lily put a hand to the stone. "The knots..."

"Of course you can't take it off; you're bound to Galloways," Ed's voice was rough with disgust. He turned to his wife, "Did she not tell you she was wed to one of them?"

"She was sick, Ed. Drugged up with the tea, I didn't know, and I never thought to ask."

"But the stone..."

"I didn't see it, Ed." Emily's voice was high, desperate. "How could she be wed to one of them? She only just arrived. I didn't see the stone."

"Well, she is, and there's nothing more to say about it. She'll have to go back."

Listening to the exchange, Lily felt her body tighten as fear gripped her. Memories of a ceremony, Joe's wedding ceremony, flashed in no particular order through her head. The central pole and the figure who called for the man and woman to come forward, the stones chosen on the beach, the chanting. And the next morning, Joe there in her bed. But it was all so hazy and she hadn't thought... hadn't connected it all together. How could they be married? Something was wrong. Of course, she must tell them.

"No, I'm not," Lily began. It was a struggle for the words to come, her mouth was so dry and her throat tight. "There was no church, not even a vicar, just some man and… and a pole." It all sounded so ridiculous, so unnecessary to even have this conversation.

"The elder of the village. Old Wilfred Black it would be at the moment," Ed informed, his voice sounding just a little less harsh. "You don't need no vicar or church at Galloways; they do it their own way and we accept it hereabouts."

Lily pulled at the knot, "I'll undo it, and no one will know. It's just a stone." Her fingers worked at the leather lace, "It's just so stiff, I can't… but we could cut it?"

Emily moved to the arm of Lily's chair, cradling the young woman in her arms, "Did you go to the beach and choose a stone?"

"Evie sent me," Lily admitted. "She didn't say why, I picked up several to take home to Mother. But there was one, a long black bullet of a stone which I rather liked and that was the one they put on a lace."

"And is there a man at Galloways who wears a stone chosen by you?" Emily asked.

"It must be Joe, I had to give him the stone."

"And he gave you this stone?" Emily's tone was soft and she reached out to the pure white sphere.

"He did and I thought it was beautiful; it *is* beautiful," Lily's eyes began to fill with tears. "I didn't know, Emily, really I didn't. It was his wedding day. Surely it had been planned weeks beforehand?"

"It was planned the moment a pretty young woman turned up unexpectedly at Galloways," Ed said, his tone bitter. He turned away from the women and pulled a coat from the stand. "I feel sorry for you, Lily. They've done you wrong, but you've a husband back at Galloways and you've no choice but to return to him. He's a decent man is Joe; you could have done a lot worse. Emily will dry your clothes and perhaps walk back with you to smooth things over and that will be it. We'll see you again no doubt and you'll have friends in us. But now you do your duty to your man at Galloways." And having made the longest speech of his life, Ed closed the door behind him leaving the two women to themselves.

No tears flowed from Lily's eyes. She just sat, with Emily still holding her. Neither of them spoke for some time until Lily blurted out, "I'm not going back there. I'll just leave now and walk to Lydd and I'll find my way home."

"You can't, love, they'll be searching for you along the coast and in Lydd."

"But I didn't mean to marry. I can't be his wife," Lily's voice grew stronger as the anger took hold of her. "I won't be his wife, not just because of this stone at my neck. Help me cut it off, Emily. If you don't, I'll do it myself. I'll not go back there."

"Don't worry about Ed, he's fearful of doing wrong and we respect the way of those who live round the Point, just like they respect ours." Emily stood and went to fetch a knife from a drawer in the dresser. "We live in much the same way as they do, but they have their ways and we have ours. Ed don't want no trouble. Now, I've got this knife and we can cut the stone off, but it don't make you unmarried, not when all them people witnessed it. And he spent the night in your bed, or you spent the night in his, to be more truthful."

"I did." Lily slumped.

"And did he...?" Emily crouched down before Lily. "Did he touch you, love?"

"I... I don't know..." Her eyes filled with tears. Anger was replaced with trepidation.

Tears ran unchecked. Yet Lily drew comfort from

85

Emily kneeling before her. The older woman said nothing as she reached in her pocket for a clean hanky and received a half-smile of appreciation. Finally, as Lily's breathing calmed and the tears abated, Emily moved to a side table and poured some port into a small glass.

"This will calm you," she said, wrapping Lily's fingers around the stem. "Now hold it steady and take a sip."

Emily slipped her fingers between the lace and the back of Lily's neck, then placed the knife so the cool metal rested on Lily's skin and the blade took the leather lace between its teeth. She moved it to and fro several times before the lace was severed and Lily felt a release from the pressure of the stone about her neck. She let the stone fall into her lap and then picked it up. Curiously, she was still drawn to its simple beauty and so she placed it in her pocket.

"He'll calm down." Emily put the knife back in the dresser. "We'll have another talk and keep you here safe. You'll be lonely though, there will be no going out and seeing the old places your mother knew. No one must know you're here. They'll be looking for you, I'm sure of it."

Lily's bedroom window looked directly out onto the shingle bank sloping down to the beach. Pulling back the thick curtain, she saw the new day brought a different view from the previous one. Fine rain and misty skies were gone, now replaced by clouds racing high across a blue sky. Waves tore at the tideline spraying white horses, which galloped with heady excitement amongst scattered shells and driftwood. Closer to the cottage a tumble of netting careered along from the direction of the Point, came to an abrupt halt against succulent sea kale, paused, lurched upwards and continued its path.

Mesmerised by this bright new day, Lily stood in her nightdress and shawl, barefoot on the wooden floor. The air, whistling around where glass met window frame, was laden with the scents of the sea and streamed relentlessly into the room. For Lily it was as if she saw life with new eyes; the final haze caused by the grey tea had lifted and she was eager to explore Dungeness, to meet those who remembered her mother and to return to Ashford exhilarated by her adventure. But of course this wasn't to be.

Ed had agreed to Emily's plea for them to protect the young woman, daughter of Alice. He had returned home, worrying he had been too harsh and fearing he had driven her back to Galloways. Lily could stay; she must stay. But no one could know and so she was confined to the home, unable to fulfil her desire to discover the area.

And so it was with mixed feelings Lily turned away from the window. She was relieved, of course she was. But now she remained trapped in another place, a loving home with kind people, but another kind of prison, nonetheless. Her spirits, lifted by the energy of the sea and wind, slumped as she pulled on the borrowed clothes.

The white hagstone nestled in her pocket. Lily allowed her fingers to wrap around it for a moment. She wondered about the man who they said was her husband; did her betrayal hurt? He seemed to be such a gentle man. Hazy memories remained of him on the beach, looking down at the hagstones in her upturned palm, and later him carrying her in his arms so she needn't struggle on the stones. He had been a part of her being befuddled by the grey tea, but Lily was sure there was no malice in his soul.

Allie, the girl named after Lily's mother, was spooning porridge into her mouth. At twenty-four years of age, she had been born just a month before Lily. Unmarried, she was another young woman from this generation who did not yet have a brood of young children at her skirts. They had compared the stories of their lives the evening before and Lily learned of a fiancé who had died in the trenches, and then of a new love who worked as a guard on the steam train.

"Did you sleep well, Lil?" Allie asked, turning and offering a warm smile. Dressed in a long black skirt and white blouse she was ready for a day's work at the tearoom.

"I feel so much better." Lily poured herself a cup of tea. Already she was feeling at home with this lovely family. "I just wish I could go out and explore. The rain has passed, and I can see the sea from the bedroom window."

"We've got to keep you safe." Allie tucked wisps of dark hair back into the bun at the nape of her neck. "It won't be for long; you don't want to go back to that husband of yours."

"He doesn't feel like a husband," Lily replied.

"It was that grey tea, had you all of a muddle. Lovely man that Joe is, though, ever so handsome, don't you think?"

"I barely saw him; he was tall and gentle, I remember that." Lily frowned, trying to recall a clear image of the man whose hagstone she still carried in her pocket. "Handsome? Yes, I suppose he was."

"He's a lovely bloke, but don't you go telling my Ernie!" Allie pushed back her chair. "Well, I'm off to work, and Ma said to tell you she's out doing the laundry at the copper."

"I wish I could help, anything to get out and see

something of Dungeness."

"There's nothing but a copper full of soapy water in a shed, and a load of gossiping women!"

Lily grinned. "The tearoom then, I'd love to come along and have a cup of tea and a buttered teacake in this railway carriage tearoom. What a place to work in!"

"Better than the washhouse!" Allie laughed as she pulled on her coat. "I'm sure you'll be along in a day or so but until then best get on with that sewing. You're welcome to my skirt and blouse but you'll want a change in a day or so."

Lily looked across to the bundle of woollen material she and Allie had cut out the evening before. "That will keep me busy and then I've an old blouse of your mother's to alter. I'm sure to have a new outfit by the time you come home."

The day passed by with Lily seeing all she could of Dungeness life from the comfort of the armchair with sewing on her lap. Emily came to and fro with tales from the washhouse. Ed appeared, slapped some fish on the side, muttered something about things to do and was gone again. The skirt took shape and was eventually complete; to show respect for the Brooks family, Lily left the hem at least three inches longer than the norm for her. Now she worked on reshaping an old blouse. Emily had said something about gathering kale and when the front door opened again Lily expected to see her narrow black boots as she glanced up from her sewing. Instead her throat tightened, and mouth went dry at the sight of a pair of pointed black and white two-tone shoes.

"'Ello Lily, my love. You going to make me a nice cuppa as I've come on the train and walked across all this damned shingle to sort out this bleeding mess you've got yourself in?"

Lily's eyes travelled up his stocky legs clad in

slightly shiny black material, to his ample waistline, broad shoulders and neatly slicked hair. She said nothing in reply. What should she say? How... how could this man... Charlie, was that his name? She thought it was. How could he help her and where was Emily? Or Ed?

"Got yourself in a right mess." He removed his jacket, slinging it over a wooden chair, and sat in the armchair by the range, legs outstretched, looking as if he was in his own living room. "Should have caught the train, not gone and got yourself married." A huge grin spilled over Charlie's face and he shook his head slightly. "Bloody foolish thing to do."

Lily said nothing. She merely put down the needle and placed the blouse on a side table.

"Not too strong, three sugars, milk and a splash of cold water." He got up and paced towards the range, then moved the kettle across to the hot plate. "There, I've given you a helping hand."

"Why..." but as the word came from Lily, the door opened again, and Ed strode in.

"Sorry about that, Charlie. Lily, I hear you've met before; came as a surprise when he told me."

"I don't miss much of what's going on in Lydd, you know that Ed." Charlie slouched back in the chair. "Now, Lil's making the tea and we'll have a chat."

Ed pulled out a chair from the table and explained to Lily, "We're at a loss as how to help, Lily. You know that. You're wed and it's as good as legal and Charlie agrees."

"Charlie agrees?" Lily repeated.

"My Ma's Ma came from Galloways; in fact she and Ma were both married in the old tradition even though the family moved to Lydd a few years beforehand."

"So you know about it all." Lily filled the teapot and

90

set out three cups.

"And with him being a solicitor," Ed continued. "I thought I'd have a word."

A solicitor? This man who appeared to be a market trader or perhaps a travelling salesman, with a briefcase of women's nylons. No, a solicitor had a hint of the Victorian era about him. A solicitor was a man who still wore a top hat and a suit jacket with tails. Exactly the type of man her mother wanted her to marry. Respectable. A solicitor didn't use all these dreadful swearwords, at least not if he came from Ashford and that was all Lily knew of life. A solicitor would drink a cup of tea with decorum, yet while these thoughts poured through Lily's mind, this dreadful man was yet again pacing about and now slurping the spilled tea from his saucer. Ed must be wrong, no she had misheard. It was the Galloways tea of course; it still ran in her veins.

"I'm sorry..." Lily frowned and waited for further explanation.

"I've come to have a talk, Lily, and I'll make no charge for it." Charlie sat down again and continued, "I feel a bit responsible for letting you go, so how about you tell me what happened, and I'll see what can be done."

Glancing towards Ed, Lily saw him give a slight nod and so she began: "It was misty when I arrived at Dungeness, only it wasn't Dungeness at all. And when Evie appeared it seemed like I was in the right place, Mary had told me to find Galloways Cottage and there it was and..."

The tale unfolded from those first moments of sitting in the armchair with Evie plying the grey tea upon Lily. Charlie asked questions occasionally, as if to clarify a point. With her eyes lowered, Lily admitted to waking up

91

in Joe's bed and her mind clearing as she used the privy in the sharp coldness of the early morning.

"Joe's a good sort and he did you no harm," Charlie concluded. "It sounds as if that mother of his was the force behind it all."

"He must have been aware I wasn't fit to know. It was all such a blur; I can barely recall it."

A silence fell upon them as Charlie considered the events. Lily picked up her sewing and pretended to concentrate on it, but her eyes kept flitting to Charlie's face as she tried to make sense of his character.

He wasn't silent for long. "Well, Lil, I think it's best I go and speak to them and get them to see sense. You're a town girl from Ashford and not at all the type of girl Joe needs. He may have placed a hagstone around your neck and you around his, but you didn't know what you were doing. I'll have a word with the elder from the place, Wilfred Black, and see if there's something to be done about revoking the ceremony. What do you think, Ed?"

"Seems the best way forward," Ed nodded. "Shall I come along with you?"

"No, best leave it to me," Charlie replied, "I've Galloways blood in me and they'll trust me."

"Fair enough." Ed stood and reached for his coat. "I'd best get back to some jobs outside while the weather's fair. I'll be seeing you soon, Charlie. Thanks, thanks for your help."

"Will they know I'm here?" Lily felt a chill running across her skin.

"No, if anything they'll think you're in Lydd or back in Ashford."

Charlie leaned forwards and grasped Lily's hand in his own. The smile fell from his face and his green eyes lost all their humour. "I shouldn't have let you go off down the Galloways Road. I'm sorry."

Shaking off his hand, Lily pulled her own back, "I should have listened, I thought…"

"You're a lovely girl, Lily, and I'll do what I can to help you." His eyes still held her own and remained serious as he continued, "You've got spirit and you're beautiful; I like that. I can't have you stuck out at Galloways married to Joe. Decent enough he is, but he's not good enough for a girl like you."

He shouldn't have held her hand; it wasn't right at all. But at that moment Lily had a hint that life was not all a big joke for Charlie and perhaps he could be relied upon to do the best for her. She said nothing while these new thoughts settled in her mind, only to be usurped by his next words.

"If I'd known you were after a husband, I'd have taken you along to The George Inn for a slap-up dinner and hoped you'd take a fancy to me!"

Chapter Nine
Joe's Story

"She's gone, Ma, and I don't know when you're going to leave it be." Joe stood and reached out for his coat. "I looked for her all day yesterday and I'll look again now, but she'll be back in Ashford. I'm sure of it."

"You're being foolish, lad," Evie sneered. "What's a young woman like her going to do with herself when she's only got her nightdress and a coat to go about in? No, she's out there somewhere and we'll hunt her down."

"Hunt her down?" Joe shook his head in dismay. What was wrong with Ma nowadays? She was so possessed with the need for a Galloways bride, it seemed all sense had flown from her. "She's not a wild animal; Lily is a lovely young woman who could be in trouble out there. How's she going to look after herself?"

"I'm glad you're thinking like that, son; like a husband who should be caring for his wife. I knew you'd grow to care for her. A pretty thing she was and nice ways about her. Nice and polite."

"There was everything to like about her, I'll agree with you there, Ma." Joe felt the loss of Lily weigh heavy upon him. It wasn't like him to feel low about life, but for a moment he had felt there might have been a chance of happiness with Lily. There had been a couple of moments when they had begun to feel close. On the beach when the hagstones were chosen, and later when he supported her during the wedding ceremony and carried her back across the stones. "It's not right, Ma. It's not right the way it was done. She didn't choose me; how could she when she had no idea what was happening? Perhaps if she chose to stay a day or so, Lily would've grown to like me for myself."

"Don't be foolish, boy. She was set on heading off to Dungeness. She weren't staying here to take a fancy to you."

"Well, best we let her go on her way. I just want to be sure she's safe."

"You're wed to Lily now, like it or not, so you'd best find her and set her right about a thing or two. Like how she wears your stone about her neck and how it's time to settle down to married life," Evie replied with force. "I'll hear no more of letting her go. We'll keep her on the tea so she's nice and mellow and when your seed grows inside her, she'll know better than to think of running off."

"I'm not happy, Ma. I got caught up in all your plans and it was foolish of me. No, if I find her, then she'll only stay if she wants to."

"If she wants to?" Evie's voice rose as she spat her words out, "If she wants to? She's got your stone about her neck and you claimed her as your own last night." Then she paused and looked her son up and down; he was too decent, too gentle for the life they led out here in this desolate land. "Tell me you took her last night, Joe? She'll be bound to you, like it or not. She'll not get another man with her innocence lost."

Poised in the doorway, Joe looked at his mother and for the first time he felt contempt. He'd known a lack of closeness, a sense of not understanding her ways, or not fully approving of them. But disgusted and repelled by her? No, he had never experienced such intensity of feeling before. "I'll say nothing of the sort to you, Ma. That's between a husband and wife and nothing to do with his mother."

"Well, think on this, Joe, if you don't bring her back, it will be a lonely life for you. There will always be a bit of a girl ready to pleasure you, but not a wife to give us the Galloways brood we need." Evie stepped towards him, ready to throw her last words out across the shingle if her son thought to leave before she was done with him. "They all saw you. Saw you pledge yourself to Lily; don't think you'll pick up another wife if one comes along."

"They'll not know of it in Ashford or Folkestone or Dover, if I happened to make a new life for myself, like I was going to before Pa and our Bert died. They'll know nothing of a Galloways bride if I left and took my chances elsewhere." Joe turned away from Evie and stepped out of the doorway, taking large strides across the stones in the direction of Dungeness.

"Shame on you, Joe." Evie's voice screeched and carried towards him on the wind which blew in an easterly direction. "May your father, God rest his soul, never hear those words coming from his only living son. May he not look down on us and see his wife deserted by a son who thought he was better than the rest of us."

With a scowl on his usually placid face, Joe moved at a pace away from Galloways and the woman who had embroiled him in her web of schemes. What had he been thinking of to listen to her, even for one moment? But Lily had touched him from the moment Ma had ushered her into the cottage. He wanted to reach out to her, to make her feel safe and cared for. Her feisty nature had been dulled by the grey tea, but it was there, he knew it. Something had pressed Lily onwards in the misty rain that afternoon she came to Galloways, a sense of adventure, a want to explore and learn about life. Joe had those needs, but they had been smothered. Not by the Galloways tea but by his duty to his mother and the family struggling to survive in the tiny community.

Backstays, the flat wooden boards under Joe's shoes allowed him to move smoothly over the stones, gliding between clumps of weeds. Instinctively his path took him inland in the direction of Dungeness, and it was not until Galloways was out of sight that he paused to consider where he was going. At first his need to make a distance between himself and Evie was his only thought. But then he realised he was being drawn to a place holding many happy memories.

Within an hour of Joe setting out, the Dungeness school building took shape before him. To his right a circle of raised shingle had once held a Napoleonic fortress and beyond it was the tiny round-topped station and then the fourth lighthouse. All images bringing reminders of happy times and places that fired the interest of a young man with a vivid imagination. As a child he had envied classmates who could get on a train and be in Lydd within minutes, or who could watch the progress of the lighthouse being built. Sometimes, on the way home from school, he had clambered up the bank of the fortress and looked down, not on the row of terraced homes now built there, but on an imaginary fort where soldiers manned 24-pounders mounted on the ramparts. At that time, Dungeness offered a wealth of experiences sorely lacking in Galloways. It was later, as he came to the age where the opportunity to go to grammar school was refused by his family, that Joe's aspirations grew to moving beyond the Point, and even beyond Lydd.

Under the supervision of Mrs Stubbs, and her band of younger helpers, Joe was one of the few who embraced the opportunity to learn in the small school. He recalled hazy memories of a teacher, a Miss Tibbs, who had taught him in his first year of schooling. She was a young woman with the severe dress of a Victorian schoolteacher, but with a warm smile and an eagerness to make lessons appealing to children. What had happened to Miss Tibbs? The five-year-old Joe had been unsure, but now he believed she was the mother of Lily. Hidden knowledge that the young teacher came from Ashford originally, and then returned to the town, came to mind.

Lily had wanted to go to Dungeness. She had never meant to be at Galloways. But Mary, Joe's cousin and the much-loved niece of his mother, had sent her there. It was as if Mary were part of the plan to have him married to some stranger, to anyone who they could lure to Galloways and keep there long enough to agree to stay. Had Lily, like himself, been drawn to the school? Was that where she went when she sought a refuge from the type of married life set out before her in the Galloways tradition? Had she run to the school, after facing the horror of waking beside her new husband the day before?

It was before he reached the school that Joe saw the figure of a man passing between the railway tracks and the lighthouse. He was a young man, well-built and as tall as Joe. There was something familiar about him, which was not unusual as most people on the Point were known to one another. But this man was from a little further afield; even from a distance it was clear he was in a smarter outfit than was usual for the area. Of course, it was the solicitor, Charlie. A man of the same age as Joe and also of a Galloways family, but how different Charlie's life had turned out. He was the first generation born of a family who had moved to Lydd. Having passed the entrance exams for grammar school, his family had allowed him to be schooled in Ashford. Whereas Joe had been forced to leave school and work on the boats.

As Joe paused and reflected on the differences in their lives, Charlie stopped and looked in his direction. Then he put his hand up to shield the sunlight from his eyes. Joe shrugged and began to walk on to the school but had barely taken a step before Charlie was hollering at him, "Joe, Joe, is that you?" Then he was waving and striding out towards him. Reluctantly Joe turned his back on the school and trudged in Charlie's direction.

"I hear you've got yourself married, Joe." These were Charlie's first words as the two men came within speaking distance.

"Where d'you hear that?" His wife was gone, and Joe didn't want to discuss it with anyone.

"News spreads and we don't get many Galloways weddings."

"No, we don't." Joe said no more, waiting to hear what Charlie had to say.

"What are you doing out here then, Joe?"

"Doing? I thought I'd come and see the old place," Joe replied, with a nod of his head in the direction of the school.

"Of course, that pretty young wife of yours, her ma was a teacher here."

"What do you know of my wife?" Joe snapped.

"I know she didn't mean to get married."

"She chose a stone." Joe reached to touch the dark bullet-shaped hagstone which bound him to Lily.

99

"I was going along to Galloways," Charlie said. "It's good to see the old place every now and then, but it was you I wanted to see, you and that mother of yours."

"Well, I'm here but she isn't. So best you go along to see her as I'm in no mood for chatting."

"If I was married to that lovely Lil, I'd be tucked up with her somewhere cosy, not traipsing about over here." Charlie grinned at Joe and received a scowl in return.

Joe didn't need Charlie coming to tell him how lovely Lily was. There he was, looking at Joe as if it was all a big joke. Did Charlie ever take anything seriously? He had a different woman on his arm every month; they were all in love with him, but he never stuck with one for long. It would have been a different story if he were Galloways born, then he'd be grateful for any girl who glanced in his direction. Life was easy for Charlie; it would have been easy for Joe had he been born off the Point.

"What do you know of Lily?" Joe snapped.

"Walk back with me to Galloways and you'll find out," Charlie said, grinning. "But you'd better listen and take notice."

Shrugging his shoulders, Joe turned his back on the school. They took a few steps in silence, but Joe could bear it no more and had to ask, "Have you seen her, Charlie? Is she all right? That's all I care about, Lily's not used to being out here."

"Have I seen her? Well, that depends doesn't it?"

"Depends on what?" Joe sighed.

"Depends on if you're coming to listen or going storming off."

"I'll listen and can only hope you'll get Ma to see some sense."

"This was Evie's idea, was it?" Charlie asked.

100

"It was her idea, but I like Lily. Who wouldn't?" Joe looked at Charlie, was he laughing at him? No, he looked serious for once. "But I wanted her to want to be here, to want me, not be pushed into it by Ma. And now... and now I just hope she's all right."

"She's all right," Charlie said. "She was found before she got herself into more trouble."

"So, she's over there at Dungeness, is she?" Joe looked back.

"Never you mind where she is. It won't make any difference to you." Charlie picked up speed as he got into the rhythm of sliding over the stones. His face was set towards the west and it was clear no confidences were to be shared. "I'll have a talk with your ma; she shouldn't have carried on as she did. She's got some answering to do and then you and I will talk some more."

Lily was safe, she must be, and Joe could only hope she would speak to him when she knew he meant her no more harm. As he moved across the stones, Joe wondered what a reunion with his wife would be like. They had never exchanged more than a few words: she had thanked him very nicely for letting her use his room, she had asked about the hagstones on the beach and of course she had stood and agreed to marry him. Perhaps not exactly agreed, but the vows had been exchanged. Lily was lovely and intelligent and adventurous. But what would he say if he could be with her now?

The two men continued without speaking. Both were busy with their own thoughts. Besides, it wasn't easy to move across the ground at a fair pace; the stones were uneven and the vegetation tough and wiry. Occasionally Joe looked across at Charlie and smirked to see him struggling. He may be of a Galloways family, but backstays needed using regularly if the wearer was to slide with ease on the wooden boards, and Charlie frequently lost his rhythm or stubbed a toe.

"What brings him here?" Evie screeched at her son as soon as he was close enough to hear her words.

"He wants a word with us," Joe muttered.

"Speak up, lad." Evie took a few steps from the doorway. "You've not found your wife then? Damned careless, that's what I say. I bet *he* wouldn't let his wife run off the day after he wed." This came with a nod towards Charlie.

"Evie, love, if some girl was lucky enough to be my wife, they'd not be running anywhere," Charlie grinned and, putting his arm around her waist, he gave Evie a quick squeeze.

"*Gerroff*! You always was a cheeky one." Evie turned and stepped back into the cottage. "I'm guessing you'll want to come in. No need for all of Galloways to hear our business."

"I do want to come in," Charlie's voice was now serious. "I've things to say and there's been some funny business going on that needs to be settled."

"There's been no funny business going on here," Evie stated, as she moved the kettle onto the hotplate. "We live a God-fearing and respectable life here. We have our own way of doing things, but it suits us very well."

"And did it suit Lily?" Charlie sat down, stretched his legs out and settled into the armchair.

"She liked it very much," Evie replied. "She was ever so thankful for the care we took of her and very pleased with the accommodation."

"Oh, Evie, you do spin a good yarn." Charlie gave a brief laugh.

Joe watched the scene from where he stood beside the central table. His eyes narrowed to see Charlie making himself comfortable. Where was the urgency to share news of Lily? There was none, for Charlie had seen her and was clearly in no rush to share news of her wellbeing. Hadn't he, Joe, waited long enough to hear about his wife? He thought so.

"Come on, Charlie. I've a right to know where she is and if she's well," Joe spoke now, raising his voice a little in order to make it clear he expected some respect from Charlie, who was in his home.

"Well, then, you'll be glad to hear that Lily was lucky enough to be found over at Denge. She wasn't in a good way, but you'll know the reason for that..." Taking a slurp of his tea, Charlie looked up at Evie, "Come on, girl, let's put a bit of sugar in here. It's as rough as Galloways Grey without it."

"I'll do it, Ma." Joe took the cup from Charlie. He reached into the back of the cupboard, extracted a jar of dark crystals and added a small amount, then added a spoonful of sugar. "But she's all right?"

"Course she is," Evie butted in. "Strong girl, that Lily is. She'll be bleeding useful when it comes to helping out on the shore. It's getting a bit much for me, but I'll be able to teach her our ways and she'll settle in nicely."

"She didn't settle here by choice and you know it," Charlie's voice lost all of its usual cheeky manner. "I'm telling you both, hagstones or not, this wedding will get no recognition beyond Lydd. But what will get the law interested in these goings on, is if a lovely young woman goes telling about how she was pressed into a ceremony and then into the marital bed." He looked towards Joe and took the cup of tea, then continued, "Look, Joe, you did well to get a hagstone around the neck of a lovely young woman like Lily but think about

103

it. You can't tie her down to life here, not when it wasn't really her choice."

"You've made a point though, Charlie," Evie reached out with her leathery hand and clawed at his sleeve. "She shared his bed, did our Lily. She's a Galloways bride through and through."

Listening in, hearing the confidence in his mother's words, Joe hung his head and turned back towards the teapot. "More tea, Charlie?"

"I will, but a bit more sugar, please. It was a bit sharp; I never did get a taste for the water coming from your wells."

Once again, Joe reached first for the black crystals and then the sugar. He stirred the tea well.

Chapter Ten
Alice's Story

"George, I don't want to make a fuss over nothing..." Alice twitched a feather duster around the ornaments on the mantelpiece, taking little care to ensure every particle of dust was removed. "But there is no way of knowing where Lily is, and we expected her home yesterday."

"She is a young woman of twenty-three, and if it weren't for the dratted war she would be married with her own family." Lily's father turned the page of his *Kentish Express*. "We have to let her live her life in the way she sees fit."

"Not if it means she takes time off work with no thought of being responsible."

"If that is what Lily chooses to do then she'll answer to her employer." George raised the paper a little so it shielded him from his wife. "It will do her no harm to consider her actions."

"But when should we begin to worry?"

"You, my dear, can worry – as you have done since she set off on Friday. I'll worry if she comes back married to a fisherman. Otherwise, I'll leave her to her own plans."

"There's nothing wrong with a fisherman," Alice tried not to snap at her husband. "They work hard and many risk their lives on the lifeboat."

"Of course they do, dear," George murmured. "I would just prefer Lily didn't marry one."

With a small suitcase at her feet and capacious handbag clutched to her, Alice stood in the hallway, one hand reaching out to the front door.

"I know you think I'm making a fuss, but she's been gone a week and not even a letter to explain why she hasn't returned." Alice opened the door and picked up her suitcase before continuing with the well-worn words, "You know both Helen and Polly have been here asking after her and I feel rather foolish not knowing where she is."

"She is at Dungeness."

"I know that." Alice gave a brief smile. "At least, we think she is. I hope she is."

The couple exchanged a brief kiss and Alice set off to the station. She had already dismissed George's offer to walk with her; this was something she must do alone. And despite her fear for Lily's safety, there was something about her return to Dungeness that brought with it a nervous excitement. It was no distance at all to walk along Jemmett Road, across the Stour and along to the station. Alice's pace was brisk and if her own mother had seen her, she may well have noted that she was not so unlike her daughter, Lily, in her zest for adventure.

An hour later, having passed though the flat lands of the desolate Appledore Dowels, the steam train skirted the villages of Brenzett and Brookland. Alice was gazing at the gable end of Midley Church. Standing tall, it was all that remained of the place of worship once serving a village on the desolate Walland Marsh. She craned her neck to study it, finding a girlish interest in the romance of a long-gone settlement. Not for the first time since Dungeness had been mentioned in their household, Alice had been caught up in thoughts of the past and the people of Romney Marsh.

Then Midley was gone and Lydd began to take form, at first just the impression of a church spire and buildings spread out below it, then individual roofs, chimneys and trees took shape. The train began to slow and there it was: Lydd Town station, an orange-brick building under a slate roof. There were still flowers in tubs and window boxes below a scalloped canopy, and there were the railway staff, now looking a little old-fashioned, part of an era seemingly forgotten by the people of Ashford.

Scanning the women with their baskets and the men in their thick overcoats, Alice searched for familiar features in the characters on the platform. It seemed as if it hadn't changed at all and as a door opened and a young man stepped into the carriage, Alice almost expected it to be Tom, or one of the other men she had known. But of course, just as she was no longer nineteen years old, the people she had known had also slipped into middle age. The young man who entered and seated himself at the far end of the carriage had been born years after Alice had left Dungeness behind her.

The engine began to pull away from the station, gradually picking up speed. How different the view was compared to that first time Alice had visited the Dungeness peninsula. The shingle ridges, topped with clumps of gorse and broom, had been obscured by a light rain. Buildings had loomed in the mist and then faded away. A young Alice came, expecting a seaside village, with visitor attractions. But within hours of arriving she had realised Dungeness was not that type of place at all.

The school appeared, and Alice's heart leapt with a love for the time she had spent there; she turned back, wanting to drink in all the details, wanting to note the changes. It looked just the same, but there was no time to see it all, and now the tiny station topped with its curved roof of corrugated iron was in sight. The engine slowed and the passengers, none of whom she recognised, began to gather bags and steadied themselves as the train shuddered to a halt against the buffers.

As she stood on the platform, at first it looked no different at all. There was the lighthouse – but of course this was the new one, built back in 1904. The old one, the one she knew, had been dismantled but, and she smiled to see it, there was the circular base of keepers' cottages still remaining. And close by were the two other white-painted bungalows in which the lighthouse keepers lived. It was in one of those Alice had first experienced the feelings of being safe and nurtured in what soon became a hostile environment to the young woman.

And there were the wooden cottages, but these were different, more of them and in the area near the station and lighthouse, rather than further along the coast. Many had curved roofs; in fact they were railway coaches. How strange. This place, once hated and then loved, was much the same as always – yet different. The wind blew in from the coast, as it did most of the time; Alice inhaled deeply. How she loved the smell of the sea, and it was never quite the same at Hythe or Broadstairs, in those more genteel towns.

The lighthouse may be a later addition and the wooden homes were of a new style, but the shingle, that was much the same as ever. The gorse was in bloom and the low-lying scrubland might look identical to any other coarse grass to be found in an area of poor soil, but Alice knew it held delicate mosses and tiny flowers with a rare beauty of their own.

It was good to be back and, in those few minutes, Alice felt the years of motherhood and housekeeping slip away. Once again, she was a young woman on the brink of an adventure and her heart soared. But, ever practical, she was there for a reason and was no longer a naive nineteen-year-old. Now she had her own foolish daughter to seek out. Where should she start? Who did one go to in a place such as this? The vicarage must be the place to start and although the vicar from her time here would have departed this stony land, his replacement was sure to be of some help.

Taking a few steps off the platform, Alice walked, and not without some awkwardness, on the stones. Then she saw it, of all things – a tearoom set on the shingle and in one of those railway carriages! Now she strode out, unhindered by the stones causing her to slip backwards with every step. This would be just the place to make enquiries. Women in teashops knew exactly what was happening.

A veranda had been built all along the front of the carriage and hanging from its canopy the word 'Tearoom' was crudely painted. Alice couldn't see through the small windows but noted layers of frilled lace hanging at their sides. The tables and chairs on the veranda were empty, but as she stepped up rough plank steps, the hum of conversation could be heard. The door was ajar, and she stepped inside.

All the original interior had been stripped out and the carriage now embraced its new life with a counter at one end and a small log burner topped with a kettle at the other. The customers, there were five of them, all swivelled and looked wide-eyed at the newcomer. They gave smiles which didn't reach their eyes and turned back to their conversations. Behind the counter, a slim young woman gave a more convincing welcome.

"Good afternoon. Just come in with the train, have you? Sit yourself down and I'll be with you in a minute."

Alice smiled her thanks, suddenly feeling uncertain in this settlement where she had once known everyone. Over the year spent here, it had slowly become not just her place of work, but her home. The log stove made the room stuffy, so she took off her coat and, in the absence of coat hooks, placed it on the back of her chair.

The tea was barely cool enough to drink and Alice had only taken a bite from her cake when the drumming of footsteps could be heard on the steps and the door was flung open wide, slamming upon the exterior wall of the carriage. A boy appeared, paused on the threshold for a moment as he scanned the customers, and on spotting his mother he shared the news.

"Oh, Ma, thank God you're 'ere," he gasped for breath. "I were out rabbiting over Denge way and… and Ma, I'm not mucking about, I swear… there were a body lyin' there on the shingle. A man, dead he was, or nearly dead… I weren't going' to find out which. I just ran, I did, as fast as I could, away from him!"

Sitting with her hand part-raised to her mouth, a piece of cake poised to be eaten, Alice felt her throat constrict and her mouth dry. It was as if she was in her first day of teaching again and the boy, Fred, was running into the classroom with tales of a body on the beach. He had also struggled to find his breath as he told the class, and he too expressed his words with a mixture of horror and barely concealed excitement.

110

"Sit down, Jack, and say it again." His mother pushed a chair towards him and, he collapsed on it, more for effect than exhaustion. "On the beach, was it? We'll need to see the coastguards."

"No, it weren't. You don't go rabbiting on the beach. It were out by them tumbledown places at Denge, just lying there."

"Well, take a sip of tea, lad, and we'll gather some men and set out there to see this body."

The tearoom became a hubbub of noise as chairs were pushed back, bags gathered and, following the initial silence, everyone began to have their say on the matter.

"I'll stay here, Ma, and have a bun." Now the boy had paled and hung back. Perhaps the enormity of his find now dawned on him.

"Don't talk silly, Jack." His ma gave the boy a slap around the back of his head. "You'll have to show 'em where it is, this body of yours. But I'll be there with you, and all the others."

Jack and his mother left, with the rest of the tearoom's customers following in their wake. The young woman tucked a strand of dark hair behind her ear, straightened her apron and set about clearing the tables. Alice ate her cake and sipped at her tea, looking just like any middle-aged woman from the town, but inside the excitement had caught hold of her. She was back in Dungeness and, although it shouldn't, this body on the shingle awoke memories and feelings she thought were gone forever.

"I don't know what you must think of us," the young woman spoke.

"Oh, it's nothing I've not seen before," Alice spoke with ease.

"Really? But with you just visiting, it's not very nice." She pushed chairs into place and brushed crumbs from the tables and then continued, "Are you visiting? We don't see many new faces around here."

"Perhaps you can help me? I need somewhere to stay but I'm not just here to visit," Alice paused, not wanting to sound foolish. "I'm looking for my daughter, she came here a week ago and hasn't returned home."

"Your daughter?" The young woman's voice was high; she pulled a chair out and looked about the room, despite the fact that they were the only two there. Then she lowered her voice and, having sat down next to Alice, she spoke. "Your daughter – Lily, is it? Oh my, you must be Alice, Miss Tibbs that was."

"So, you've met Lily?" Alice felt the tension release from her body. "She's not come home, and I didn't want to fuss but..."

"Well, she's fine now, but it's not all good and she's staying with us." Allie began to untie her apron strings. "I'd best take you over to ours, Ma will be there and between them they can tell you all about it."

"What luck I found you then. But Lily, is she hurt or…?"

"She's not been well but is on the mend. And Ma, oh, I forgot you didn't know – I'm Allie, named after you, and my ma, she's Emily. Emily Brooks."

"I can see the resemblance!" Alice recognised the slim face, slender frame and large eyes. "But your hair – you've got your father's colouring, not Emily's."

The two women walked past groups of railway carriage homes, some still in their original form and others boasting newly built extensions in the form of verandas and rooms at the back, doubling the original size. For Alice, this was a new Dungeness, a changed

112

landscape. Yet it fitted in, for the homes were still wooden and they stood in undefined plots of land.

"It was all empty here before," she tried to express her thoughts.

"There's been quite a change in the last few years," Allie told her. "They pulled these old carriages off the end of the tracks and set up home here."

"But who? Who would think to do that?"

"Those who had no jobs at the railway anymore and couldn't afford a home. And sometimes people who just heard there was a chance of a home here. There's all sorts of new people come to live here."

"How very strange." Alice reflected on this for a moment. What was it like for these new people who came to live in this bleak land, and in a railway carriage of all things? "And do they... do they like it here?"

"Some do and some don't – and those who don't either leave, or they make the best of it."

They left the new part of Dungeness village behind them and continued walking towards the east. Now the cottages were familiar to Alice as she recalled who had lived in each one. There was the vicarage and, a little inland, the Webbs' home. Nearing Allie's family home, she remembered Emily and Ed coming to live here, having moved around the Point from Denge. There was Tom's place, looking to be in good order as usual. Did he still live there? Of course he would; where else would he be? The Bartons, the Brooks and the Webbs, they would all be here still and for generations to come.

Since her arrival in Dungeness Alice's emotions had danced about, from fear for her daughter, uncertainty, to the elation felt when old memories were stirred up. Now they approached the Brooks' wooden cottage and – could it be? Yes, there she was, Emily, pulling a wet net across the stones, lying it flat to dry. Other women

113

were going about their duties: pumping water from the communal well, gathering dry washing from the lines, tending the vegetable plots. Alice scanned their figures, but the slim frame and bobbed hair of her daughter could not be seen.

"Your Lily won't be here; she has to stay inside," Allie informed.

Alice's eyes widened and she felt the chill of the wind on her skin. "She's been ill then? I should have come earlier, but her father said..."

"No, no. You're here now and Ma will tell it better than I could, besides it's not my story."

Watching the women at work, Alice saw Emily turn and straighten her back, then shield the sun from her eyes, clearly wondering who was with her daughter. She stepped across the stones, still unsure of the newcomer. Watching her progress, Alice saw surprise and bewilderment before a huge smile spread across her friend's face.

"Oh, Lord above, it's Alice! And there's me taking His name in vain again in front of the vicar's daughter!" Emily flung her thin arms around Alice and the two women held each other tight for a moment before breaking away and studying each other. "How long has it been?"

"Twenty-eight years."

"It seems like yesterday that you was here, and Ed and me were just setting up in this cottage."

"And here we are with our own children all grown up and Lily here with you..." Alice left her worries unsaid, knowing she would soon learn what kept her daughter here in Dungeness.

"You've come to find her then." Emily's smile faded. "Come along in and have a sit down, there's plenty to tell."

Chapter Eleven

Reaching into her pocket, Lily's fingers wrapped around the cool stone and explored the hole where the leather had been threaded through. How strange it was to have Mother appear in this place and to listen in on the shared memories between her and Emily. How unexpected to note Mother's lack of surprise as her story unravelled. Back in Ashford, in the comfort of the front parlour, would this story have ever been believed? Yet it seemed Alice accepted the odd customs of Galloways and the ways of those who lived on the shingle point.

There had been concern for Lily's welfare, disgust at the way she was lured to Galloways and put into a hypnotic state with the grey tea. Then pride, yes really, a look of pride in Alice's face as the tale of Lily's escape unfolded and the joy when it was confirmed it was indeed Emily who had rescued her daughter. There were tales to tell, Alice admitted. She would tell her daughter about the time she'd spent in Dungeness, starting with the body found on the shingle.

"And can you believe it?" Alice spoke, almost with glee in her voice. "I had only just sat down for a cup of tea when a young lad raced in, telling of a body he had found. It was as if I was nineteen again!"

"No!" Emily's hand went to her mouth. "Washed up by the sea, poor soul. It's not happened in a while."

"Not the sea," Alice replied. "He was clear about

that. It was inland because the boy, Jack, he was, had gone rabbiting."

The talk flew back and forth between the two women. Lily saw in her mother the young woman she had once been when she had lived and worked here for a year or more. Alice was to stay for a night or two, it was agreed without the words being spoken. She would have Lily's bed and Lily would share a room with Allie. Then Emily, who rarely sat still for long, started preparing the evening meal.

It must have been an hour after Alice's arrival when the door opened, and Ed walked in. He stood in the doorway, the great bear of a man in his thick overcoat and his eyebrows knitted together as he studied Alice.

"My God, can it be? Not Miss Tibbs, Alice?" Taking a step forward, a smile stretched over Ed's face. "Of course it is, but thirty years older like the rest of us! And you're back here at Dungeness."

"Hello, Ed." Alice stood and gave him a great hug.

Lily frowned. She thought of the friends and relations who came and went over the years. A polite handshake or a gentle pat on the arm, this was how Mother greeted someone.

"No need to ask what you're doing here." Ed smiled and shook his head a little. "This daughter of yours has got herself into a right lot of trouble."

"She certainly has," Alice agreed. "But no doubt it will be resolved, although I can't imagine how."

"I'm afraid things have taken a turn for the worse." Ed's eyes darkened. "There's been an accident, or something of the sort." Then turning to Lily, he continued, "It's Charlie, he was found between here and Denge and he's in a bad way."

Guilt weighed heavily on Lily. It lay like a blanket upon her slender frame, numbing her emotions. Whatever led to Charlie being found unconscious, it was due to her thoughtless ways. If she had seen beyond his jocular manner and not made judgements about his character, then perhaps she would have listened when he advised her to take the train to Dungeness. But would Lily really have taken heed of his words when she had merely laughed at her own mother's talk of there being no road to Dungeness?

For the past five days, Lily had been kept in the Brooks' cottage during daylight hours. Unable to even leave to use the shared privy, she had met no one from the local community and spent the days repairing clothes and helping Emily with the cooking. As the sun dipped beyond the hills at Rye, Lily had explored a night-time world. With Emily or Allie, she roamed the landscape and wondered about the people who were merely shadows beyond curtained windows or a featureless figure who passed them by during their evening treks.

This man who had been found barely alive was now at the Royal Navy Cottages, having been taken there on a stretcher. Lily knew nothing else. Only that if it were not for her and the Galloways wedding, Charlie would be sitting at some bar or music hall in Lydd with his friends around him and perhaps a wife or girlfriend waiting at home. And so, already knowing the tracks and the shadowed buildings, Lily slipped out while the older women gossiped, left the cluster of fishermen's cottages and set out to see the injured man for herself.

Dusk had fallen upon the land and, as always on her evening rambles, the landscape was all shades of grey – from the silver sparkles of wavelets on the sea to the almost black crevices between the stones.

Buildings were merely shapes, their features dulled. Lily knew of their inhabitants from stories told by Emily and Allie, and distinguished their homes by the shape of the roofline, distance from the tracks and their varied extensions.

The sea breeze was brisk but thankfully the sky was clear, enabling Lily to pick her way over the stones and past clumps of kale or ragged weeds with ease. It took ten minutes or so before she neared the lighthouse and the railway carriage homes. Although her shawl covered her head and disguised Lily's slim body, she moved a little inland, not wanting to be exposed within the lighthouse's shaft of light. Yet from a distance, she marvelled at the burst of colour the rhythmic beam of light gave to the scene and was comforted by its presence.

From the railway station, Lily followed the raised track-bed in the direction of Lydd and before long a mass of stone rose to the west. This place had caught her imagination when Allie had first explained: it was the remains of a fort, one of many in the area built at the time when Napoleon threatened the south-east coast. Now only the shingle circle of the outer fortress remained and snug within its centre was a terrace of cottages, home to Royal Navy staff who worked in the shore signalling station. Lily was unsure of why, in a place as small as this, such a number of cottages were needed to house these men. But that was not her concern. In one of these cottages, Charlie was being tended, its being the closest place to where he was found, and this was all she need be worried about.

An opening had been formed in the circle of stones and Lily stepped through. Pausing for a moment she was surprised to see a substantial terrace of rendered cottages, as good as any you would see in Ashford or

Folkestone. Clearly the Royal Navy didn't house their men in converted railway carriages or any form of wooden dwelling. Each house had fine sash windows; there was an array of neatly-ordered chimney pots and dormer windows in the slate roof. To one end, the terrace ended with a larger and more elegant home, boasting both a bay window and a porch; this must be the chief officer's home, Lily surmised, and so she set off towards its front door and rapped firmly upon it.

The woman answering the door frowned as she looked out into the darkness. "Yes, who is it?" She was a small, neat woman, who straightened her pearl-buttoned cardigan as she stared out at Lily.

"I'm looking for the man who was found injured or dying… I'm not really sure. Is he here?"

"He's here, but we weren't expecting… not unless you're the doctor and I doubt that." She stepped back, opening the door to allow Lily into the hallway. "I'm sorry, my dear, it's been such a shock to have him brought here and in such a poor way." She paused, looked towards a door which was slightly ajar and continued, "Were you wanting to see him or…?"

"I'm not quite sure." Lily, who had set out with such determination, was uncertain of exactly what she wanted. "I just… I was wanting to know how he is. I mean, is he conscious… or –," and now the words came in a rush, "he is still alive, isn't he? I didn't know what to expect, but I had to come."

"Oh, my dear, he's not dead but I couldn't say if he'll pull through or not. That's why they called for the vicar to come and he's sitting with him now. I've just made tea; come and sit down with me for a moment. I wondered if he had a wife, but there was no-one to ask, and he's not able to speak." The older woman placed her hand on Lily's elbow and guided her into the parlour.

119

"I'm Edith Browning, and I'm sorry, I don't recognise you. We've not been stationed here long."

"I'm Lily, I'm not his wife, or anything really. But it is my fault he's here."

The parlour was all that Lily was used to in her own home. A coal fire burned in the grate and warm light was cast from the lamps. The curtains were a thick brocade of golden velvet and a square of golden-brown patterns carpeted much of the wooden floor.

"Sit yourself by the fire, Lily." Edith gestured to an armchair. "I'll pour the tea. I imagine you've had a fair walk to get here and I've not much to tell about his condition."

"Is he conscious?" Lily leaned forward, smiling her thanks as the tea was placed on a side table.

"He's not woken since they carried him here." Edith placed herself in the chair opposite Lily.

"Oh dear, I was hoping... I didn't know what to think."

"It's not your fault, dear; why ever would you think such a thing? Something has happened to him; he has been taken ill for some reason, but it can't be your fault."

"He's not injured then?" Lily frowned. If there has been no accident, what had caused him to lie unconscious on the shingle?

"Injured? No. He doesn't appear to have been in an accident. But he's not well and we are hoping the doctor will be able to tell us what's happened."

Gazing into the fire, Lily reflected on Edith's words. It was now Friday and on Monday, Charlie had set off to Galloways in order to speak with Joe. Had he ever reached the settlement, or had he been taken ill on the way? Had he returned to Lydd and then left again on some other business or indeed on the same task? There had been no word of him in all these days, leading the Brooks and Lily to wonder about the result of his visit to Galloways. The thought of him lying there, probably hours away from death, caused a lump to form in Lily's throat. It seemed almost impossible that he could have been alone on the wastelands for four days.

"Forgive me, dear, but I'm still at a loss as to what brought you here?" Edith voiced her confusion.

"I'm..." How could she tell of the Galloways wedding? Lily couldn't bring herself to share her shame with this stranger. "I'm staying here at Dungeness, with one of the families. My mother once lived here for a year and I was curious to see the place for myself. Charlie, he's a solicitor, perhaps you knew? He came to give me some advice, and that was the last we saw of him. I had some trouble you see, when I first arrived, and he was going to help me."

"I'm not one to pry, dear, but whatever happened to him, please don't blame yourself." Edith stood and patted Lily on the shoulder before gathering the teacups and placing them on a tray. "We can only pray for his recovery and perhaps then we'll learn more about what happened. Now are you feeling brave enough to see him? He has the vicar with him; my husband went for the doctor."

"Yes, I'm ready. I need to see him."

"He's in the dining room." Edith led the way back into the hall. "We couldn't possibly carry him upstairs, so the men brought down a bed-frame. I was thankful they were here. It was the fishermen, you know, who carried him here."

A lamp glowed in the corner of the dining room, with the only other light coming from a lone candle on a low table beside the bed. Both the vicar and the body in the bed were almost shrouded in darkness. It was clear the room had been hastily rearranged in order to make space for the bed, which stretched out below the window, while the table was now pushed against a wall.

Rising from his chair, the vicar spoke. "No change, I am afraid. His breathing is shallow and pulse as weak as ever. I had hoped that once he was in the warmth..."

"We can only hope the doctor arrives soon." Edith walked to the bedside and gazed down at the unconscious man. "I do hope this doesn't distress you too much, dear. He is at rest; we can be thankful for that." She moved aside and Lily took her place beside Charlie.

At first Lily thought he had passed away: Charlie's body was still and his face so peaceful. Then she heard a slight exhalation of breath and saw his chest rise and fall within the striped nightshirt. She studied his features, the four-day old stubble on his chin, the slightly aquiline nose and his hair which someone, possibly Edith, had washed and brushed so it lay neatly rather than being slicked into place. Expecting to see some sign of distress on Charlie's face, Lily turned to Edith and asked: "Is this how he was when they brought him here? He looks so peaceful."

"We've had to clean him, poor man. He'd been lying there for a day or two, or so we believe; he wasn't looking his best." Edith placed her hand on Charlie's and held it for a moment, "I'm sure he'd have not survived another night, but he's warming up now, don't you think so, Vicar?"

"God willing, he's a fighter," the elderly man murmured.

"We had to borrow a vest and nightshirt from one of the men; my husband is a slim man, you see, and nothing of his would fit this poor man," Edith said, as she reached under the covers and moved a hot water bottle. "I mustn't burn him, but he needs the warmth."

"Could I sit with him? Just for a while?" Lily asked. He looked so alone, so vulnerable, just lying there. She felt a need to place her hand on his and comfort him. Or was it herself needing the comfort as he knew nothing of her being there?

"You do that, dear." Edith turned to the vicar. "A cup of tea in the parlour, Vicar?"

Twenty minutes must have passed while Lily sat there beside Charlie. Perhaps she should speak to him? Would he hear her words passing through his dreamlike state?

"We've been wondering where you were. Ed said he was going on the morning train to see you. They've been keeping me in all this time, not wanting me to be seen. It's just at night they allow me to take a walk, but never alone. One of them takes me out and I see Dungeness under the light of the moon, and the lighthouse. It's been quite mild and dry too; I expect you're thankful for that. Or you will be when you wake.

"My mother is here. Not for the first time. She used to be a teacher at the school. It was a long time ago, before I was born."

What else could she say? Lily knew nothing about this man. She got up and placed a shovelful of coal on the fire, then moved the hot water bottle. Then she stood by the bed, scrutinising his face. Did his eyelids flicker? A little, perhaps.

Then new sounds came as first the front door was opened, and muffled voices could be heard in the porch, followed by the inner door opening and footsteps in the hallway. A tall man in a smart navy coat, salt and pepper hair, and a neat moustache walked in, followed by a younger man clutching a leather bag. As the first man paused and looked at Lily in surprise, Edith rushed in behind them.

"This is Lily, a friend of Charlie's. She's come to sit with him."

"Not really a friend..." Lily's voice trailed away. "I just wanted to..." She stepped away from the bed, but, reluctant to miss out on the doctor's words, moved to the corner of the room and pressed against the dining table.

"Just myself and the patient, please." The doctor placed his bag on a chair and turned to survey the gathering of spectators behind him; even the vicar had returned and hovered at the doorway. "Perhaps just your wife, sir." He looked towards Edith and continued, "If you wouldn't mind assisting."

And so, the Royal Navy Officer, the vicar and Lily moved through to the parlour and awaited the doctor's verdict.

Chapter Twelve

"In my opinion this man has been taking the unripe seed of the Jury's Poppy, either by his own hand or it has been forced upon him," the doctor announced to the four people who stood before him, having summoned them back to the bedside. "How he came to have it in his body is for him to tell us, or for the coroner to decipher."

"Jury's Poppy?" Lily whispered and, as she said them, she heard the words repeated by the others beside her.

"Jury's Poppy," the vicar repeated. "An insignificant enough flower beside the large red flowers we see, or our own beautiful yellow specimens we have here on the Point. But for some of those who know of it, the Jury's Poppy can be a temptation."

"And not in a good way," the doctor continued. "Their unripe seeds exude a milky liquid. In small doses they can relieve pain and are harvested for this reason. In larger doses they first relax the person who takes the liquid, and if the dose is increased the danger begins. I've been called to cases such as this before, where too much has been ingested. Although it has to be said that those who use it generally have an understanding of how much to take before it becomes unsafe. Its medicinal uses are well known hereabouts."

"His organs are failing?" the vicar asked.

"Charlie wouldn't have lived many more hours once

the night set in." The doctor put his stethoscope back in his bag. "You know of this poppy then, Vicar? And you are right, I fear his organs are failing. Both the heartbeat and respiration are slow, his cough reflex will be weakened and so it is imperative he lies a little more on his side. The next few hours are crucial. You are keeping him warm." He shot a smile towards Edith. "And I recommend someone sits with him through the night. I see he has a crucifix by his side, and no doubt prayers have been offered. This man is in good hands and all any of us can do is wait."

"Is there nothing else we can do?" Edith asked.

"Nothing but keep a bedside watch." The doctor reached for his bag. "I'll return in the morning. There is no need for me to stay. If he passes, it will be in peace."

The naval officer walked the doctor to the door.

"It doesn't need the four of us to watch by his bedside," Edith said, as they stood looking down at the bed. "Lily, I know you'll want news. Will you come back in the morning? Although I don't like to think of you out on the Point at night; perhaps you could walk back with her, Vicar?"

"Of course," the vicar replied and, turning to Charlie, he bowed his head, placed a hand on his chest and murmured a few words.

Looking down at the man who seemed to be at peace, yet might not survive many more hours, Lily knew she couldn't leave him here with these kind people who were strangers to him. She wondered about his family in Lydd and why no one had come to be with him. Did they know of this?

"I'd like to stay. I'll sit with him here through the night," Lily said. "I feel it's what must be done."

"You're a grown woman and, painful as it may be, if you have feelings for the man, then of course you must stay." Edith smiled her understanding. "I'll fetch a blanket, you'll feel a chill as the night passes, and you are in need of sleep."

"No, it's not that I have feelings other than a responsibility. I've only met him twice, but I feel I need to be here. Thank you, I can doze a little in the chair."

"I'll come back not long after first light," the vicar said. Then turning to Lily, he lowered his eyes a little and placed his hand on her own. "God, give this young woman strength; give her the words she needs to comfort this man. Let your presence come into this room and carry love with it. Encourage her and give her your support as she sets out on her vigil through the night. Amen."

An armchair was brought into the dining room and Edith ensured Lily was comfortable. "I'm a light sleeper, you only need to call up the stairs if you need me," the older woman told Lily. "If there is any change, and we know he may well pass away in the night, don't hesitate to call."

Lily smiled her thanks and settled down in a position where she could see Charlie's face and the steady rise and fall of his chest. The hours passed, accompanied by the steady ticking of the clock on the mantelpiece. Occasionally she stood and paced around the room; sometimes she slept for a short time. It was at two o'clock in the early morning when Lily woke with a guilty start, having fallen into a deeper sleep. Charlie had shifted his position a little and his eyes were open, looking straight at her. For a moment fear clutched at her stomach; she thought he had… But then he frowned a little and, as he closed his eyes, it seemed his breathing was a little stronger.

Morning came and with it the signs that Charlie was gaining strength. There had been other times in the night when he had lain awake for a few minutes. Lily, unable to lift him but sure that his mouth must be dry, had gone to the kitchen and returned with a clean cloth. She dipped it into a glass of water and squeezed some into his mouth. The nod of gratitude was barely noticeable, but as his green eyes looked into hers, it seemed an understanding passed between the pair of them.

It was at six o'clock in the morning, when Lily sat with a fresh cup of tea in her hands and the sun was sending shafts of weak light through the gaps in the heavy velvet curtains, that he spoke.

"Where am I?"

"You're in the Naval Officer's house."

"You going to make me a cup of tea then?"

Lily frowned. She couldn't possibly sit him up. Perhaps with the help of Edith's husband? But even while these thoughts raced through her mind, she saw his eyes were closing again and sleep overcame him.

When Edith came, an hour later, she entered the room with trepidation and then her eyes widened in surprise to see Charlie gazing back at her. "Oh, thank the Lord, he's awake."

"And asking for tea!" Lily smiled.

"You had us all worried," Edith said to him.

"Sorry. I was at Galloways and felt a bit odd..."

"They found you near Denge," Edith told him, instinctively tidying the bedcovers.

"I don't know..."

"It doesn't matter for now," Lily said. "You're awake and that's enough for us. The doctor will be with us in a few hours and he'll advise on how to care for you."

"You're my nurse?" He attempted a grin.

"No, I'm… I felt responsible."

"Now that's enough of that." Edith shook her head. "It's done now, and it looks like Charlie will recover. Lily, we've not spoken about your family but there must be people worrying about you?"

Lily slumped a little. "Yes, I should go to them, and perhaps come back later?"

"You do that, dear, and we'll have news by then," Edith replied. Looking down at Charlie, the women smiled to see he was sleeping again.

This was Lily's first opportunity since her arrival to see Dungeness in the daytime. The rising sun was soft behind a light mist; grasses and broom carried a lustre from the early morning dew and sunlight cast mellow tones on the shingle. The stones were no longer all shades of grey, from a silvery white to charcoal. Now daylight showed them also bearing tones of beige, fawn and taupe. Lily was able to see the whole sweep of the bay, from the flat shoreline of Romney Marsh through to the gentle hint of far-off hills at Hythe and Folkestone. Yet none of this was seen very clearly; this time Lily was drugged, not by the grey tea, but by lack of sleep. All her attention was fixed on the ground and passing over the stones, while keeping herself steady.

Now the enormity of her night-time adventure was at the forefront of her mind. It seemed as if Charlie was to recover and, although she still felt herself to be fully responsible, her thoughts were with the family she had left behind. They would all be frantic with worry and Lily could offer no excuses for her inconsiderate behaviour.

As she reached the lighthouse and the railway carriage homes, Lily noted activity in the distance. The fishermen and their families were preparing to launch their boats and would be out fishing all day. She didn't see the tall figure of a young man, partially hidden behind a salon carriage-home. Lily's attention was all on reaching the cottages of the fishing community before her fragile strength expired. She didn't think to look behind her and had no awareness of Joe stepping out from behind the railway carriage and following her footsteps along the seafront track.

Alice left for the mid-afternoon train that day. Watching from the cottage window, Lily felt unusually subdued. Yesterday she had seen glimpses of the young woman her mother had once been, hints of an adventurous character. But today, following a long anxiety-ridden night, all sense of mischief had washed away from her mother. It seemed as the tide lapped at the upper reaches of the beach and turned, so Alice's thoughts turned from all the fun to be had here at Dungeness, and she could only dwell on her daughter's wrong-doings.

Now it had been agreed that Lily would continue to stay with Ed and Emily, she felt a need to be sure of Charlie's recovery and a strange desire to face her husband and to insist on being released from the union. But while Emily had shown an understanding, acknowledging the turmoil Lily had encountered in the past week, Alice had been firm in the belief that no harm could come to her daughter once home in Ashford and it was by far the best option to return and put this foolish episode behind her.

And so the relationship between mother and daughter had been strained as the perfunctory embrace was performed and Alice departed for the station. Lily, still tired from a lost night's sleep, settled by the range in the easy chair. When the door opened her first thoughts were that this was Emily returning and she,

Lily, must have been sleeping as the time had passed so quickly.

"Lily."

She felt no fear on seeing him standing there. Joe had never offered anything but kindness and Lily sensed there was no malice within him, just a deep sadness.

"How did you...?" She turned to face him, straightening her blouse and skirt.

"I saw you yesterday morning, walking over here."

So he had been prowling around, looking out for her. They had said he would; that the Galloways family would not let her go. And there, around his neck, was the hagstone binding the pair of them together. Lily's hand felt for her own smooth white stone hidden in the folds of her pocket.

"You're looking well," Joe continued.

"I've had time to recover from the grey tea which was plied upon me." Now Lily stood, not wanting to feel at a disadvantage by having him standing there so tall while she slumped in the chair. "What were you thinking of? You seem like a decent man, so why press the tea on me? Why take a guest into your home and... and allow such a thing to happen?" Her anger rose as Lily finally faced the man who she had apparently married in the Galloways tradition.

"We all drink the Galloways Grey and it does no harm."

"Does no harm?" Lily scowled. "I was unaware I was at my own wedding."

"You weren't used to it," Joe muttered. "A cup here and now soothes the body."

"But I was given cup after cup by that mother of yours."

"You were," he admitted. "I should have stopped her, and I see that now. I've never met anyone like you, Lily. You're different from the women I meet on the Point, or even in Lydd. You're beautiful and intelligent and interesting too. I saw a chance to have someone special and I hoped you'd grow to love me."

"It wasn't the way to get someone to love you," Lily's tone was scornful. "I thought you were a good man, kind and decent. But this… this is no way to get a wife. And is that how you see me? As your wife when we know so little of each other?"

Reaching for his stone, Joe said, "I won't remove this until there's no hope. But in Galloways and hereabouts we are bound by the ceremony."

Remembering Charlie, who had set out days ago in order to speak with Joe and Evie, Lily wondered what had come from his talk with them. Not liking to press him to speak of it, Lily had merely reassured herself that the solicitor was gaining strength when she had visited with Emily the evening before. Charlie was still tired and although he mentioned being at the cottage with Evie and Joe, his manner was vague and Lily could only hope he would recall the visit over the next day or so.

"And what brings you here now?" Lily walked to the window; there was no sign of Emily returning, having walked her mother to the railway station.

"I was hoping we could talk and perhaps you would consider coming home with me in a day or two. I've had strong words with Ma; I've had enough of living the life she chose for me. I've got plans, Lily. Plans we never spoke of. I'm leaving Galloways and I'll find work in Lydd or Ashford or wherever you want to be."

This caught Lily by surprise. She had assumed Joe, Galloways born and bred, had an unbreakable bond with the small fishing settlement in this barren land. She considered him for a moment; what type of life would he live in Ashford or one of the towns? He was a fine looking man, tall and broad, with a good straight nose and soft brown eyes. The young women of Ashford or Folkestone would flock to this man with his honest face and gentle ways. But where did a fisherman work if he left the coast? And what would he do of an evening? Perhaps a game of shovelboard or darts before returning to his rooms in a shared house?

"Is that what you want?" Lily felt compelled to ask. "Not for me, I hope, not because you expect..."

"Not for you, but perhaps you've shown me I need to follow my own dreams," Joe replied. "I did well at school. Could have gone to the grammar in Ashford but she wouldn't let me, Ma wouldn't. Said it wasn't for a fisherman to go off and turn posh. I would have gone away later, when I was old enough to make my own choices; then Pa and my brother died, and I had to stay to look after her."

For the first time, Lily was beginning to understand the man who claimed to be her husband. She recalled moments of togetherness during her time in Galloways and now she learned that he had an intelligence, not immediately apparent, and dreams of a life beyond the Point. Did this man appeal to her sense of adventure? Did he offer something quite different from the neat young men with their slicked hair and well-fitting suits, shiny shoes and natty ties? She thought of the Lily who paced from home to work to coffee shop, thwarted and frustrated with life, reaching for a cigarette to sooth her irritable manner. Would he offer her the project she longed for if she were to play a part in rescuing him from the life that trapped him? Or just as Joe longed to be free of Galloways, did she want to be free of Ashford?

"I never thought," Lily began. "I mean, I assumed

your life was here."

"So did I," Joe replied. "But I'm going back to tell her, to tell Ma that I'm off. And when I'm settled, I'll find you and you'll see I've still got the hagstone around my neck, even in Ashford, and you'll be glad of it one day. I'll show you, being married to me is not a bad thing."

This was a new Joe. A more confident man; a more attractive man. But would she really change her mind? Lily didn't, couldn't, believe she would put aside her misgivings because, deep inside, she would always know. She would know that he allowed Evie to press the grey tea on her until she could barely walk and had no awareness of the marriage she was taking part in. And whatever changes Joe made to his life, Lily would carry this feeling of discomfort with her.

"Will you go now, Joe?" Lily asked. "Will you go back to Evie or have you come to drag me back and force me to submit to your plans?"

"I'll go because I want us to be friends and you to be with me of your own free will, just as it should be."

"Perhaps you could start by apologising?" Lily replied.

But Joe's reply was lost under the sound of the door opening, the stamp of boots and rustle of material as Ed removed his bulky jacket, worn to keep out the wind and rain while at sea. For a moment all three stood and looked at one another before Ed bellowed his rage.

"You! You dare to come into my home with all your bloody trickery." Stepping towards Joe, Ed's face reddened as he grasped at the front of Joe's jumper. "Don't tell me you've come to claim your wife. By hell, you'll never drag her past me, I'm telling you."

Lily felt her mouth dry as she looked on, horrified at the anger she saw in Ed. Joe's eyes darted towards her and his skin blanched. Though just as tall as Ed and

134

twenty years his junior, the younger man shrank away, fearful of what was to come.

"Have you nothing to say for yourself?" Ed roared.

"I..." Joe coughed a little as if to clear his throat but the fist at his chest only twisted the wool of the jumper tighter. "I meant her no harm."

"No harm?" With ease, Ed swung the younger man around until he stood near the open door. Then he began to push him backwards.

Struggling to keep his balance, Joe stammered, "I'm going."

"Ed, Ed, listen." Lily found her voice, "He came to talk; he'll go now."

"Has he hurt you? Did he mean to take you back with him?" Ed barked at her.

"No, no. He just wanted to talk."

Ed let go and Joe, unable to keep himself steady, fell backwards in the doorway to the cottage, landing partly on the shingle ground. He was on his feet in a flash and, although he showed none of the rage which came so readily to the other man, Joe spoke with a force that surprised Lily. "You've a right to show a temper if you don't want me in your home, Ed Barton. But I'm telling you, while she stays on the Point, Lily is my bride and I've every right to claim her. You know that and so did Charlie who came snooping around. She's removed the stone from her neck, but there were enough witnesses to see it placed there." Taking a step out of the doorway, Joe looked as if he were about to turn but, before he did so, he threw a few more words in Ed's direction, "And I've a feeling she holds her hagstone close."

Ed took a step towards the man who threatened the peace of Lily, whom he saw as part of his extended family. Lily, seeing his fury, rushed to place a hand on his arm and spoke, her voice soft so he needed to pause in order to hear her words. "He's going now, and he caused me no upset. Let him go, please."

Turning to look down at her, Ed gave a brief nod. "Very well, I'll just see the bloody fool on his way but there will be no harm done." Stepping out of the cottage, he took two long strides across the shingle and bellowed his final words out in the direction of Galloways "You, Joe Stoneman, you'll not take her back to Galloways, married or not. I'm telling you I'll not have it. I'll damned well make sure of it."

Chapter Thirteen

"I'm going back to my nets," Ed said to Lily, as he snatched his jacket from the hooks on the wall. "He's gone now, but best you have a talk with Emily or Allie about him coming here. I don't like it; but it's done with and he'll not be back in a hurry. Be careful; now they know where you are, there's no knowing what tricks that Galloways lot will try next."

The sound of stones being crushed upon each other could be heard as Ed strode between the cottages, and he was gone. His temper, which came in a flash, had dispersed and Lily was sure all would be fine when he returned. Nervous of settling back in the chair to rest, she looked towards the railway station and was rewarded with the sight of Emily returning. There would be time for the pair of them to talk through the recent events and put it all to rights before Ed returned.

"I must go and see Charlie again," Lily announced on the Sunday morning, as the women sat around the breakfast table. "I can't stop worrying about him. He was awake yesterday morning, but still so weak. The doctor would have visited again and there must be more news."

"I'll walk over with you," Allie said. "My Ernie is coming here for dinner; there's plenty of time for us to go to the Naval Cottages first. You can't go on your own, not now Joe knows where you are."

"We don't know what plans they may have," Emily added. "But no need for you to hide away. I know your family would prefer you back in Ashford and it makes sense, but I'd like to hear from Charlie if he did speak to them and find out what they had to say for themselves."

"I imagine Charlie won't be well enough to speak about it," Lily replied. "I just hope that, when he is able to talk, he remembers what happened."

"Perhaps we'll go there before church and if the Captain and his wife want to go to church, then we can sit with Charlie," Allie suggested. "They usually go but I'm sure Mrs Browning won't want to leave an ill man on his own."

"No, she won't." Lily drank the last of her tea and pushed back her chair. "What can I do to help, before we go and find out how he is?"

An hour later, Lily found herself relaxing in the company of Allie as they made their way to the Naval Cottages. She was being introduced to a novel method of crossing the shingle.

"Is this really easier?" Lily grinned as the wind whipped at her short, bobbed hair. Her sturdy boots were slipped into leather straps, which in turn were nailed onto rectangular pieces of flat wood. The wood was not much larger than the boots and, although these enabled them to move in a skiing action across the stones, they lacked the length of skis.

"Not at first, but in time..." Allie laughed, sliding ahead and looking back. "You step down with these and your weight is spread out more; you're not digging the toe of your boot into the stones and slipping back."

"But they flap about so!" Lily lifted her foot and the backstay hung at an awkward angle.

"Put your foot down then!" Allie shook her head and raised her dark eyebrows. "They're not meant to be dangling about in the air, are they?"

Lily grinned and persevered. It was good to be out in the fresh air with Allie. By the time they reached the ring of raised stones, which was the old Napoleonic Fort, both girls were rosy-cheeked, and Lily's heart was pounding from the exertion. They propped the backstays against the outside wall of the porch and Lily knocked on the door of the Officer's House.

Edith Browning answered the door; she looked tired but gave a smile when she saw Lily. "I thought you would be back today." Stepping back, she allowed the young women to walk into the hallway. "Come on through and we'll have a little talk before you see him."

"Is he all right? He's not worsened?" Lily tried to keep the tension from her voice.

"No worse, my dear. Just rather sleepy," Edith reassured her, as she led the way to the parlour.

"This is Allie," Lily introduced her friend. "I am staying with her family here at Dungeness." The two women exchanged greetings and Lily continued, "If you wanted to go to church with your husband, we could sit with Charlie."

"That's kind of you." Edith gestured for them to sit down.

It was pleasant with the sun pouring in through the bay window. Lily saw Allie looking around the room, her curiosity aroused by this home. With its sash windows, patterned wallpaper and decorative details, it was so like the houses Lily was familiar with, but unlike a typical Dungeness cottage.

"There's not much to tell," Edith said. "You saw Charlie was awake yesterday morning, but he still sleeps most of the time. We take it in turns to sit with him in the day, and last night we made several checks. We've both read to him from the newspaper, but whether he really listens or not, it's hard to tell. I'd say that he's never awake for more than an hour. The doctor tried to ask what happened, if he knows who gave him the Jury's Poppy, but Charlie doesn't seem to remember what led to him being there, left for dead."

"Does he speak much?" Lily asked.

"No, he tries to tell us what happened, but then he doesn't seem to recall it," Edith frowned. "He clearly has some memories and they are confusing him. I don't push it much. The police will be here tomorrow, and I think that will distress him."

"And the doctor?" Lily wondered.

"He was here yesterday morning and again early this morning. He's happy enough. But he says we can't be sure that Charlie won't suddenly fail. But with every hour we grow more positive." Edith stood up from the armchair and continued, "Shall I make a pot of tea and then you two can sit with him while I go to church? It will make a pleasant change for Charlie to see some pretty young faces and will do me good to get out of the house for an hour."

Charlie was sleeping when Lily and Allie moved silently into the dining room. The blinds were still drawn and so the light was dim: a contrast to the bright, sunny parlour. They sat and waited, listening to his steady breathing. It must have been fifteen minutes before he stirred and they watched as he opened his eyes and slowly moved his head, then frowned as his eyes focused on them. As the recognition came, a smile spread over Charlie's face.

"Am I in heaven?" he asked, his voice a little uneven, as if he was unused to speaking.

140

"Still a flirt then!" Allie replied in mock despair.

Charlie closed his eyes again for a moment, and when he opened them again, he continued, "Thank you for coming to sit with me. How are you, Lily? Not been drinking the grey tea again?"

"I'm fine, thank you," Lily said. "We're more worried about you and the Jury's Poppy seed."

"I'll be fine in no time. The doctor is pleased with my progress."

"Charlie, do you know what happened?" Allie asked.

"I was talking to Lily and then I went to speak to Evie and Joe," Charlie began. "But I have a feeling..." He paused, frowning as he tried to place things in order. "Yes, that's it; I met Joe beforehand. He must have been looking for you. He doesn't like me, Joe doesn't."

"Why?" Lily wondered, but then she recalled Joe's frustration that he had missed out on a grammar school education.

But Charlie's thoughts had wandered. "I was talking to them. Felt a bit odd."

"What did you speak about?" Allie asked.

"It must have been about Lily; I don't remember..." Charlie's eyes closed, and his breathing changed. He was asleep.

The young women sat in silence for a while, not liking to speak. Allie poured their tea from a tray provided by Edith and they sipped at it.

"Don't trust him, Lily." Charlie's words made them jump. "She made my tea; but he added the sugar. It wasn't sweet. Go back to Ashford. Keep safe."

Then he was sleeping again and didn't wake before the Captain and Edith returned.

When did the whispers of a death reach Dungeness?

141

Who first knew of the young man's body, with head injuries, found lying midway between Galloways and Lydd? Perhaps he was still a little closer to his home at Galloways. He lay alone, in a landscape where a thin layer of earth began to take hold over the stones and grass put down roots through poor soil. Not far away, was a stout pole, which the Lydd sergeant soon removed from the scene. The wood bore traces of blood and, on further investigation, some fine strands of wool.

It was Ed who brought the news to Brooks Cottage on the Monday afternoon. He burst into the living area, his face ashen and blurted out the words: "My God, have you heard? He didn't deserve this." Then looking at the surprise on the faces of his wife and Lily, he continued, "You've not heard?"

Lily's heart clenched and her response came out as a strangled cry, "Not Charlie? He was getting better." She turned to Emily who ran to her side, "I told you, didn't I? We spoke to him, Allie and I; he was getting better. Although the doctor said..."

"Not Charlie," Ed said. And then a silence hung between them, just for a few seconds as Emily and Lily waited to hear and Ed prepared himself to tell. "Sit yourselves down," he told them, and they did as he said.

"It's news from Galloways and I believe it to be true." Ed ran his hands though his wiry hair. "It's Joe, and I know you barely knew him, Lily, but the two of you had unfinished business. I don't know how you're going to feel about this. He was found on the road to Lydd – and it seems that he was murdered."

"Oh, my Lord," Emily gushed, as she clutched Lily to her. "When?"

"He was found not long ago, and they think he'd

been lying there since the evening before."

"He were a weak man, but not bad." Emily's hand gripped hard on Lily's arm. "Oh, Lily, what must you think of us and all these terrible things happening?"

It seemed to Lily as if the blood had drained from her body; she felt stunned, her body taut. How should she respond? How should she feel? A connection had been made between the two of them, just forty-eight hours beforehand. Yet still she doubted his character. For all he spoke of regret at his life in Galloways and his part in the wedding, he had still known of the plan to trap her; he had still allowed her to have the grey tea pressed upon her. It showed a weakness that did not impress Lily. And what was it Charlie had said, just yesterday when they sat at his bedside? *Don't trust him.* Those were his words. And something about the tea, not grey tea but the sugar not being sweet.

"Was it the Jury's Poppy?" Lily forced the words out. "Is that what happened to him, but he wasn't found in time?"

"No, it wasn't." Ed spoke slowly, as if making sure Lily understood. "He was hit around the back of the head. There is no doubt of it. The weapon was left nearby."

"The weapon?" Lily and Emily repeated.

"A pole or stout piece of wood," Ed told them. "Whoever did this, he was young and strong. You'd have to be, to fell a big man like Joe Stoneman."

"And where is he now?" Lily asked.

"They will have carried him to Lydd," Ed informed. "There will be an investigation over this; there's no doubt about it."

It was over. The man who claimed to be her husband had died. How many days since the wedding? Lily counted them in her head: nine days. She had married a man whom she had known a day, shared a bed with him and then ran away. Now, nine days later, she was a Galloways widow, no longer a bride. But when she left this place and returned home to Ashford, she would be neither. It would be as if it had never happened.

"Should I go to see his mother, the rest of the family?" Lily asked Emily.

"It would be the right thing to do," Emily replied. "We'll go tomorrow or perhaps the next day. Give them some time."

Lily spent a restless afternoon and following day, prowling about Dungeness. She watched from a distance the boats go out, and the old men sitting on benches repairing nets and fixing crates. At home Emily kept her busy, hauling the washing from the lines and draping it over a large wooden rack near the range. Then the next day they ironed and folded. Later, Lily kicked at the stones as she walked to the tiny village shop near the lighthouse and railway carriage homes, and attempted to smile and give a friendly greeting to those who stared at her, wondering who this pretty young woman was.

What had Charlie meant by the tea having sugar, but not being sweet? Was he suggesting that it was Joe who gave him the Jury's Poppy? Finally, Lily decided to go back to see Charlie, but when she arrived at the Naval Officer's home neither Captain nor Mrs Browning were at home. A daily help answered the door and told Lily that Charlie had been steady on his feet after waking in the morning and much brighter. And so, when his brother had come to see him, the two of them had returned to Lydd on the afternoon train. Lily scowled her frustration; if only she had called by an hour before, she

144

could have seen him.

As she stomped back to Brooks Cottage, the sky, which had been bright and with cotton-wool clouds racing along up high, was now an ominous purple in the direction of the Fairlight hills. It suited Lily's mood very well.

"This is Hazel Barton, she lives nearby with her husband, Tom. He's a fisherman too and they've been good friends of ours since before Ed and I came to live here." Emily introduced a woman whom Lily immediately liked. She was perhaps a little younger than Emily, with a pleasantly rounded face, blue eyes and blonde hair streaked with grey, swept back in a loose bun at the nape of her neck

"I used to work at the school with your Ma," Hazel told Lily. "I moved out there and we lived together in the schoolhouse."

"Of course, Mother was talking about you when she was here." Lily felt rather guilty, "I'm sure she would have loved to see you but I'm afraid she was so worried about me. Has Emily told you?"

"She's told me some of what brought you here and you've not had a nice welcome," Hazel replied. "We thought it best if the three of us went over to Galloways this morning."

"We'll have some tea and then walk over there." Emily poured boiling water into the old brown teapot. "I'm not sure what we'll find, but you can be sure they'll be grieving badly over Joe."

The clouds hung low and grey over the Point as the three of them walked to Galloways. The air was damp and clouds threatened rain, yet let them pass along without suffering a drenching. As they walked a little inland from the coast, the dark carcasses of homes

145

which were Denge appeared to their left. Lily's stomach felt heavy as hazy memories of her desperate flee from Galloways, and subsequent hideaway in an old shack, came to the forefront of her mind. If it were not for Emily, then would her own body have found the strength to move onwards to Dungeness before the man who called himself her husband dragged her back to his home?

The tall coastguards' tower was the first building to show itself as they neared Galloways. And then the cottages, at first just a muddle of low roofs, took shape as individual buildings. Twisting snakes of smoke rose from chimney pots, the bleating of goats carried on a light wind and the creaking hinge of a privy door made an eerie noise. There was no person to be seen; no one came forward to find out who was approaching this place which mourned the loss of a young man. A man needed to work the boats and father a brood of Galloways' young. The people of this small community had shut themselves away beneath the dark cloud of their grief. Lily steeled herself to lead the other women to Evie's and it was she who rapped on the door.

The woman who answered the door looked familiar. She was one of those who had gathered around Evie during the wedding, Lily recalled. In fact, she had supported Lily as they walked somewhere, or rather as Lily floundered, unable to keep herself steady with the grey tea swimming in her veins. Most likely they had been walking to the ceremony. It was hard to place events of that day in any order. For a moment, the two women stared at each other and then Evie's sister spoke: "It's the bride." And turning to announce it to whoever was in the room behind her, she repeated the words, "It's the bride come back to be with us."

The door was opened wider to admit Lily, Emily and Hazel. As their eyes adjusted to the dim light within the shuttered living room, they saw the hunched figure of Evie rise from a chair and walk towards them. "Is that you, Lily? Come to comfort me?" She held her hand out to clutch at Lily's arm.

"I thought I should come," Lily replied, placing her own hand upon Evie's gnarled fingers. "It's been such a shock. I'm so terribly sorry for you all."

"Your coming brings me comfort," Evie said, leading her towards the table. "Sit down, my dear. And your friends too. Dungeness folk, are they?"

"Emily Brooks and Hazel Barton," Emily told her. "Lily has been staying with my family."

"Emily Brooks." Evie craned her head forward to study Emily's face. "Oh, I know you, Emily. I remember you as a young girl, with your red hair. I remember your mother too, living there at Denge; God bless her soul."

The woman who had answered the door, Lily recalled her name was Ivy, moved the kettle onto a hot plate. "I'll make a pot of tea," she said.

"Brown tea from the shop in Lydd," Emily said, her tone sharp. "None of your Galloways Grey."

"We find the grey is a comfort," Evie began.

"You'll give us brown or none at all," Emily cut her short.

"We're sorry for your loss," Hazel's words sounded formal, out of place for these people and their strange ways.

"Just when his wedding brought us so much comfort," Evie said, seemingly forgetting the bride had fled within hours of the ceremony. "Lily liked it here; she liked the room he made so nice for her. And he was a good man. A good hard-working man."

"Till he got that foolish notion," Ivy muttered.

147

"He'd have come home to me," Evie replied. "What was Joe going to do in one of those big towns? He would have come back and settled down in no time."

"Where was he going?" Lily asked.

"To Ashford or Folkestone or some place." Evie shook her head. "We were all having tea, Joe and myself and dear Mary, who had come visiting. And my sister, Ivy, she were here too, weren't you?"

Ivy nodded. "That's right. He told us the news that he'd found you, Lily, and had a nice talk. We were all so pleased and then he spoiled it all."

"Just when we were all so happy for him," Evie continued. "We were so shocked; you should have seen Mary sobbing. Said it was all her fault for sending Lily to us. Then she just got up and left, couldn't bear to be around him anymore. Went to her ma, I assume. My cousin that is, who lives just past the privy and the goats' pen."

"There was no talking to him; he were that stubborn," Ivy added. "Said he'd stayed here long enough."

"He'd have come back. I know it," Evie said. "He would have turned back soon enough."

"Lily just wanted to come here, to say she was thinking of you," Emily told them.

"Of course she did." Evie nodded, "And will you come again?"

"I'm... I'm not sure when I'll be going home," Lily began. "Perhaps, I could..."

"Because there's only one thing that could bring pleasure to us at the moment," Evie paused and took a long drink of her tea and then reached out for Lily's hand. "If only a baby could come of your union."

"A baby?" Lily frowned "I don't think so."

"It's what we pray for," Ivy murmured.

Chapter Fourteen

"Lily, love, you don't have to go, you know that," Emily said, as they neared the railway station. "I'll not say it again, and I can hear the train coming, but you don't have to... No one would expect it."

"I just feel I should. It will bring an end to all this... all this terrible business."

"It will," Emily smiled. "And I know I keep asking, keep checking. But you know I'd do the same. I'd face it just like you are and I like you for it."

"Thank you." Lily's tone was sombre. "Thank you for finding me and not sending me back there and letting me stay, and well... everything."

"Oh Lily, me and Ed, well, we've told you how your ma helped us, her and Tom, and Ben and Connie. They all played their part, but it were tough on Alice, her not being used to our ways. We liked her for that and so when you came into our lives, it gave us the chance to do something for her."

"I can't believe I was lucky enough to be there, in your old home at Denge, on the day you chose to visit."

"It were strange. It calls me, that old place does." Emily's eyes had a faraway look as she gazed over the shingle ridges towards the deserted settlement. "Not often, but sometimes, I go there and have a think about how my life turned out. No regrets, you understand. It's been good livin' here at Dungeness. It's been a proper home to me and the family too, that's how it is to us."

"How strange to think my mother thought of staying here, not just for the year, but for always and maybe to marry..."

"I thought it for a time. But your mum and Tom, well they were from different worlds. Not like Denge and Dungeness, or even Lydd. There she were with all her learning and a vicar's daughter too, and Tom... well you couldn't meet a more decent man, but no, they were too different and they both had the sense to see it."

Lily had met Tom Barton within the last week. Broad and tall, with more grey than blond in his thick head of hair, he still had a twinkle in his vivid blue eyes. Lily could see he had been a handsome young man. At nearly sixty years of age, he was taking a more sedate role on the fishing trawlers now. Like Ed, Tom knew it was time to let the younger men do more of the hard work. He was friendly, seeming pleased to meet Lily, welcoming her to Dungeness, His wife, Hazel, spoke of happy memories; she had been an assistant at the school, sharing the schoolhouse with Alice.

The women reached the platform just as the train gave the final turn of its wheels before nudging at the buffers. The wind was brisk, bringing with it a chill from the north-east, whipping the steam away from the chimney and racing with it across the Point. The sky was a bright blue and, far higher than the steam, wisps of clouds hastened to cross the coastline and reach the cliffs at Fairlight.

"We're going then," Emily stated.

"We are," Lily agreed, as she reached to open the coach door.

The train from Dungeness to Lydd left early in the morning and the one coach was still half-empty. It offered the people of Dungeness the chance to travel to Lydd or beyond and, as long as they were back at Lydd town station by mid-afternoon, they could travel home that same day. Within minutes the train was slowing into Lydd Town Station, causing Lily to reflect on her foolhardy decision not to return there on her arrival exactly two weeks beforehand, but to walk to Dungeness instead.

The two women stepped onto the platform and Emily led the way past station staff and passengers, then out to the main road.

"It's a little early, but we can buy some groceries in Hutchings' General Store and some meat for supper at Hughes'." Both women carried baskets ready to fill with anything needed from the shops in the town. "Your ma couldn't believe it," Emily continued, "she never thought to see a shop in Dungeness and we're lucky to have our little store there by the lighthouse, but it's very small, don't you think?"

"It is rather, but how marvellous to be able to buy your fresh fruit and vegetables there," Lily smiled her agreement. Although boasting large windows through which customers could look at the variety of food available, the shop itself was tiny. Lily had often walked to the villages in the countryside near Ashford, such as Kennington and Willesborough, but never had she seen such a modest village store.

By now they were in Lydd town centre and walking past the church before turning into Coronation Square. Lily was drawn to the long façade of Hutchings' Store with its three large windows displaying all manner of items from material to boots, groceries and saucepans. Its frontage onto the street was as smart as any in Ashford, yet it seemed to hark back to the era before the war. Emily, almost cowed by the splendour of the gentleman who stood at the doorway to welcome them

151

in, entered the shop, her back straight and basket held before her.

"I need some thread and buttons," Emily informed Lily, as they manoeuvred their way past displays of shoes and boots, then bags and hats.

Marvelling at such a selection of goods, all displayed in dark wooden cabinets and on highly polished shelves, Hutchings' Store reminded Lily of Dixons back home in Middle Row, where such a variety of items could be bought under one roof, rather than in the individual shops. Although this substantial shop was on a smaller scale than those in Ashford town centre, coming here with Emily reminded Lily of shopping trips with her mother.

On leaving the store, the two women walked across the square to the butcher's. Carcasses of sheep and pigs hung from hooks along the front of the shop, making a narrow entrance through which to enter. Higher up, running along the length of the second floor, were rows of dead rabbits, their white bellies turned outward, and birds, still waiting to be plucked.

"We'll choose a nice bit o' mutton and leave it here all wrapped up 'til later," Emily told Lily as they squeezed past the bodies of pigs and into the shop.

An hour later saw the two women sitting at a table by the window of The George Inn. Curiously, they looked a little like mother and daughter with their red hair and grey eyes, although admittedly Emily's hair was streaked with grey and Lily's chin less pointed. Lily stretched her legs out and looked at her feet in their T-bar shoes; it was the first time in two weeks she had exchanged her rough boots for shoes. Emily, Hazel Barton and Lily had walked across the Point to Galloways just two days beforehand. Now the fight to

152

claim Lily was over, they were able to collect her belongings and today she wore her own clothes again.

"It's nice just sittin' here watching the people pass by," Emily tried to make conversation, sensing that Lily's spirits were low.

"Did my mother ever come here, do you think?"

"I know for a fact she did, because it were the day she got her fringe cut," Emily replied. "I didn't know her then, but she told me she came with Hazel and it were her first time in Lydd after coming to work as a teacher." She took a bite of her toasted teacake. "Now are you going to eat some of yours while it's nice and warm? You've got to try, Lily. Don't do no one any good to go hungry when there's decent food in front of you."

Lily took a sip of tea and ate some of the teacake without tasting it. She gazed out of the window, watching the people of Lydd pass by: women with shopping baskets, children scampering along and old men with pipes and newspapers folded in their hands.

"Look at that, Lil. Now there's a sight." Emily leaned forward to watch the soldiers of the Royal Tank Corps march by.

They did all look rather smart, Lily admitted to herself. But she had seen enough of khaki uniforms during the war. Six years on and, unlike many of her friends, there was no flutter of interest in these young men.

Another hour passed, with little conversation as they watched life go by from the window of The George. They had previously strolled from Coronation Square to the Rype, following Lily's footsteps of two weeks before when she had walked the length of the green. Emily had pointed out various places of interest as they walked: the old Tithe Barn where Ed had taken her to see shows, the terraced house in which the retired teacher

153

of Dungeness School lived, the pub where she and Ed had eaten dinner as a newly-married couple. Had Emily travelled much further than Lydd, Lily wondered? They had been by train to Littlestone on many occasions, Emily had told her, and to Rye too, just a few times.

But whether they walked on the Rype or drank tea in The George, both women knew they were waiting for time to pass. Eventually, they looked at each other and knew the moment had come and, although no words were exchanged, chairs were pushed back, the waitress was thanked, and they stepped onto the High Street. Looking along the road, Lily could see the tall church tower and felt all her energy sapped from her body as the bell began to toll for the twenty-nine years of a life taken too young. It resonated through the small town, causing passers-by to turn in the direction of the parish church and silence to fall on the lips of those who had been chattering as they went about their daily business. With her body heavy and a slight feeling of nausea rising in her throat, Lily walked on, one step at a time towards the parish church of All Saints.

There was a small gathering outside the double doors at the base of the tower. Too small a gathering. A man had died, taken from this earth before his time, yet only two dozen people came to mourn his passing. On entering the churchyard, Emily and Lily slowed, content to hang back and keep a distance from the others. Looking up at the tall tower, Lily took in the details: the decorative perpendicular window, echoing the shape of the doorway below and higher still, the smaller windows, and then the castellated top with pinnacles of differing styles.

Keeping a respectable distance from the mourners, yet closely observing every detail, was the town's police sergeant. Lily gave a nod in his direction, having met him the day before. Beside him was another man, not in uniform, yet smartly dressed and with an air of dignity. A senior police officer, most likely. They would be looking for clues, watching how people reacted, waiting for the unexpected. Lily had read a few crime novels: she knew how they worked.

The clock showed ten o'clock and, as they readied themselves to continue, someone bustled by, pushing against Emily in her hurry.

"Sorry, Mrs Brooks. Sorry." It was Mary from the tearoom, niece of Evie. Her face already blotched, she was clutching a capacious lace-trimmed handkerchief.

"Come on then, love." Emily had her arm firmly linked through Lily's. "Let's get this done."

All eyes from the group at the doorway were now on the newcomers. Lily recognised the young women, Jennie and Martha. There was Mary, and others, vaguely familiar. But the men, they all looked much the same as one another with their rough skin, unshaven faces and ragged hair. Their ages differed but it was clear they all had a tough life, facing the harshest of weather and making little money for their efforts.

"Let me through then," a sharp voice came from amongst them and they parted to let an old woman step out. She was small, with a crooked back and olive-coloured skin. "Come along then, Lily. You'd best walk alongside me. It's only proper." And so Evie stretched out her claw-like hand and pawed at Lily's sleeve.

With a glance at Emily, Lily allowed herself to be taken and the whole group stepped through into the cool darkness of the church. There was something comforting about the slightly musty smell of old wood and stone. Something familiar about the soft light and shadowed corners. Lily had never been in this church, yet she felt she knew it. Fixing her eyes on the large window above the altar she studied the detail in the intricate stonework. The nave was long, and the pace was slow, until finally they gathered in the pews nearest the front and stood in silence. It was only at that point Lily allowed her gaze to rest upon the coffin with its simple wreath of wildflowers. The wooden box in which Joe's body lay encased.

"I've got this for you, Lil." Evie pushed something cool in Lily's hand. The black hagstone. "It's only right you keep it with your own. That's our way."

Lily gave a slight nod and her fingers wrapped around the smooth oval shape. Her own white hagstone was in her skirt pocket; who would have thought the Galloways wedding would have ended in this way?

With her parents and brothers, Lily attended church on a regularly and, in recent years, she had been to several funerals. She was familiar with the process and went through the motions expected of her. But her thoughts were on those shared moments with Joe. She had so few memories of him that each one now seemed to hold a special significance. There was the time of her arrival in Galloways when he had so kindly prepared his room for her to use. Then the finding of the hagstones on the beach and knowing he had taken care to choose the pure white stone for her. The wedding ceremony was hazy yet came with a warm sensation of feeling safe with him. Then, their last meeting, the time when she began to learn about him and, when he left, for a while she had wondered… *what if?*

Afterwards, walking away from the open graveside, Lily's attention moved to the soft pink blossom on the flowering cherries in the gardens bordering the churchyard and the fresh green leaves, newly unfurled from their buds. There was a warmth in the light breeze

156

and signs of fresh beginnings all around as nature began its new cycle of life. Perhaps the time had come for her to move on with her own life? Two weeks had passed since she had arrived at Galloways. Sometimes it felt as if she had been there for a lifetime, that the old Lily belonged to a different era. Then it was as if she had only just arrived, having still seen so little of the Dungeness her mother knew so well.

"It must be time to go home," she said to Emily.

"I knew you'd be thinking it," Emily replied. "But you know you're welcome to stay a little longer. There's always a bed for you with us."

"I just feel..." Lily paused, wondering how to express herself. "It seems that I've been to Galloways, then I was hidden away at yours, then Charlie was ill and Joe, well, you know about that. I feel that I've not seen Dungeness properly. So perhaps a few more days and I'll have seen it all?"

"You've certainly had your share of trouble since arriving." Emily led the way along the path and through a gap in the churchyard wall leading onto the High Street. "Why not stay another week and go home then?"

"Yes, I'll do that. It will seem like the right time."

But would it? Life at home in Ashford would give Lily no satisfaction. Young people who grew up during the war had become older than their years. Not only those who fought had suffered, but also those who stayed at home and saw, from a distance, the pain suffered. Visiting convalescing soldiers and packing aid parcels was all useful but had left her feeling as if she hadn't done enough. Joe had felt the same in some ways; he felt that he had been deprived of an education and wanted new challenges. He had no such opportunities, but what could she, Lily, do with her life on her return?

Dearest Father and Mother

At last your wayward daughter will be returning home and I know you will both be relieved to have me back in Ashford with you. I come free from the union with the man who claimed to be my husband, but the news comes without the jubilation you would expect. Joe came to see me just the once; his visit was unexpected but caused no bother. He was in no way argumentative, despite declaring himself to be married to me, and I found him to be a gentle person, although clearly misguided. He spoke of leaving Galloways, and sadly his wish to leave was granted that very day, but not as he planned. The dear man was killed that evening by an unknown hand. The funeral was yesterday; Emily and I went, despite her concern it would be upsetting for me. How bleak my heart felt to hear the bell toll for his twenty-nine years. A sound we heard time after time in Ashford during the war years.

I now have his black hagstone on the leather with my own white one. I shall keep them always and hope they serve as a lesson to listen to those who seek to advise me. I am sure you will now both shake your heads in despair of my ever being responsible. In which case I will keep the stones as a reminder of my adventure on the Dungeness Point. I have met some lovely people and learned about Mother's time here.

I plan to return home next Friday, catching the early train and being back by mid-morning. Father dear, I know you'll never understand the ways of this remote place, but I do promise to stay on the train all the way to Ashford and not walk any way until I step out of the coach at Ashford railway station!

With love to you both from your daughter, Lily

Chapter Fifteen

"We'll go along to church this morning," Emily announced over breakfast.

"Oh of course, but... to Lydd?" Lily thought of the grave and Joe lying there amongst his ancestors. Too young, like so many of his generation.

"No love, just along to the school, like it was in your ma's time."

Lily grinned. "Of course, I was thinking..."

"Well, he's going to be on your mind, but it will pass." Emily reached for the teapot.

"They'll all be talking," Allie commented.

"Of course they will," her mother agreed. "It's what people do. They gossip about one thing and then soon enough their minds have moved onto someone else's troubles."

"It will be the mystery of what happened that keeps them wondering." Lily frowned. "It makes no sense, first Charlie left out there in the cold with no injuries but drugged by the poppy seed. Then Joe, well I just can't, I mean I try not to imagine what led to him being injured like that."

"A bash on the head is no accident, you can be sure of that," Allie added.

"That's for the police to think about," Emily said. "And they will be, but I can't see they're related. No, it were different with Charlie, him not being hurt at all. I mean he were ill enough from being left out there, but not injured."

"I wonder if they'll find out who did it." Lily stood and began to gather the used dishes from the table.

"I'm sure they'll try their best," Emily replied. "And it won't be appreciated if the police are pestering us decent people as we go about our days. Anyway, Ed will be back in a while; he's just seeing young Edward off on the boat and we'll all walk over to the school together."

In her bedroom, Lily shook out her blanket and straightened her sheets. Reaching into her handbag, her fingers closed in on the slim smoothness of her cigarette holder. Strange how she had thought she needed to smoke, that it soothed her. Since retrieving her belongings from Evie's cottage, Lily often looked at the enamelled cigarette case with five remaining within it, and the glossy black holder. But the need had gone and, on reflection, Lily didn't want to be bound to tobacco in order to soothe her troubled mind. Standing on the beach, with the scents of the sea and the wind catching her breath, or trudging inland over the shingle ridges until not a soul was in sight – these were her new ways of calming her mind and setting her thoughts into some order.

It wasn't the cigarettes her fingers had been seeking, they now touched on the intricate detailing of a hair grip and she withdrew it from the bag. Lily brushed her hair, noting that its short bob had lost its definition and her auburn hair now curled around the pale skin of her neck. What had happened to her modern look? She gave a wry smile, looking down at the hem of her dress, the one worn on the day she had travelled to Dungeness, and showing an inch or two more of her slim calves than the borrowed clothes worn during her time with the Brooks family. Should she wear her own dress, or the simpler costume more suited to this place? She would wear the smarter dress just for the morning, for church.

They walked in a sprawling ribbon of churchgoers along the track to the school-church. There were the Bartons and other fishing families from the nearby cottages. Young Edward's wife, Grace, joined the family group with a toddler in her arms. The older men spoke now and then about repairs needed to boats and equipment, and agreed to meet after their midday meal for a pint of ale at The Pilot. The women gossiped, still finding things to speak of when the men had fallen silent.

For Lily this was a time to fully appreciate the vastness of the shingle headland. Most of the cottages clustered around the lighthouse and railway station then trailed along the coast; this was the area she was beginning to know. But to walk inland, as she had done a couple of times in the last few days, gave a new sense of freedom. The track undulated as it followed swathes of ridges, formed over centuries as stones were deposited by the sea. Any plant life was sparse: a clump of gorse, the occasional spiky broom, but mostly just patches of coarse grasses and delicate mosses. There was a beauty in this desolate landscape, but not the obvious beauty of a flowering fruit tree or a climbing rose. No, this was something more unique and less obvious; it appealed to Lily who was interested in experiencing anything different.

The wind was strong, pushing them along and pressing upon the ragged plants. The walk back would be hard work; Lily already knew that silence would fall on the group as the salt-air pressed upon them, almost

161

causing them to choke on it. But for now, as their backstays slid along, they moved with relative ease across the stones.

On nearing the schoolhouse, Lily felt her curiosity rise. She had seen the outside on several occasions, but now she was to see the schoolroom where her mother had taught for a whole year. The building was surrounded by a picket fence, with no other properties in sight, its being at least twenty minutes' walk from the fishermen's homes, and the railway carriage homes placed near the beach. It was a substantial building for this shingle landscape. What had inspired someone to build a school of stone, with a high slate-topped roof and additional accommodation for the teachers, when the people of Dungeness lived in such humble homes?

"That was Alice's room." Hazel Barton pointed to one of the three rooms attached to the main building. "And I was in the room next to her. She was alone at first, horrible it was for her, stuck out here. Then they came up with the plan that I could have a room too, so that was it. Alice and I shared together for a year. When she left, Ruth came and lived with me, and then of course we both married, and it was all change again."

"And Mrs Stubbs?" Lily remembered the name of the headteacher who had taught alongside her mother.

"Mrs Stubbs, well, she lived in Lydd as she married Mr Stubbs. The policeman he was. She must have taught here for another ten years after your ma left, then she retired and she's still living in Lydd with her husband. Getting old now, the pair of them are."

They passed through the gate in the picket fence, the people Lily's mother had known in her time here, all twenty-five years older – the Bartons and the Webbs, and the Brooks of course. Some of the older ones had passed on and others could no longer struggle across

162

the uneven ground to the school-church. But now the younger generation joined them, including Lily from Ashford whom they accepted as one of their own.

"We have the curate now, comin' from Lydd," Emily informed Lily, as they rounded the end of the building and entered the school as the children did, through doors at the back. "We don't have anyone regular here now; they come and go the curates do, and the vicar, well, he stays in that big church, he don't come to see us lot on the Point."

There he was, a young man, so different from the elderly vicar who had been a friend of Lily's grandfather and the one who had invited her mother to teach at Dungeness. He stood there, a mere fledgling, with his ash-blond hair and pale eyes a contrast to the black cassock hanging to his feet. Lily gave him a nod and a smile as she passed by and into the school-church.

Inside, the first impression was that this room smelt of a school. Was it the ashes in the grate, the rows of wooden desks or the decades-old odour of children's damp coats and sweaty socks? Lily couldn't be sure but memories of her own school days flooded back. The ceiling was cavernous and the windows high; the walls had a map showing the British Empire and various drawings of wildlife and plants; King George V looked down upon the churchgoers, and a blackboard on wheels was being pushed aside. There were books and boxes of paper and pencils. Was it so very different from the time when her own mother was a teacher here? Lily thought very little would have changed and, as she helped move the desks and set up the chairs, she knew her mother had done the very same.

A small altar and the window behind were revealed as a curtain was pulled back at the east end of the schoolroom and, as an elderly man pressed upon the keys of an upright piano, the curate stepped onto a small platform.

Hazel, sitting behind Lily, gave her a tap on the back. "Mrs Stubbs, she stood there to teach, and your ma and us helpers, we stood about to help. But when Mrs Stubbs went on the train, at half-past two, it was your ma who stood there teaching."

"Welcome, we have come today in the presence of God," the curate began, and the congregation settled to listen, "...to hear and receive his Holy word, to pray for the world and for ourselves. Especially at this time we think of our neighbours in Galloways who have lost one of their young men, and we keep them in our thoughts on this day."

The service ended with the Lord's Prayer and, as desks were lifted back into place, the curate moved amongst his people. Hazel gestured for Lily to join her in the doorway, which clearly led into the teachers' accommodation.

"It's not locked; I'll show you where Alice lived."

"Won't they mind?" Lily asked; her sense of adventure flickered.

"There's no one living there all through the week. Miss Coombes, she stays with her family in New Romney at the weekends, and her helpers just walk in each day." Hazel lifted the latch on the door and it swung open; the bolt had not been drawn across on the other side.

They stepped straight into a living area. A huge old-fashioned stove lay dormant, yet the central table with a collection of books on it and the easy chair with the bag of wool beside it, showed that this room was still used. It was clean and tidy, with no signs of modernisation over the past years. Lily could well

164

believe that the cross-stitch in a frame and the crude watercolours had been on the walls since her mother's time. It had a comfortable feel about it though and was a spacious room. She could imagine the teachers and helpers all gathering around the table before the school day began and then again in the dinner break. Lily was curious to see the rooms beyond the other doors, but this was someone else's home and so she stood in the centre, taking in all the details before stepping back into the schoolroom.

"All ready for school tomorrow," Hazel commented, as they walked past desks and chairs towards the outside door.

On the threshold, Lily gave one last look at the room and smiled to note the school motto *Play the Game* displayed on the wall. She pulled the door shut and, as they rounded the east end of the building, felt the full force of the brisk wind.

Lily was sitting on the shingle bank looking out to sea, watching the shapes of the Dungeness fishing boats take form as they neared the coastline. Young Edward Brooks had been out since the early hours of the morning and it was his boat she was hoping to recognise soon. The wind was brisk, giving an energy to the sea as huge waves rolled in, and white horses galloped as they raced to the shingle. The sky was a bright blue and up high pure white clouds raced with a speed to match the breakers below.

This was invigorating; the wind blew straight into her face and the salty taste of it was on her lips. Lily wore Emily's shawl but refused a hat, liking the way her short hair tumbled about in all directions. This was her fourth day in Dungeness since the funeral and now the troubles of the last few weeks were fading. The news of

165

Charlie was that he was recovering back home in Lydd, perhaps a little weak, but with no lasting damage. From Galloways, she knew nothing; Lily's connection with the place was finished.

The scrunch of footsteps on the stones caused Lily to turn and she smiled to see Ed. "Look who just came knocking on the door for you," he said, as another man caught up with him on the shingle bank.

"Hello, Lily. I couldn't be sitting around a moment longer." Charlie grinned down at her as Lily scrambled to her feet.

"But you shouldn't be… it's too far." Lily stared at him, her eyes round. "You're too ill."

"I'm not as fit as usual, but a walk to Dungeness and a train ride back won't do me any harm," Charlie replied. "And after you and me have enjoyed a nice chat over tea and cake, then I'll be ready to head back."

"Oh tea… of course," Lily took a step towards the cottage.

"No, I didn't come here to get you to make me a cuppa." Charlie reached out as if to take her arm, but merely shrugged as Lily neatly sidestepped his move. "We'll walk along to the tearoom where your Allie works and I'll treat you."

"Well, Alice couldn't object to you taking tea with a solicitor," Ed commented as Lily threw him a look, a plea for help. "Now I've got nets to mend, or I'll have Edward complaining."

Charlie had set off, leaving Lily to scurry after him. Following the line of cottages at the top of the beach, it took about fifteen minutes to reach the railway carriage homes and teashop. Charlie led the way up the plank steps and opened the door to the café.

On glancing in, he turned to Lily. "We'll sit out here, shall we?" He gestured to the tables on the veranda. "It's a bit breezy but we can talk in private."

Lily nodded. She wanted to ask about the poppy seed, and did he have any thoughts on who might have done such a dreadful thing to Joe, who seemed so gentle. They had only spoken of inconsequential matters on their walk, such as how Lily was liking her stay with the Brooks and life here at Dungeness.

"A pot of tea and..." He glanced at the cakes on display and then at Lily. "Fruit cake? Victoria sponge?"

"Sponge."

"Two slices of sponge, Allie."

"How are you, Charlie?" Allie asked from behind the counter.

"Oh, you know me, tough as anything. And now I've got a lovely young woman to take out to tea."

"Well, isn't she the lucky one!" Allie grinned as she lifted the heavy kettle from the range.

Lily shook her head in disbelief. What was it that Ed had said? Oh yes, that her mother would approve of Charlie. Now that did make Lily smile, knowing her mother's distaste for anyone who wore such vulgar things as pointed shoes!

"I like it that you came to see me; you stayed all night, they said." Charlie reached across to take Lily's hand. Sitting on the veranda, they were looking out on the ramshackle collection of carriage homes; beyond, a ribbon of sea sparkled.

"It was all so awful, and to think it was my fault." Lily moved her hand back a little so only their fingertips touched. "We thought you would die."

"Not me," Charlie smiled. "It wasn't good though. I remember feeling a little woozy, but I thought I'd be fine

167

with a bit of fresh air. Thought they'd been giving me the grey tea, and I'd need a lot of that to knock me out."

"But it was Jury's Poppy."

"Nasty stuff."

"And do you think… do you think they wanted to kill you?"

His face was serious now, green eyes looking directly into Lily's grey, "I don't know. I like to think they didn't. They wanted to scare me, and I hope that's all."

"They wanted to stop you from talking about the Galloways wedding. From trying to get them to see sense about it."

"It seems like they did, but I thought I was smarter than that. I thought I'd notice if they were up to their tricks." Charlie looked away, as the door to the tearoom opened and Allie appeared with the tea tray.

"Look at you two out here with all this wind coming off the sea." Allie balanced the tray on her hip, and put the teapot, cups and plates of cake on the table. "You don't want to come inside?"

"Things to talk about in private, Allie. Not private from you, you're practically family to Lily, but you know…"

"I know all right, Charlie." Allie arranged the plates before them. "Lily was so worried about you and then there was that other business…"

"You were worried, were you?" he grinned at Lily. "It's about time a beautiful woman worried about me."

"Oh, Charlie. I bet you've got plenty of girlfriends back in Lydd," Allie laughed as she turned away.

"I haven't." There was that serious look again, the one that puzzled Lily.

"Of course I was worried." Lily changed the subject. "You got hurt because of me and now Joe is dead, and I can't think why. He came to see me, did you know?"

168

"Joe did?"

"It was when you were in the Naval Officer's house; he came to the Brooks' cottage." Lily looked into the distance, recalling the short time they had spent together. The time when she began to get to know the man who called himself her husband. "He said he was planning on leaving Galloways."

"Oh, was he?" Charlie frowned. "Evie wouldn't have liked that. She wanted him to stay there. Doesn't approve of anyone leaving."

"But during the war, he must have been gone then?"

"Oh, no, he was needed to bring in the fish." Charlie shook his head. "She made sure of it."

"And you?" Lily wondered.

"I was there, on the Front. I don't talk about it now. Time to move on with our lives."

"I would have been there if I could," Lily told him. "I'd have been a VAD nurse or something useful. But I was too young; all I could do was package up aid parcels and serve cups of tea in the hospital."

"It all helped, Lil." Charlie reached out for her hand again. "Really it did."

They sat in silence for a moment. It was as the last crumbs of cake were eaten, when Lily poured their second cup of tea, that Charlie voiced his thoughts.

"You'll be off soon, I guess. But Lydd's not so far away from Ashford and I like you, Lily, you know that. So when you've got over all this upset about Joe and blaming yourself for everything, I'm going to come and find you and take you out somewhere nice. Somewhere a bit posher than this place."

"Oh, I rather like it here." Lily ignored his serious manner. "But you're right, I'm going home on Friday. Back to my job and my family and my... my boyfriend."

169

Chapter Sixteen

"Tell us about this place you disappeared to, Lily."
Charles reclined on the picnic rug, took a long drag on
his cigar and expelled the smoke in her direction. "You
went for Easter weekend on some mad escapade and
didn't return for three weeks. Shoddy behaviour, too
bad."

"We thought you'd run off with a fisherman!" Tommy
sniggered as he looked out from under the brim of his
straw boater. "It certainly gave some jolly good
entertainment when we met for tea at The Saracen's
Head last week." On receiving a nudge from Sarah, he
continued, "At least it would have done if we hadn't all
been so worried about you."

"You could have written," Helen said. "Take no
notice of them, but we were worried."

"I… well, it wasn't planned." Lily looked out over the
Eastwell lake. The trees, whose leaves were only just
thinking of unfurling when she left, were now displaying
fresh growth in all shades of green. Families of ducks
with their young gave entertainment to these young
people, and birds flitted about overhead. Above the
treetops the crenelated tower of the decaying St Mary's
Church peeped. "And mother knew..."

"She gave nothing away when Polly and I called
around to ask after you," Helen persevered. "Now come
on, Lily, give us all the news. Did you fall in love?"

These were Lily's friends: a group of young men and women who had escaped the horrors of war. All in their early twenties, they were too young to have suffered on the front line, but to say they had escaped was perhaps an injustice to them. Charles' brother had been killed in action, his body lost in the carnage of war, and his name remembered on the Thiepval Memorial. Helen's father, a local doctor, suffered badly from the traumas he had experienced, and relived the memories of all those casualties he had failed to help in time. Polly had a neighbour who went to war a confident young man, only to return with something called shellshock; something not to be spoken about. All twelve of these apparently carefree young people could tell stories of family members or friends lost to the Great War. But they chose not to tell, not to talk.

Instead they worked during the day, often following in the footsteps of their parents: the men were in banking, medicine, law, or working towards managerial roles. The young women were teachers, clerical workers or stood behind the counters in department stores. In the evenings they sometimes met at the Beaver Road cinema and pretended not to admire its grandeur or to be enthralled by the improvements in filmmaking since it opened in 1912. The young men occasionally met in a public house and dallied with the type of women they would never consider marrying. The women frequented the town centre tearooms, where they spoke of the frustrations of being young in this small town and planning a move to London, or some other place where life could be lived at a faster pace.

At the weekend, adventures such as this trip to Eastwell were planned. Sometimes they walked, but today Charles was showing off his brand new motorcar:

171

an Alvis with bright blue bodywork and a folding roof, very much like a pram hood; and Oliver had borrowed his father's more sedate MG saloon. They arrived in style at Eastwell: picnic hampers and rugs crammed in the back of the cars, the young women seated on the knees of the men. Giggling and joking, they poured out in the narrow lane and set up a picnic before sprawling on the rugs, eating and chatting idly.

"Come on, Lily; it's not like you to be a bore," Charles persisted. "Tell all."

"You can't just go off to wherever for three weeks and not tell us about it," Polly added. "You didn't, did you? You didn't fall in love?"

"Of course she didn't," Sarah replied for her friend. "Lily doesn't just go about falling in love."

"And what sort of place is it, this Dungeness?" Oliver asked.

"Oh, it's nothing but a load of old stones," Helen reported. "Not much else. Some fishing huts and that's about all."

"There's a railway; that's how she got there," Sarah informed. "It's the sort of place that's a century behind the rest of us! All Victorian, with skirts to their ankles. The men fish and the women well – they gut the fish and breed children."

"What on earth did Lily do with herself?" Charles almost sneered.

"Oh, she befriended these women: taught them poetry and fine needlepoint. Useful skills!" Oliver replied.

"Lord, she can't have been in such a place! Not Lily, it's all a ruse, I'm sure of it." Charles reached over and took a sip of sparkling wine. "She eloped with a Frenchman or someone terribly handsome and made

172

up this tale of Dungeness. Come on, old girl, where are your usual retorts? Tell all."

Lily looked at them all, most of them friends for the last decade. Educated and well-to-do. Pleased with their cars, shorter hemlines and tailored suits. Was any one of them better than the Brooks or the Bartons or the Webbs, who worked hard, cared for their families and welcomed a stranger into their homes? "Oh, I did go to Dungeness. Nothing much to tell," she said, in a careless manner. "It was different, not like any place I'd ever seen. Stony, windswept, desolate."

"Lily, whatever did you do there?" Polly asked. "What possessed you?"

"I went to visit some friends of my mother."

"Gosh, the story intrigues," Sarah gushed. "Your mother?"

"She taught in the school there," Lily explained. "Before she was married."

"A school? It's nothing like we imagined then. But, Lily, three weeks?"

"I was ill, the flu." Lily rested her head in her hands.

"You poor darling."

"But did she have the flu?" Charles nudged Polly sitting beside him. "I'm certain Lily is pulling our legs. There's a mystery here. And what's that ridiculous thing about your wrist?"

"This?" Lily raised her arm a little and turned the pair of hagstones on their leather lace. "Oh, these are my hagstones."

"What a scream!" tittered Sarah. "That's a love token, if ever I saw one!"

Polly grabbed at Lily's wrist and held it up. Pulling herself free, Lily rose to her feet and put her straw hat firmly on her head. "I've had enough of sitting about. I'm going to the church. It's half-ruined and quite romantic."

173

She had walked a dozen steps on her own, leaving the others to their cigarettes and idle chatter, content with her own thoughts, when there was a light touch to her elbow."

"Do you mind? I've heard of the marble figures and would love to see them." James was new to their set. A cousin to Charles but with none of his brashness. "I won't ask a thing about your time away. I won't even speak if you prefer to be left to your own thoughts."

"There's just nothing much to tell," Lily lied.

They walked along, gaining glimpses of the lake through gaps in the trees surrounding it. As they neared the small church its tower began to show through the trees and soon the unkempt condition of the whole building was clear to see. The roof looked to be in poor condition and a dense mass of dark green ivy crept up one side of the tower and seemed intent on conquering the upper reaches, easing itself under the tiles and claiming the church as its own. On entering the graveyard through a gap in a low stone wall, Lily was dismayed to see long grasses and weeds amongst the toppling headstones.

"How sad it is, yet I am drawn to this place. I wonder about the people who used to worship here." It was uncharacteristic for Lily to express her secret thoughts and feelings. "What a lonely place it is for them now."

They walked past the headstones, frequently pausing to decipher old lettering, to ponder over the names and ages. Some died so young and others so old; James and Lily spoke of the unknown people whose lives had long passed on from this earth. Lily found herself not minding the gentle company of this man whom she had barely noticed before.

After circling the small church, Lily stood at the doorway. "I always like to see the marble monument, and you said you'd like to?"

"I would." James hung back a little. "That is, if you don't mind."

"It's fine." Lily looked back at him as they entered the dim entrance at the base of the tower. "She, the Countess of Winchilsea, is in a chapel off to this side." They walked briskly though the nave and into a chapel.

There she was: far too grand for a place such as this, with its musty smell, cracked windows and water-stains on the floor and pews. Emily Georgiana, in almost pure white marble, reclined on a chaise longue, with classical pillars for its legs, and sumptuous drapes. She was dressed, not in the style of her time, but in that of a Greek goddess. Bare feet peeped through the folds of her dress and her arms were unclothed. Was it likely, Lily mused, that Emily Georgiana ever sat down to read with no shoes or slippers upon her feet? The sculptured hair, running in neat waves then coiled at the base of her neck, was not unlike Lily's own short bob, restyled since her return to Ashford.

"I wonder why..." James began. "Look at her so grand and this side-chapel is in better condition than the rest of the church, but it's a miserable place for someone such as this Countess."

"She must have some connection with the place," Lily replied. "But look at this *'Who died July the 10th 1848 aged 39 and was buried in the chancel of Ewerby Church, Lincolnshire'*. I often wonder what reason there was to have her monument here."

"It's a mystery," James replied. "And one worth exploring."

"Perhaps it is," Lily agreed. "But for now, we had better return to the others."

They walked in silence, through the tired old church, the ragged churchyard and out into the dappled sunshine of the lakeside walk. Even from a distance, before their companions could be seen, their chatter and laughter could be heard above the rustling of the leaves and the birdsong.

"And what is it like at Dungeness?" James asked. "I mean, really like. I won't make fun of you."

So Lily told him a little about the stony Point, which at first appeared barren, but where beauty could be found in the tenacious little plants or the colour of a pebble. And how the people, although humble and often uneducated, were brave, hard-working and welcomed a stranger into their homes. On their return to the others, Lily found that the conversation had moved onto new things of interest and she was able to sit, listening to their banter but not truly feeling a part of it.

The following weekend saw the same group of friends meeting in the village of Willesborough. This time picnics were carried in bags and stout shoes were worn, as they set off on a waterside hike. But first they strolled from the motorcars, parked not far from St Mary's Church, where Lily's maternal grandfather had been rector, towards the countryside. While chattering about inconsequential matters, they reached the end of the road at the Corn Mill and began to navigate the uneven ground beside the river.

Walking in groups of two or three, they followed the course of the river as it twisted and turned. Sarah fell in step beside Lily and spoke to her. "I've changed my mind about Tommy."

"Marriage?" Lily queried.

"Of course," Sarah replied, her voice high and excitable. "He's so jolly good-looking, I wouldn't want anyone else to snap him up, just because I was thinking it through."

"Oh, I thought you were quite decided."

"I was, and now I've changed my mind again."

"And that's what you want?" Lily asked. "To set up home, do all those household chores and have babies?"

"We'll have a daily help, of course, and everyone says that Tommy is so eligible. We'll have gorgeous babies."

"I'm sure it will all be perfect." Lily gave her friend a quick hug and a kiss on the cheek. "Congratulations!"

"I'll tell him later," Sarah said, flashing a smile. "And then there'll be a party to organise. I'll give up work so the wedding can have all my attention; there will be so much to do.

"Oh, you haven't told Tommy that you have changed you mind?"

"I've only really just decided, but the poor thing must be put out of his misery. Look how desolate he is without me."

Lily looked across to Tommy who was walking beside James. They paused to look more closely at the river, pointing and chatting about something. The sun shone through the treetops, casting a dappled light on the ground. The river was shallow with numerous weirs; water sparkled as it rushed along between stones. Lily liked Tommy; he was a decent sort. He worked in a bank; a favourite with staff and customers, he was now in a management role. It had become clear that he and James were fast becoming good friends, and Lily believed they had taken up fishing together. James said something and Tommy gave him a playful punch on the arm, they laughed and moved on.

"How good of James to comfort Tommy," Sarah commented.

Turning away from the river, James saw Lily watching and walked over. "We're planning our next fishing trip," he told her. "It's good fun – although we don't keep the fish; we let them go again."

"Oh, isn't that the reason for it?" Lily thought of the baskets of fish brought in on the boats at Dungeness. But that was different; James and Tommy merely fished as a hobby.

"It's relaxing," James said. "Sitting there on a rug by the water, watching the wildlife. Perhaps you'd like to come along sometime? Not everyone, too much chatter." He gave her a smile, "We'd never catch a fish with Charles and Oliver about."

"No, we make quite a crowd. Enough to frighten the bravest of fish." Lily considered going out one afternoon, just the two of them. "I'd like that, thank you."

"It's not always easy to plan, but do you work a half-day on a Wednesday?" James had not long finished at medical school and worked beside his father, who was a general practitioner in Kennington, a village close to Ashford.

"I understand, and I do work a half-day. It would be nice to do something different."

They walked in companionable silence for a while, Lily was watching Sarah and Tommy, who were walking along in deep conversation.

"I hope she's not going to upset him," James said.

"Oh?" Lily was surprised, not expecting him to comment on their friends. "No, I don't think so."

"He's a decent sort," James observed. "Probably for the best she refused him. He can do better and seemed

178

quite keen on my sister when they met last week. She's perhaps a little young, but a lovely girl."

"Tell me about your family," Lily replied. She watched on as Sarah and Tommy parted and, when her friend walked past her sometime later, she seemed a little less exuberant than usual.

That afternoon they picnicked beside one of the weirs with Breeches Wood behind them. Then, after retracing their steps until they were able to cross by a footbridge, the group of friends followed a path across the fields to Sevington. Finally, as they crossed the Stour again by the Corn Mill, they walked back into Willesborough, now a little weary but having enjoyed the outing. Lily, no longer the centre of their entertainment, found herself enjoying the afternoon as she sought out the company of the less high-spirited of her friends.

They parted with not only plans for the following Sunday, but with a suggestion from James that just the two of them could take the train to Hythe for the day on Saturday. Lily found herself agreeing, without a hint of reservation.

Chapter Seventeen
Emily's Story

"I'm going to see Lily," Emily told her daughter, as she placed a small carpet bag at the front door. "I can't say why but I just feel I should do something.

"I know, Ma." Allie poured her mother a cup of tea. "You're not one to sit about waiting for something to happen. Will you eat before you leave?"

"No, just the tea. It's all I can manage at the moment." Emily watched her daughter push the tea across the table. She was a good girl. Well, young woman now. A mixture of herself and Ed: with Emily's slim body and pointed chin, but her father's dark hair and eyes. None of his temper, thankfully. Allie stayed impassive, where Ed was prone to fiery outbursts. And that was the problem: he had often been seen to act first and think later; it was known throughout the Point.

Still standing, Emily drank the tea and rinsed her cup. She gave her daughter a quick hug and picked up her bag. "I don't know if I'll be back today, so I've got an overnight bag. What it would be like to stay in the town, I can't imagine, love. But I never thought I'd be here without your Pa. Not till it was God's will for one of us to be taken."

"It's shocked us all, Ma. You do what you think is best and if Lily brings you consolation then go to her. It's only right she knows of this anyway."

It didn't matter to Emily that the sea-mist was rolling in over Dungeness. Carried by the wind, it came in thick swathes. If she had cared to look, she would have seen it curling in upon itself, twisting and turning, as it moved inland before dispersing over the countryside of Romney Marsh. Fishing boats sat on the ridge, like sentinels awaiting their moment. This was the fourth day of the mists, the fourth of boats being beached by order of the weather, and the fourth day since Ed had been arrested early one morning.

The police had come when the sun was still low in the sky – a faint glow beyond the blanket of mist, making such little impact on the day. From the railway station, they had slunk along the beach track unrecognised. They rapped on the door of Brooks Cottage and pressed upon the latch before anyone had a chance to answer it. Their presence filled the room, as they stood in their black belted coats with brass buttons: the Lydd sergeant in his helmet and the inspector in his flat peaked hat. Wooden truncheons were at the ready; they expected trouble from the man they came to arrest for the murder of Joe Stoneman. But Ed, normally so vocal when wronged, had been led away, head bowed and silent.

Sitting on the train, Emily kept her eyes lowered as they passed through Lydd, then Brookland and Appledore stations. She didn't want to make eye contact with anyone. Didn't want to be recognised as the woman whose husband was in the cell of Lydd Police Station. With her eyes firmly fixed upon her folded hands, Emily refused to even look towards the nearby police station as the train eased out of Lydd. Had she tried, she could have glimpsed the Victorian brick building on the main road. She hardly noticed the mist thinning as the train journeyed across the Appledore Dowels before taking the gentle incline as it pulled away from the Marsh.

It was only as she neared Ashford that Emily began to take an interest in her surroundings, for she was naturally curious, with a liking for new experiences. She had been to Rye several times, in her Sunday best and a smart felt hat. Quite smitten by the beauty of the small town on the hill, where houses jostled for space within the ancient town walls, she had explored cobbled streets and marvelled at the stories of French raiders who ransacked the town and stole the church bell. With their children, she and Ed had travelled to Hastings, where they had enjoyed the pier and traditional seaside amusements. And, numerous times over the years, Emily had been to Littlestone, at first with Ed and then with the children as they grew up. But she had never been to Ashford, although she had wondered about the town and what was to be seen there.

As the train came to a stop at Ashford station, the depression which had cloaked Emily for the past few days began to lift. It was all so grand with four sets of tracks running through and a footbridge to take passengers from one platform to the other. The canopies were deep, the ironwork ornamental and the brick buildings decorative with classical details. For Emily, used to the fresh coastal air, the smell of steam was an assault to her senses: she could taste it, smell it and her eyes smarted as grey plumes belched from the chimney and a gust sent it over the platform. And the people – there were so many of them – calling out and rushing about. For a moment she stood, not knowing quite what to do next.

"Can I help you?" An elderly porter approached Emily.

"I… I'm not sure." Emily looked about her in wonder. "I'm visiting, you see. I need to get to Jemmett Road and I'd like to walk, if it's not too far."

"It's no distance at all." He beamed at her, his face round under his cap. "You'll need to cross the footbridge, go out over there and you'll see the town to your right. Now, you have to turn left, away from the town, and walk straight down Beaver Road. Take a right turn when you see the church, and when you reach the end of the road, you'll be in Jemmett Road."

"Thank you. What a relief, it sounds easy enough."

"Oh, it is. And you'll know you're there when you see the park with its railings and gates."

Of course, they lived by a park. So Emily set off, her spirits lifting at the thought of seeing Alice and Lily in no time at all. She walked at a brisk pace, out of the station, past the motorcars, motorised bus and horses with carts, all awaiting those who were about to appear from the busy station.

The next thing to attract her attention was the large number of sheep being herded along the very road she was expected to walk along. She was forced to wait for them to pass by and couldn't help voicing her thoughts out loud, "Oh my Lord, look at all them sheep."

"Driven all the way up from Romney Marsh, poor buggers," an old man informed her, as he stood back, resting upon his walking stick and looking on.

"Well, I never, I've just come from there meself, but I were on the train."

"It'll get no better for them after they've been to market," the man replied. before turning away.

The Romney Marsh sheep plodded on and Emily was able to walk along the street, lined with red-brick terraced houses. It was a busy road and she had to sidestep waste from both sheep and horses, as well as contend with delivery boys on bikes, and the occasional motorcar. How anyone could walk with ease from one place to another in this town was beyond Emily.

On reaching the church, Emily noted it was not as ancient as those in New Romney, Lydd or Rye. It was attractive in design; built of ragstone under a slate roof, with neat rows of small lancet windows and a small bell turret. Now she walked the length of a slightly narrower road, feeling a little hemmed-in by the rows of Victorian terraced houses. They were built for the railway workers; Emily recalled Lily telling her about the area in which they lived.

Finally, the iron railings of Victoria Park could be seen and there was Jemmett Road with its semi-detached houses. Emily knew to look for one opposite the park gates, and there it was. She checked the number and, feeling a little uncertain, walked up the path to the front door. It was terribly posh: all those panels on the door and the coloured glass, the fancy brickwork and patterns made from wood. Well, she knew Alice would live somewhere a bit special; it wasn't going to be a place made of planks and no proper path leading to it.

"Oh, Emily, what a thing to happen!" Alice reached across the table and took her friend's hand. "And have you seen him? How is he?"

"I've only had word from young Edward, and that's just that they say he's settled." Emily looked towards the gas oven. "Oh my, fancy you not having a range like the rest of us!" Her eyes had been dancing around the room since she had first been ushered into the kitchen. It was the oven which interested her the most.

"But they have no evidence?" Alice asked.

184

"Just that someone heard Ed shouting, someone from outside the cottage heard him shouting at Joe." Emily looked straight at Alice now, "He's always been one to have a good rant, but as for hurting someone, he'd never do that."

Alice thought back to the Ed she first knew: the man who had been broken, thinking his wife was dead. She recalled his previous life, when he and that no-good cousin had gone aboard boats in distress and robbed them. He hurt people then, left them for dead, just for a bag of grain or the boots on their feet. But that was all so long ago and he had only stolen to feed his family, not for any other gain. Once the people of Dungeness gave him a chance to fish alongside them and live an honest life, he took it. And when he joined the lifeboat crew, he was able to save lives rather than allow them to perish in the turbulent grey waters. Alice had seen Ed Brooks at one of the lowest points in his life; she had seen him angry and raging when he was a younger man. But she never felt he was someone to use physical violence; he roared a lot, but he would not kill a man.

"Lily will want to know about this." Alice stood and started to tidy away the teacups. "I suggest we walk to the town and meet her as she takes her midday break. We can have a little something to eat in a café and talk this through."

And so Emily's bag was put in the small spare bedroom. Then she marvelled at the tiny closet with the high-flush lavatory, its cistern on decorative iron brackets, before walking down the elegant staircase. Finally, the two friends stood in the hallway, Emily's grey eyes wide as she looked at the detailing in the cornicing and the coloured light dancing on the walls as the sunlight passed through the glass set into the window above the front door.

"We'll walk through the park," Alice announced, as she closed the front door behind them.

They spoke a little of distant memories, frequently punctuated with Emily's observations: the decorative railings, the orderly flower beds and the magnificent fountain – they were all so grand and so very different from her own world. In her limited experience, only Hastings compared: it was highly ornamental on the seafront and in the parks.

Small bridges crossed streams and the Stour before Alice led the way onto a footbridge passing over the railway tracks leading into the station. Now the greenery was exchanged for iron railings, coated with soot-lined crevices, and the view to her right was of the station, with two great metal beasts slumbering at the platforms, and all the rooftops of the station buildings. There were sidings, stretching out like fingers from the station, and sheds and great piles of coal. Beyond this was the brown-brick engineering works, with smoke drifting from tall chimneys and yet more sidings. Tracks arched away in different directions, one back to Romney Marsh and the others to destinations unknown to Emily.

To the left, the Romney sheep were gathered in the market, along with cows and horses, in various pens. And across the tracks from the market and the great cylindrical gasometers, it appeared as if there was another railway station, with yet more sidings and tracks leading to other towns, and then most likely on to London. Alice and Emily had passed over the bridge and the jumble of industrial Ashford and, before Emily had taken it all in, the buildings became tall and quite grand as they walked up the hill towards the town centre.

"This is where Lily works," Alice said, as she stopped outside an elegant building.

"The National Provincial and Union Bank," Emily read. "My, look at that."

"We could go and ask for her?" Alice suggested. "I never have before, but I believe she takes her break at this time."

Shying away from the tall wooden doors with brass fittings, Emily replied, "I'll just stay and look at the street, if you don't mind."

"I'm going to leave my job, Mother. Yes, I know it's a decent place to work and there are poor people struggling to earn money at the moment. Well, let one of them have mine. I'll go to Dungeness with Emily and I doubt I can be of any help, but she needs me and I need to be there. If I can be of use in some small way, then I must try."

As they sat in Lightfoot's Café, set on the corner of the High Street and Castle Street, Emily looked on. There was Alice, seeming to be as much the vicar's daughter as she had all those years ago when she first came to Dungeness. And Lily, young, irritated by her life and seeking adventure. They thought they had nothing in common because Alice barely remembered the days before she had the responsibilities of being a wife and mother, and her daughter didn't know enough about her own mother's past.

Emily knew about the frightened young Alice who had arrived at Dungeness and could have got on the next train and gone straight back to Ashford. Instead she had stayed, in order to discover the mystery of the body on the shingle. And then Alice did her best to

187

enable that person and her husband to better their lives. The young woman washed up on the beach, nearly dying on the stones, was Emily. She knew better than anyone how determined Alice could be when she needed to be. She saw in Lily more of her mother than either of them suspected. But this was a new century and women were more confident; Lily was part of this new generation and the time had come to make changes.

"Lily, they won't keep your job for you." Alice warned, as the waitress placed plates of cold ham, fried potatoes and pickle before them. "What of your character reference?"

"Mother, I don't want them to!" Lily replied. "I really can't tolerate it a moment longer. I'll go to Lydd and we'll sort out all this nonsense, and I'll come back home and find something useful to do. I want to do something worthwhile, to help people."

"We can talk about it while she's with me," Emily suggested.

"We can," Lily agreed. "But first I must speak with the police about Ed. I was there when he shouted at Joe; it was over in a flash. He knew Joe was a good man."

"Emily will stay with us tonight and return home tomorrow," Alice told her daughter. "Will you follow on in a day or so?"

"If I could race to the station now and be sure of reaching Lydd before the last train to Dungeness, then I would," Lily declared. "But no, I'll be leaving with Emily tomorrow."

Emily smiled her gratitude. She couldn't think what Lily could do to help, but she felt sure something good would come of her return to Dungeness. "I'll look after her, Alice. She won't get caught up in anymore trouble."

188

"It wasn't you who caused all this," Lily reminded her. "If I had listened to Mother and Charlie, then I would have arrived safely and not got caught up in Evie's foolish plans. Joe would be alive. Charlie would never have got harmed. Ed would be home safely with you."

Toying with the last of the food on her plate, Emily shook her head. "You can't carry on blaming yourself for everything that happened after you took a wrong turning and headed off to Galloways. Blame Evie if you want to cast blame. You made a mistake and that's all, Lily."

"I've an idea," Alice said. "Why not offer to help in the school while you're there? Not as a teacher, but as an assistant. Children hardly ever come along from Denge, Galloways or the cottages lying further away from the school. Could you do anything for them, Lily? Do you think you could make them see it is important to have some education?"

"Perhaps I could," Lily replied. "I met two young women, Jennie and Martha, they were too old for school, but they thought nothing of having an education. If I could encourage people like those two, now that would be worthwhile."

Plates were cleared away and an offer of pudding declined. Lily must return to work and Emily, having eaten her first proper meal in days, had no appetite for anymore.

Pausing outside the National Provincial and Union Bank, Lily flashed a smile at her mother and Emily. "You won't believe it, but after all these years I think I may have an idea. Something I could do to make a difference, to be of some use somewhere. Let me think about this and there is someone I need to speak to, then perhaps I'll be able to share it with you. But first," and she reached out for Emily's arm, "we must do something to save Ed. He is innocent, of that we are certain; we just need to prove it."

That evening Emily saw Lily take writing paper and envelope from a drawer and seat herself at the small mahogany table in the bay window. Was she doing the right thing in taking this modern young woman back to Dungeness with her? Was she being foolish in her notion that Lily could in some way help?

Dear Helen,

I got such a ribbing last time for running off with no explanation. I have none this time, just that I must go again to Dungeness. Mr Simpson at the bank was rather displeased; I have left my job with immediate effect. When I return, I plan to do something useful with my time.

The others can make of this what they will, but do give my apologies for not being on Sunday's outing.

Your friend, Lily.

Dear James,

I am terribly sorry, but I have to cancel our outing to Hythe on Saturday. I was very much looking forward to it. I am going back to Dungeness for a week or more. A friend needs my help, and I really can't say any more in a letter. Only that I wouldn't be rushing off without good reason. The others will gossip awfully, and I have no intention of sharing the reason for my going away with them. I will tell you a little of it when I return, in the confidence that you will listen sensibly and not make fun of it.

With my best wishes, Lily.

Chapter Eighteen
Alice's Story

Alice slumped in the armchair, sewing on her lap. Not that she was going to sew; it was just best to have it there. To make it seem as if she were about to do something useful.

"Who's there to see you anyway?" she muttered to herself.

Winnie, the daily help, had completed her duties and George wouldn't be home for lunch for at least an hour. Having just returned from walking with Emily and Lily to the station, Alice felt rather lost. How did she feel about Lily's second visit to Dungeness? When her daughter set off on the first visit, it brought back so many memories. They jostled for position in her mind, each one seeming more important than the other.

At first, she thought of how much more capable and grown-up Lily was compared to the nineteen-year-old Alice. And then she thought about how irresponsible and reckless it was for Lily to travel to this unknown place with no plan. Then she felt a little envious of Lily setting out on an adventure, before thinking that it would be good for her to see somewhere so different. So her thoughts continued to conflict, causing her to be a little short-tempered all weekend.

Now, having seen Lily in the home of Ed and Emily, Alice began to wonder if her own daughter was better suited to Dungeness life than she had been. Foolish thoughts because Lily was only visiting, not considering a lifetime of living there. But she was returning, and only yesterday she had left her clerical job; now Lily was free to live and work wherever it suited her. Would Dungeness suit her restless spirit?

After a fretful night, and with the sun casting its golden rays through the window warming Alice in the chair, her eyes began to close a little. She was nineteen again and running away from her responsibilities as a teacher. No, that was not what she ran from; she ran from the people of Dungeness and their secrets. She ran because a young woman's body had been lying on the shingle and she couldn't help. Was the red-haired woman dead or alive? Alice didn't know and there was no one she could trust to tell her. This was the first time Tom had held her in his arms.

Tom held her in order to shout at her, to make her see sense, to order her back. Yet it was then that she first betrayed herself. It was there, in the black of the night, with only the shingle and stunted gorse to witness their fight, that her heart first lurched at a man's touch. Nearly thirty years later, Alice allowed history to take a different course:

"I'm engaged to be married," she screamed at him, brandishing the ring as proof.

Tom took her hand, looked at the ring and dismissed it. "Where is he now then? Back in Ashford? If you were my woman then you'd be with me."

"If I were your woman?"

"Then you'd stand by me and help me deal with all this bloody mess. You'd not be running off." His hand was still gripping her wrist and now he took both her

192

wrists in his hands. "If you wore my ring, then I'd not let you go."

They stood for a moment, their breathing ragged, barely able to see each other's features as the clouds raced over the surface of the moon. Her throat tightened a little in trepidation of what was to come and she waited, mouth slightly open, her gaze on his face. He leant down and kissed her, softly at first. And then, without needing to check her response, with more passion, the tip of his tongue exploring her mouth.

They parted slightly and he cupped her face with both hands, before kissing her more gently. "Is that how he kisses you?" Tom asked.

"No," she replied.

Alice moved slightly in the chair, luxuriating like a cat in the sunshine. That wasn't at all how she behaved, but if only she had... Then she was in the shack at Denge, the previous home of Ed and Emily. But they weren't there, Emily was ill and staying with the Webbs; Ed was... she didn't know where. And she, Alice, had come with clean blankets for the bed. She was disturbed by that rotten Jake Brooks. But what if it had been Tom who walked in to find her bending over the bed, ankles showing, her skirt tight about her gentle curves?

Alice turned and sat on the edge of the box-bed, lips slightly parted, eyes shining to see him there. Her skirt was still gathered up a little, allowing him to see part of her slim stocking-clad calves. She should pull it down, but she had seen him looking, appreciating her. There he was, grinning at her, his fine white teeth showing, eyes shining, and, as he ran a hand through his unruly hair, the dark-blond curls fell back in an unruly manner.

193

"Well, Miss Tibbs, not the prim teacher now. What brings you to this man's bed?"

"You know very well, Mr Barton." She held his gaze. "I am helping prepare this room for the return of Emily."

"And you look so damned good doing it, that I wonder if I should wed you, just to see you showing your legs as you neaten the blankets on our own bed!"

"Marry me? But –?"

"I like the way you're helping the people here. You've not just come to teach, you're touching our lives and fast becoming one of us."

"But Albert… my intended..."

"But Albert? He can take his pick of any number of dull young women. But you should remain here with me. Don't you think?"

If only it had happened like that. If only it had not been Jake Brooks who disturbed her that day, and when Tom arrived it had been to see that vile man about to force himself upon her. What happened built a divide between the pair of them for, although her virtue was saved, a man's life was lost. Ben Webb had been there too and one of them, she never asked who, had been the one to throw Jake from her, and in doing so Jake's head had cracked on the table as he fell backwards. They never spoke of it again and it was not until the body was found, when a storm whipped the shallow covering of stones from him, that Jake Brooks' body was taken from its hide and buried in a pauper's grave in Lydd. The discovery of his body, and the proper burial that followed, gave Alice a little peace. But the memories of that afternoon lived on.

"Miss, Miss, look there's a man walking under the rainbow." Dora tugged at Alice's sleeve. "I think it's Mr

194

Barton. Ma thinks he's ever so handsome, but he's ever so old, maybe even thirty. What do you think, Miss Tibbs?"

He wasn't thirty. He was about twenty-five or perhaps twenty-six. Not thirty. He had wanted her to walk across to Denge with him. "I've got some news for Ed and Emily; there's a cottage here for them at Dungeness if they'd like it. So perhaps you'll come and be a part of letting them know. We've two hours until sunset, plenty of time to be there and back. And I'd like to spend some time with you."

"With me?" Alice's heart glowed. The school day was coming to an end; she would be free to leave in ten minutes. But not in her severe black dress, her teacher's outfit. She almost skipped to her bedroom within the schoolhouse and changed into a soft tweed skirt and cream blouse. The dress was cast upon her bed, not carefully folded away in the clothes press as it should be.

They walked across the shingle together, with Tom telling Alice about the cottage. Then he slipped his hand around hers, they looked at each other, and continued in that way until they neared Denge. It felt right, his fingers entwined with hers.

Alice stirred in the armchair. "Foolish thoughts," she murmured. "We weren't walking; we were on backstays. You can't hold hands and move along like that. And if you did, it would be awkward, not romantic.

Something happened. Something had stirred within her, and a general dissatisfaction with Albert began to take hold. This was coupled with a growing attachment to her life at Dungeness, the people she had met and the new experiences. A commitment had been made though, and together she and Albert were planning their

195

married life in their own home: one of the railway workers' terraced houses overlooking the green at Newtown. But on her return to Ashford, she learned that the plans had changed.

"Bad news." Albert bowed his head slightly to portray the burden of telling. "I was told just this week that Mr Baldwin is to retire at the end of July, but his replacement comes from Manchester with a family of five children. His need for a house is greater than ours."

"Might there be another opportunity?" Alice's mother asked. "You deserve a house, Albert; they must see that. A good worker must surely have a house when he marries?"

Alice listened in, her spirits sinking. She had become quite attached to the vision of those brown brick houses, all in an orderly line with their own little front paths and inside water-closets. They were to have their own allotment too which Albert would tend at weekends.

"There is a chance of a flat, but Mother says, and I must agree, why would we live in a flat when she has a decent house with space for us all?"

So, that was the plan. To live with Albert's mother. A good plan and what most young couples expected. But Alice couldn't picture it. What would her role be in a place where his mother already had her routines in place?

It was at that moment a new arrangement began to form in Alice's mind. It only took a visit to Albert's mother and afternoon tea in the parlour, and the decision was quite fixed in her mind.

"Albert, we must stop and talk for a moment." Alice pressed on his sleeve slightly and nodded towards a

196

bench set under an old oak tree. "Let's pause here and speak of our future; so much has changed."

"Just for a moment, my love. I wouldn't want us to catch a chill and we can't be sure the wood doesn't harbour some damp."

"Albert, I am fond of your mother, and of you of course, but I worry for our future. I've changed. My time at Dungeness has taught me to make decisions for myself and to feel a pride in helping others. I meet all kinds of people and see the good in those who lack our education and manners. I am a better person now, but I am not the woman you wanted to marry."

"Oh, Alice, my love, you need not worry. Tell this Mrs Stubbs of your decision to stay here in Ashford and you'll soon forget all these foolish notions."

"But Albert, I have no intention of forgetting them. I want to stay in Dungeness, and perhaps for longer than planned." Alice steeled herself to say her final words: "Albert, I would like you to release me from our engagement."

"Enough of this foolish talk, Alice. You'll soon settle back to normal life." Albert laid his hand on her arm. "But in the meantime, think a little of the pain you cause me."

"I do think of it, really I do," Alice felt her throat tighten as she persevered. "But I truly believe it is better if we part. I won't make you happy, Albert. I am quite certain of it."

Moving his hand from her arm, Albert stood, as if to emphasis his role in their relationship. "I've been too understanding, too tolerant." His voice deepened and eyes darkened. "Enough of this, Alice. I should never have allowed your father to send you to that place. Anyone could have gone to teach those… those

197

ragamuffins. But to send a young lady… it should never have even been considered."

"No, Albert, you are wrong." Alice felt the fury rise within her. "And to hear you even speak like that makes it clear we cannot continue our engagement for a moment longer."

Albert's body stiffened. "Very well, Alice. I was prepared to overlook some of your recent behaviour, to trust Mother to guide you. But if that is how you wish things to be." He pocketed the ring Alice offered. "I will give you a week – exactly a week and not a day longer – in which to reconsider your nonsensical behaviour. Then you will take the ring back and nothing more will be said about it. Your parents will be very disappointed. Very."

Alice stood and walked away, without looking back at the man whose gaze followed her every step.

"You foolish girl; a handsome young man such as Albert will have a new love by the time you come to your senses," the words poured from her mother's lips. "He is all you could want for in a husband: well mannered, respectable, with a steady career and an orderly mind."

"Albert is dull and thinks nothing of my wishes."

"He thinks only of your wishes and comfort." Mrs Tibbs turned to her husband. "Did you not know the type of place you were sending your daughter? Did you not think of the influences that would prey on her innocent mind?"

"I only thought of her doing good deeds," Reverend Tibbs replied. "I am deeply disappointed in your daughter."

"It's not too late… he will understand." Mrs Tibbs began to usher Alice towards the door. "Go now, be

198

contrite and he is sure to forgive you rather than suffer any further embarrassment."

"I'll take a walk by the water-meadows," Alice replied, as she pulled on her boots.

It was another two years before Alice redeemed herself by forming an attachment to George. In him she found a man who suited both herself and her parents. For Alice he offered a gentle and giving personality: he cared about the less fortunate and chose to teach in a school where he could truly make a difference. She was attracted to his red hair and slightly stocky figure, his friendly smile and his extended family of siblings, nephews and nieces. For her parents, he offered a well-to-do accent, a good education and a small inheritance which allowed him to buy a modern family home near Victoria Park. But before she once more became the daughter her parents wanted, Alice returned to Dungeness declaring she would stay there for at least a year and return only for short visits.

"It's nice over Littlestone way, with tall houses overlooking the bay… and a decent path along the seafront," Tom began tentatively at first, and paused before continuing, "...and a fine hotel where they do a nice midday meal, so I hear. The train goes there from Lydd and it's a pleasant stroll to the promenade."

Alice looked up at him and waited.

"So, I wondered, Alice… if perhaps next Saturday…?"

"That would be lovely," Alice replied.

"Good. Well, I'll knock for you at just before ten o'clock?

"I'll look forward to it."

Alice's stomach was all butterflies that Saturday morning. She fussed over her hair, paced up and down, tidied the schoolhouse and adjusted her hairclip again. When there came a knock on the door, she was ready to set off on a new adventure.

"It's an hour's wait in Lydd for the New Romney train." Tom sounded apologetic. "I thought we could go for tea? And then have a bite to eat at the hotel on the seafront in Littlestone."

"It sounds lovely." Alice smiled up at him.

It was all very pleasant: the walk down the tree-lined avenue to the seafront, the tall, terraced houses, the Grand Hotel and the stretch of greens alongside the promenade.

"This is just as I imagined Dungeness to be," Alice told Tom.

"What a disappointment!" He slipped his hand around hers.

"No, not at all." Alice looked up at him. "Well, perhaps at first!"

All too soon, they were forced to return to the station. "This time we are straight to Lydd and onto Dungeness," Tom explained.

"It's been a lovely day." Alice's heart felt full to bursting; her hand tingled to be wrapped within his. Was this what falling in love felt like?

On the short train journey back to Lydd, they were alone in the compartment. When Tom looked at her, Alice yearned for him to kiss her, imagining him to be a far more passionate man than Albert. When he leaned in to press his lips against her own, his kiss was firm, leaving her aching for more.

"We could perhaps take the train to Rye next weekend?" Tom's expression was serious as they *parted outside the schoolhouse. "That is, if you'd like to."*

"I'd like to very much." Alice gave a smile and tried to hide the true extent of her happiness.

The sound of a motorcar's horn, as it passed the house, roused Alice from her slumber. "Sleeping in the daytime; I'm becoming an old woman," she murmured. The thoughts were pleasant, albeit rather foolish. But it didn't hurt to daydream for a moment about the long-gone romance.

The story of Tom and Alice was nearly over, though. There were perfect days over the summer, when the sun shone down upon them and the weather seemed to always be fair for picnics and outings on a Saturday. But as winter came with the strong winds and rain, and the miserable sea-mists, their times together became less frequent. There was no pleasure in long outings so they caught the train to Lydd and played out their romance under the curious eyes of the Dungeness women, who also used the extra Saturday train as a convenient way of taking a trip to the town and filling their shopping baskets.

Alice still enjoyed her teaching position at the school, and the company of Hazel. She visited her parents occasionally, staying in Ashford for a few nights, but was always content to return home to Dungeness. As December came and she thought about her planned Christmastime visit to Ashford, it was time to speak about her future with Tom:

"We've known each other a year now," Tom began, as she nuzzled up beside him on the small sofa in his cottage. She had just cooked their supper and now they were pleasantly full. With a tankard of ale and a sweet

sherry on the side table, they were able to relax with the warmth of the radiating heat from the stove.

"Mmmm," Alice replied, running her fingers along his forearm and tracing the lines on his hand.

"So best I come along to meet your parents and we'll talk about a wedding in the spring, or sooner if you'd like it."

"I'd like it," she smiled up at him. Then she asked, although she knew there was no need to, "And the school... could I continue there? But Mrs Stubbs already leaves early, and I should be here to cook for you."

"I fend quite well for myself, with Connie coming in to do my washing and giving the place a sweep through. Besides it would only be for a few months... and then perhaps?"

"A family?" Alice frowned. "I wonder what that would be like?"

But try as she might, she couldn't imagine it. Not here at Dungeness. On her last visit to Ashford she met her cousin, Doris, and they had strolled along the streets of Willesborough, then down to the water-meadows, with the new baby in luxurious cushioned comfort. The large wheels and springs enabled Doris to push her baby daughter along with ease. It was all rather pleasant, and these walks were part of the baby's daily routine. But as a fisherman's wife in Dungeness, how would she fill her days? There would be plenty of jobs to do, of that there was no doubt. But with her teaching position finished, and her husband out on the boats for many hours at a time, could Alice really be happy there? And could she really make her husband happy? Dungeness suddenly became a very lonely place.

Alice pulled herself up from the armchair. George would be home soon and expecting a meal on the table. She'd made the right decision, of that she was certain. It was best for Tom too; he needed a wife who was used to life at Dungeness. Yes, Alice had done very well and made good friends, but it wasn't quite the same as living there forever. When their relationship ended, she was desperately lonely; her heart ached for him. Every day she longed to knock at his door and beg him to find a way of making it work for them. She stayed another three months, then left Dungeness one morning, with the persistent drizzle soaking through her coat and the wind pushing at her back, just as she had found it in the autumn of 1894. When George had come into her life, Alice knew she had made the right choice.

Chapter Nineteen

Lily watched Emily seeming to shrink into her seat, as the train halted in Lydd Town station. No one got into the carriage and Emily's eyes lost some of the haunted look. The mist, a thin film over Lydd, now thickened with every turn of the engine's wheels and even the school, so close to the tracks, was partially obscured by it. Peering through the window, Lily searched for the lighthouse, but there was nothing to be seen, or perhaps just a sliver of black pointing upwards; it was hard to be sure.

There was a clunk as the engine's wheels came to a stop at Dungeness. The women stepped onto the platform, then stood watching the tank engine's wheels start a slow reverse turn as it began pushing the carriage back towards Lydd. Soon the great metal beast, with its belly full of a roaring coal fire, had moved away. Only the taste and smell of its steam remained to mingle with the mist. With the engine gone, the silence was now punctuated by the long blast of the foghorn, and when that passed, it seemed that they had come to a place devoid of life.

"We'd best get back," Emily said, clutching her bag to her.

Lily picked up her own small case and hung her handbag from her elbow. They walked in silence, Emily taking the lead, past railway carriage homes which loomed through the mist. Occasionally, a scrunch of footsteps on the stones told of a person nearby and a figure would begin to come into focus, only to fade away again. A chill dampness settled on their skin. This near-silent place with undefined features and everything shrouded in a soft quilt of mist, was worlds away from the early summer sun, the fresh green leaves and the sparkling river in the countryside near Ashford. It was a little like the world of silent films, experienced by Lily in the Beaver Road cinema.

It took a quarter of an hour to reach the timber cottage, and on reaching it Emily left her bag by the front door and announced to Lily, "The boat won't be out in this mist. I'll go along and see if Edward has any news."

"Shall I…?" Now she was here, Lily wasn't quite sure what Emily wanted from her.

"Of course, best you hear it straight from him."

Edward Brooks lived just a few steps away. "Back from the big town then," he said, as he answered the door. "Thanks for coming, Lily. Lucky you did as the police want to speak to you."

"Me? I suppose they do." Lily thought back to the last day she had seen Joe. "I was there when your father shouted at him. It was just words of course, and I'll tell them so."

They were ushered to sit around an old table of scrubbed pine. "Tom and I have just been talking it through," Edward said, nodding his head in the direction of Tom Barton who already sat at the table. "Have you stopped for tea yet, Ma?"

"No, we came straight here," Emily placed the blackened kettle on the hotplate of the stove. "Sit down, Lily. It will be all right; you just need to tell them what you saw. There's no harm in that."

"It's better that Lily goes to see them, rather than the police going all the way to Ashford and causing a fuss," Edward observed. "Your ma wouldn't care for that."

"Gosh, no, she would have a fit!" Lily thought of curtains twitching and her mother's embarrassment.

"Hazel said she'll go along with you to see the police," Tom told Lily. "It's not something you'd want to do on your own."

Lily liked Tom's wife, Hazel. She was someone who knew her own mother well from their days working and living at the school together. "I'd like that," Lily replied. "Unless you wanted to come, Emily?"

"They won't let me see him and I've had enough of that inspector, him that's come along from Folkestone to deal with all this," Emily replied. "No, I'll stay here and you go with Hazel. It will be an early start if you go on the first train."

Over tea, they spoke of everything Emily had seen in Ashford, and it seemed to take her mind off her husband. It was now five days since Ed had been taken to Lydd for questioning and there was no hope of his being returned to them.

"We went into Lydd and spoke to Charlie yesterday," Tom told them. "He can get word of Ed, whereas we're told nothing. He says there's not much evidence to go on. Just the word of two fishermen who came with their rods to fish off the beach. They came sniffing about the cottages, looking to use our well, and that's when they heard the row."

"Not Dungeness men?" Lily questioned.

"No, and I'm glad of that," Edward replied. "I wouldn't like to think of our neighbours betraying Pa."

"They wouldn't do that," Emily's tone was sharp. "I'd like a word with those two and to tell them what a good man your father is."

206

"That wouldn't help, Em," Tom said. "The police wouldn't take kindly to you tampering with a witness."

"Well, best the police find out who did it."

"They've been having words with Charlie, too," Tom continued. "Wondering if there is a link between the two incidents, but I can't see there is."

The talk moved on to the weather and the mist which persisted in smothering the point. Five days was enough, they all agreed. It was no good at all to have the boats marooned on the beach and no fresh fish for themselves or to sell. Then Emily and Lily returned to the cottage to complete household chores and await Allie's return from work.

The following morning, Lily and Hazel travelled in the lone railway carriage, hauled by the stout little tank engine, to Lydd. Hazel told Lily about the winter of 1895 when the sea froze along the edge of the beach and the lifeboat went out in treacherous conditions.

"One day they'll speak about the mists of 1924," Lily mused.

"I don't know how it can be that nearly thirty years have passed," Hazel replied. "Most of our parents passed long ago, and now our men sit fixing nets and sails, waiting for the boys to come in with the catch. But they're not boys anymore; our own sons are grown men."

Despite the silver running through Hazel's fair hair, and her skin, which was rougher than Lily's own mother's, there was still a youthful exuberance in the older woman's manner, especially when she recalled the days of working alongside Alice. She was gentle, with a sunny smile and blue eyes which shone.

"I had an idea, something I've been wondering about," Lily said, as they came to a halt in Lydd Town station. "I'd like to ask you for some advice after we've seen the police. It's about my future and a plan I have."

"I'm curious now," Hazel smiled. "I can't think what help I could be, but I'll try."

They walked along Station Road, feeling the warmth of the early morning sun through the light mists which would disperse over the next hour, while at Dungeness they persisted in hanging low over the sea and shingle landscape. With no words exchanged, Lily led the way from the main road, and past some pretty cottages to a gate leading into the churchyard. They paused to reflect at the mound of fresh earth with the small wooden grave marker bearing Joseph Stoneman's name. Then Lily and Hazel went to the local shops and had some produce set aside for collection later.

"I was thinking of going to see the solicitor, Charlie. He might have some advice," Lily began. "Would you know where to find him?"

"There are some offices in an old house in the High Street," Hazel began to lead the way. "It wouldn't hurt to see what he has to say. He's the only one who has been allowed to see Ed."

A small woman with a round face and hair scraped back in a bun, looked up from behind a desk as Lily pushed open the door and stepped off the pavement into the ancient building.

"I've come to see Mr… er, Charlie?" Lily said, aware for the first time that she didn't know his surname.

There were two inner doors, and before the secretarial worker could begin to query the reason for Lily's visit, one of them opened.

"Good morning, Lil. How are you, darlin'?" A big grin spilled across Charlie's face. "Come to see me? I knew you would!"

Shaking her head in mock dismay, Lily entered the small office. Charlie gestured for her to sit in a chair while he settled himself behind a large desk.

"You're back then."

"Emily came to Ashford," Lily began to explain. "She wanted me to know about Ed being in the police station, and for me to be here with her. And now the police want to speak to me, so I thought it best if I came to see you first."

"It's that inspector from Folkestone; he's come along interfering in things he knows nothing about," Charlie said. "They even wanted a word with me, knowing I'd been along to Galloways and that there had been some trouble. But those Naval people set him straight, saying I was in no fit state to go about knocking anyone around."

Lily frowned. "Of course not, and you've been a victim too."

"Oh, I'm all right now and they wanted to know all about that, too. What was I doing lying there nearly dead?" Charlie shrugged his shoulders and grinned. "Well, if I knew that then maybe I'd have been able to help myself a bit better. But it was Evie or Joe who fed me the Jury's Poppy. Now I ain't going to speak bad of a dead man and that mother of his, she's suffering enough."

"What do you think they want with me? I hardly knew him."

"Like it or not, Lil, you're his widow and they'll just want a little chat about what you heard when Ed gave him a good telling off that day, and if you knew of anyone else who would do him harm."

209

"I just don't want to make it worse."

"You just tell them that Ed was upset, coming across Joe like that." Charlie moved from his seat behind the desk and sat in the chair beside Lily; reaching out, he took her hand. "Listen, Lily, you just need to tell them what you saw and it will be fine. He was trying to protect you, keep you safe in his home and look what happened: Ed went out and along came Joe. He had a bit of a shout and settled back to fixing his nets or helping young Edward with the catch; never mind what he did, the temper had passed. That's how it is with him: he has a roar and then it's forgotten."

"I know," Lily said. She stood up, pushing the chair away. "I'll go and see them."

"Come and see me afterwards? Or shall I come with you and we'll have a cup of tea when you're done?"

Lily grinned, she couldn't help liking him despite his pushy ways. "Thank you, but I've come with Hazel Barton, so I have company."

"I'll keep trying!" Charlie grinned. "I have a feeling you're going to grow to like me one day."

The police station was a substantial red-brick building. Built at the end of the last century, it had bay windows, typical of the late Victorian era, and a slate roof. It stood alongside Station Road, not far from the railway station. The heavy wooden front door was ajar, so Lily pushed it open and stepped into a large entrance hall. A young police constable stood behind a desk with an open ledger before him. He wasn't much older than Lily, causing some of her nerves to fade.

"Hello, Harry." Hazel took a step forward. "We've come to see Bill and that inspector who's come along from Folkestone."

"Good morning, Mrs Barton and Miss..." He looked at Lily.

"This is Miss Lily Stevens from Ashford," Hazel informed. "She's come to have a word about this terrible injustice dealt on Ed Brooks."

"Very well," Harry's expression was grave. "I'll just tell them you are here."

Lily stood looking at the plain walls, high ceiling and decorative coving. The desk was solid and plain in style; the only picture on the wall was one of King George V and his consort, Queen Mary. A grandfather clock gave a steady tick; time seemed to pass slowly. She could hear a muffled conversation coming from one of the nearby rooms.

Then the young policeman returned and ushered them through to a large room at the front of the building, with a tall bay window through which the early morning sun was shining. Both men were standing and shook hands as they introduced themselves. The inspector was a slim man with a neat moustache; his hair was dark and neatly slicked into place, and his suit a well-fitting tweed, double breasted, with a sharp pleat to the front of the trousers. His eyes looked hard as he scrutinised Lily.

"Ah, the widow," he said, as their hands joined briefly. "I'm Inspector Morgan, been sent here to sort out this shocking business, and this is," he nodded towards the town sergeant, a pleasant, slightly rotund man, in the dark uniform of a police officer, "Sergeant Banks."

"Good morning," Lily kept her voice cool, immediately taking a dislike to the inspector. "This is Mrs Barton, from Dungeness. A friend of both the Brooks' family and my own family."

211

"She'll have to wait in the entrance hall," Inspector Morgan looked at Hazel. "If you don't mind..."

Hazel cast a helpless look at Lily, who attempted to smile her reassurance.

"Now, Mrs Stoneman, if you'd please be seated." The inspector nodded to a chair. The two policemen placed themselves in chairs behind the large table, which had orderly piles of paperwork on its polished surface.

"It's Miss Stevens," Lily replied.

"I see. The marriage was somewhat unusual, but recognised hereabouts, I understand?"

"I believe it is, but it is a marriage I did not consent to, so I prefer to be known as Miss Stevens," Lily said. She felt uneasy about giving Inspector Morgan any more bait than necessary.

"You didn't consent to marrying Joe Stoneman on..." he glanced at his notes before him, "April 19th of this year?"

"I didn't."

"Yet interviews with the deceased man's mother and other members of the Galloways community state that you married at a ceremony unique to the settlement. I have indeed queried this arrangement, but both the town sergeant and the mayor confirm that a Galloways wedding is an accepted procedure hereabouts." The inspector narrowed his eyes and held Lily's gaze, "I am a conventional man, Mrs Stoneman, and I like things to be carried out in accordance to British law and tradition, but in this case I have put aside my misgivings and accepted this marriage as binding."

"I did not consent. I was unaware it was a wedding ceremony involving myself. No one told me and no one asked." Lily felt her body tense; she would not be told how it was by this man with his cold eyes and

212

condescending manner. "I arrived just the day before and they drugged me before the ceremony."

"Are you making a formal complaint, Mrs Stoneman?" the inspector asked.

"No, the man they called my husband is dead," Lily replied, all fear lost, and fired by the urge to defend both her own name and that of Ed. "I am here to speak in defence of Mr Brooks, who you are keeping in your cell for no good reason."

"For no good reason?" the inspector repeated. "That will be for me to decide and, later on, the magistrate."

Lily said nothing and waited.

"Married or not, you left Galloways on the morning after the wedding and went to Dungeness, to the home of the Brooks, who are friends of your mother. You stayed there for several days until Joe Stoneman sought you out. What happened during that time? How did Ed Brooks feel about your being there and the marriage?"

"At first he said I should go back. But we talked with his wife, Emily, and he soon agreed I should stay with them."

"Why would you stay with them? Although known to your mother, they were strangers to you, were they not?"

"They were," Lily agreed. "But I was ill. I had been drinking the grey tea, not realising it was blurring my senses. I thought I was ill with influenza or something similar. I was weak, tired and confused. So I stayed with them and Emily cared for me."

"The grey tea?" Inspector Morgan queried. "Are we in a fairy tale?"

"Galloway's Grey," the sergeant began to explain, "is a brew made from a plant unique to the area. It is

213

known to have soothing properties, but for those who partake of too much, or are unused to its effects, it can dull their senses, causing them to be unable to make rational decisions or be aware of what is happening around them."

"I learn something new every day I spend in this backwater," the inspector's voice was laced with contempt. "Very well, your senses were dulled by the Galloways Grey. You stayed to recover; let us now move on to Ed Brooks' response to your marriage."

"He was surprised."

"Surprised?" Inspector Morgan raised his voice a little. "Ed Brooks – he was angry, wasn't he? Furious that a lovely young woman such as yourself should be lured into the bed of a chancer such as Joe Stoneman."

"At first he was upset, as anyone would be," Lily cautiously agreed. "But rather than get in a temper, he came here to Lydd and sought legal advice."

"Was he known for getting in a temper?" the inspector snapped back at her.

"I wouldn't know," Lily replied coolly. "I have known him such a short time."

"Now, let us move to the day when your husband paid you a visit. Who else was in the Brooks' home with you?"

"I was there alone."

"And your husband arrived. Tell me about it."

"He said he was sorry, that he wanted me to return to Galloways. Joe told me he wanted to leave the point, to live and work in a local town. He wanted to prove his worth and for me to choose to be with him rather than be pushed into it."

"Charming!" Inspector Morgan gave a short laugh. "Fine words for a man who forced a woman to marry him."

214

"It seemed very decent of him." Lily ignored the inspector's apparent humour. "We talked for a short time and then Ed – Mr Brooks – came back from fishing or helping with the fishing. He was shocked to see Joe. Who wouldn't be?"

"So shocked that a fury descended upon him," the inspector stated.

"No, he said Joe should leave and asked me if I was all right," Lily replied, deliberately keeping her voice calm. "I said I was fine, that we had talked, and Joe was leaving anyway."

"All very civilised. So why did Ed Brooks shout..." Inspector Morgan glanced at his notes. "Shout 'You'll not take her back to Galloways and I'll damned well make sure of it,' and shout with such venom that it could be heard by strangers on the beach?"

"It was because..." Lily looked him straight in the eye. "It was because Joe shouted out to him that I would want to return to him, that I had feelings for him, or something like that. And so Ed responded. And then it was over. We returned to the cottage, Emily came back from the railway station and we discussed the matter. Any anger that Ed Brooks may have felt was gone."

215

Chapter Twenty

"I used to come here with Alice," Hazel said as she and Lily sat over lunch in The George Hotel. "It wasn't so very different then from how it is today."

"How strange to be here with me now," Lily mused. "I wanted to ask you something. It's about my future; I had an idea about doing something useful. I have been wanting to do something worthwhile for so long, but I never knew what it was that I could do."

"And now you do?"

"I think so," Lily said, frowning. "At least, I hope so. You see there are so many people who have missed out on an education. All those children who live in the countryside or far from schools — and there is one excuse after another as to why they rarely attend. Then they become adults who can barely read or write. They have children and they can't help their children with their schooling. Perhaps, as parents, they don't show a commitment to sending their own children to school."

"You want to help those people? The adults?"

"I think so. I want to help them all, but perhaps if the adults can make changes in their lives then it will help their children too." Lily's mind raced as the ideas flowed. "I met two young women, Jennie and Martha, at Galloways. They were perhaps seventeen years old and they told me that they had barely been to school. It all sounded like such a joke to them; it was as if they just couldn't make the effort to do that journey across the stones to the school. And I can hardly blame them; it's a miserable thing to have to do in bad weather. How many others are like that? How many adults, young ones and older ones, who live here on the point, have very little education?"

"When I was there at the school with your ma, there were some children we barely saw from one week to the next, and it will be no different now," Hazel told her. "Those new ones to the area, living in the converted carriages, they usually go along, and those from the lighthouses and the Naval cottages. It's not so far for them. But I see it with the families living near The Pilot and even further away along the coast, they make any excuse not to walk all the way out to the school. It's not easy; I did it myself with my brother and sister and there's no fun in trudging over the shingle ridges."

"And do you think the adults would welcome some education now?" Lily's eyes searched Hazel's face, looking for her reaction.

"I think some would and others would worry about looking foolish." Hazel frowned. "It's a good plan, Lily. But I can't see them paying."

"No, I'd be doing it because it would be worthwhile, to make a difference. My father's mother, my grandmother, left me some money," Lily began to explain. "Not a huge amount but enough to live on, if I was careful, and so I could do this. I could help these people if they wanted it."

"Well, I think they would," Hazel replied. "But they'd be cautious, unsure. It couldn't be like a school."

"No, I thought I would visit them in their homes. It would be just the two of us, at first."

"Perhaps as they grew in confidence, you could teach friends or neighbours in groups of two or three?" Hazel began to warm to the idea.

217

"But how would I know who to approach?" Lily looked up and smiled at the young waitress who served their shepherd's pie. "It would need careful handling."

"I think," Hazel paused to consider, "I think you should go along to see Miss Coombes at four o'clock one day. She'll know of the children who don't go along to school as regularly as they should. Find out who the children are then I'd bet it's their parents who need the help."

"You're right!" Lily smiled. "I'd need to think of how to approach them and to buy in some supplies of slates and chalk. Then I must have my reading books sent from home. Could they start with a slate, or should it be paper?"

"Perhaps paper. They wouldn't want to feel as if they were children. It's more expensive though."

"Yes, but if it encourages them to write then it's worth it." Lily pushed shepherd's pie onto her fork. "No point in putting them off by treating them like small children."

"You're right." Hazel nodded. "This has to be done in a thoughtful manner."

They ate in silence for a moment before Hazel continued, "I thought you were here for Ed and Emily. Are you thinking of staying?"

"I must be," Lily grinned. "When the idea came to me, just a few days ago, I thought of doing it in Ashford. But it was Jennie and Martha who inspired me, and the stories of Mother teaching here at Dungeness. It feels right to stay – that is if Emily will have me!"

"Of course she will," Hazel smiled. "Let's have a cup of tea after we finish our dinner and then we'll go and pay Mrs Stubbs a visit. She was the headmistress for many years and will remember Alice. She may well have some ideas."

218

Mrs Stubbs lived in a tall Victorian terraced house on the Rype. It suited her very well, Lily thought, as she too was tall and stately. Her iron-grey hair was pulled back in a severe bun, she wore metal-rimmed spectacles and, although her hemlines were free from her ankles, Mrs Stubbs' blouse was buttoned up to her neck and adorned with a large polished stone in a decorative setting. Her face was a little severe, but it broke into a smile when she recognised Hazel on her doorstep.

"My dear Mrs Barton, and I know this isn't your daughter, but I heard rumour that our dear Miss Tibbs had been to Dungeness and her own daughter is visiting."

"I'm Lily Stevens, Alice Tibbs is my mother," Lily replied, giving Mrs Stubbs a warm smile.

"Miss Stevens, how lovely to meet you." Mrs Stubbs extended her hand. "Come in; shall we have tea?"

"That would be nice, thank you," Hazel replied, and they stepped through the hallway into the front parlour. "We came to talk to you about something in particular, but I had a feeling that you would like to meet Lily."

Ten minutes later and Mrs Stubbs had produced a notebook. "I would say that you'd do well to start with half a dozen women from Galloways and Dungeness. It must just be women; it wouldn't do at all for an attractive young woman like yourself to be spending time with young men of limited education."

"It will be women," Lily agreed. "Men have more chances to learn later on, through their work for example. I want to make a difference to the life of women. When the men are at the pub, their wives and daughters should be able to read a book or write a letter if they wish to."

"The young women you have mentioned, Jennie and Martha, they are now about seventeen years old.

In my time at Dungeness School, they attended infrequently and I doubt there was any improvement when I retired. Jennie had an older sister, married with children of her own, I believe. What was her name, Mrs Barton?" Mrs Stubbs looked at Hazel, her pen poised over the notebook.

"Annie," Hazel supplied the answer. "She's still there at Galloways."

"And if Annie was interested, then perhaps she would be more inclined to help her own children learn." Lily felt a surge of excitement. "I am beginning to feel that this could work. That I could do something really useful. Do you think so, Mrs Stubbs? Could I make a difference to their lives?"

The older woman studied Lily for a moment. "I do believe it could. We have three names for women at Galloways. Start with Jennie and Martha; they are the same age and can learn together. The other one, Annie, may be resistant. She has young children and a home to look after. She will make excuses. Let her hear about it from the others; let her become curious before you offer her the help."

"Gosh, I'm glad we came here!" Lily said. "You are such a help, Mrs Stubbs."

"And in Dungeness, there's a family living near The Pilot with a daughter still at home." Hazel said. "She was at school with my four, but hardly ever there. I'd say she was the same age as my Bobby, about twenty; she works in The Britannia. Molly, she's called; I think you should put her name down. She's got a cousin; no, two of them. One's married; her husband works on the boats and I often see her about. May her name is and the sister is... now let me think – Rose."

"And with those three, which is the best one to approach?" Lily asked.

"This time, I think I could introduce you to May. She's a lovely young woman, a little older than you perhaps. I have a feeling she would be willing."

"So, we have six names to start with," Mrs Stubbs concluded. "There will be more, I'm sure of it. I wonder if Miss Coombes would be happy for you to order the pencils and writing books through the school? She will have all the contact details."

"I'm going to ask Mother to pack up some of my own reading books," Lily said. "And I've bought a notebook here in Lydd today. I need to start planning."

"You have Mrs Barton nearby, but do come back and show me your plans," Mrs Stubbs replied. "I may be able to give you some tips."

"I'm sure you'll be a great help, thank you."

"We've got a train to catch now, but how about us coming back in a week's time?" Hazel suggested. "You'll have time to plan and see Miss Coombes beforehand."

And so, it was all agreed. Hazel and Lily set off across the Rype, arriving at Lydd Town station in time for the 2:15 to Dungeness. Lily felt more alive than she had done for some time. At last she felt the satisfaction of planning something worthwhile. But as they neared Dungeness, she recalled her true reason for being there and that was to support Emily while her husband remained in gaol, with the prospect of standing before the magistrate within a few days.

Emily was eager for news; but what could Lily tell her that would give any reassurance? She saw the desperation in Emily's eyes, and noticed how the older woman seemed to have aged within the last few weeks. Her face, usually slim with its pointed chin, was now gaunt and her clothes hung from her thin body.

221

"They wanted to ask about Ed's temper, and I couldn't deny he had been angry," Lily began. "But I told them it was over in a flash; he had a shout, and it was all over."

"That's how it is with Ed," Emily said.

"I tried my best to help." Lily's spirits were sinking. "I went to see Charlie beforehand, to see if he had any news or advice; he said to make it clear that Ed flared up but it was over as soon as it started."

"Was there any other news? Did Charlie have anything else to say?" It seemed as if Emily were pleading for reassurance.

"I'm sorry, there was nothing," Lily replied. "But it does seem that they have no evidence other than the word of these fishermen. And Joe was murdered the next day. Ed didn't get into a rage and hunt him out. This was a whole day later and there is no reason to think that anything happened to get Ed all fired up again."

Emily pushed a letter across the table towards Lily. "It's from that inspector; Ed will stand before the magistrate next Wednesday. He'll plead not guilty of course and Charlie says it will be months before it goes to trial."

"Months to prove him innocent," Lily attempted to sound positive. "And he is innocent so he will be freed."

It was when Allie returned from work and the three of them sat down to supper, that Lily mentioned her plans. "...And so, I was hoping I could stay here for a while. I can't say how long but I really want to make a difference to the lives of these women, and their children too."

"I hoped you were going to say that." Emily smiled. It seemed as if some of the anguish had been swept aside, just for this moment.

"Someone of my own age about the place," Allie grinned. "I like the sound of that. Can you help me make some more fashionable dresses? Perhaps something like the new one you brought back from Ashford with you. And maybe Ernie has a nice friend; we could all go out together."

"She's only just got over all the trouble she had when she arrived here, so let's not rush anything," Emily replied, before Lily could respond. "And there was talk of a young man in Ashford; what about him, Lily? He sounded nice."

"James, yes, he is nice." Lily thought of the walk around Eastwell Lake and the ramble along the riverside. James had been a good companion; she suddenly felt a little regretful that the outing to Hythe had been cancelled. "He seems like a decent chap, and there's really no reason why we couldn't still meet; Ashford is no distance by train." But in her heart, she knew their friendship, which was so new, was unlikely to blossom with her being in Dungeness and him in Ashford.

"And some of these young men have motorcars," Allie said. "Does James have one?"

"No, he doesn't. But I believe his father does."

Well there's no need for Lily to worry about romance; she'll know when she finds the right man and maybe she already has," Emily offered her advice. "You'll be here for a while then, Lily. Especially if you want to educate some of them women who can't read or write a word."

"If you'll have me, then perhaps six months or longer," Lily suggested. "I'm going to see Miss Coombes after school, but I'll have to wait until after the weekend. It only seems right to tell her my plans and I am sure she'll have some advice to offer."

"You stay as long as you like and you'll still be here when Ed returns," Emily spoke as if she truly believed he would. "We'll have a fine party then."

Dearest Father and Mother

I hope this letter finds you both in good health. Here at Dungeness we are ill at ease, knowing that Ed is shut away in Lydd Police Station. What must it be like for a man who has only known the open seas from his fishing boat or the wild expanses of the headland here? The only good news is that there seems to be such little evidence against him. Everyone speaks of him having a temper which flares and then is gone within minutes. Poor Joe met his death a whole day after their brief altercation. It seems that this inspector brought in to solve the crime will struggle to convince a jury that Ed is guilty. We can only hope and pray this is the case.

Just before I left Ashford, I spoke of an idea I had. An idea which meant I could fulfil my longing to be of some use, to do something worthwhile with my life. In the short time I have spent here, my plan is beginning to take shape. I am hoping to educate the women of Dungeness and Galloways who have such little learning that they can barely read or write. In turn they cannot support their children's schooling and often take little care to send them to school regularly. I have spoken to Hazel Barton and Miss Coombes, the current headmistress at the school here. And, Mother dear, you'll be delighted to read that I have also met with Mrs Stubbs, who remembers you with kind thoughts. I found her to be a little severe at first, but highly supportive of my idea and eager to be kept informed. Miss Coombes was interested and offered the use of various books in the school, as well as enabling me to order paper and pencils through their suppliers.

I plan to stay here for several months, as I am sure you realise by now, and I can only hope you are happy that I have found a vocation. It is no distance at all by train and I will visit so often that you will barely notice I am gone! I know you both worried about my character reference when I left the bank, but I am sure Mrs Stubbs and Miss Coombes will happily supply one if needed. For now, I intend to draw money from dear Grandmother's legacy to me and I am sure she would approve.

I'll leave you now as I want to send this letter with the afternoon train, so must make haste.

Your loving daughter, Lily.

Chapter Twenty-One

Lily had been to Galloways twice before; the first time had been unplanned and the result of her impetuous ways. The second had been to visit a family in mourning, who named her the Galloways Widow. The community still mourned, and Lily still suffered confusion and distress over the events following her first meeting with Evie and Joe. This time, on her third visit, she was bolstered with her good intentions and determination to make a difference to the lives of young women.

Would they welcome her interest in their lives? Lily didn't know, but she did know that even if they allowed her to tell them of her plans then it could prove hard to win their co-operation. She walked to Galloways with Allie, a young woman born on the point; someone whom Lily hoped Jennie and Martha could relate to. They decided against taking anyone else with them, although Hazel Barton had offered to come to give support.

As they walked to Galloways, Allie's father lay on the wooden bench in the cell at the police station, accused of killing Joe Stoneman. Trapped and lonely, covered with a thin rag of a blanket, Ed stared up at the square of sky he saw through the tiny, barred window. But the people of Galloways were wiser than Inspector Morgan with all his special training and the long words he knew. Ed Brooks had been known to them all their lives; they knew he had a fiery temper and could bellow as well as anyone. But they also knew he was all fire and there was no true fury in him. They knew he would not kill and his temper would have burned out long before he could have trekked across the shingle to hunt out Joe. There was no evidence against Ed, only the words of strangers who happened to hear his angry words. Words of support for Ed and his family had come from the people of Galloways within a day of his being arrested. His daughter, Allie, was welcome there, along with Lily, the Galloways Widow.

Brisk winds now raced across the shingle peninsula, dispersing the mist and whipping at the sea, forcing it to end its period of lethargy. As soon as the tide allowed, fishing boats were sliding down the steep bank and breaking through the waves. Away from the beach, delicate grass-heads danced and tiny flowers opened up. The walk to Galloways was punctuated by Lily's exclamations as she spotted the smallest flowers and the delicate mosses, which somehow clung on to life amongst the sparse soil.

Despite the turmoil of the past weeks, and the worries over Ed's future never being far from their thoughts, it was impossible not to be exhilarated by the wind. It caught in their throats and pressed upon them, yet the battle was invigorating. The sun shone and clouds raced along as they tramped over undulations in the shingle, past the shells of the shacks at Denge and then on to Galloways.

It seemed only right to visit Joe's mother first, so Lily had to rein in her eagerness to seek out Jennie and Martha. She endured being pawed at by Evie, who seemed more withered and bent than just those few weeks ago when she had first welcomed the newcomer into her home. They drank brown tea, with Allie watching Evie's every movement, just in case… To Lily's embarrassment, Evie asked after her health. And it was when the possibility of a Galloways baby was mentioned, they knew it was time to leave the old woman, and to ask where Jennie and Martha might be found.

"They called by earlier, asking if I needed anything," Evie said. "What dear girls they are; we all care for one another here. You'd have liked that, Lily, if things had been as we planned. Now, if you go along to the beach front, you'll be sure to find them. They were out gathering kale and the grey leaves, and were promising to bring some back for me."

"We'll soon spot them." Allie drained the last of her tea.

"And perhaps we could call back in to say goodbye before we leave," Lily added with reluctance.

A smile broke out across Evie's wizened face. "You're always welcome here, Lily. You know that. My Joe will rest in peace knowing you are keeping an eye on his old ma."

They found Jennie and Martha easily enough; the girls were walking from the beach, back towards the cottages. They carried baskets of leaves in their arms and exchanged looks of surprise upon seeing Lily.

"Come to see Evie, have you?" Jennie asked, pushing windswept locks of long dark curls from her face. "That's nice of you."

"But what's she doing with *you*?" Martha glared at Allie.

"My pa didn't kill your Joe, and you know it," Allie replied. "He's all fire and no heat; everyone knows that hereabouts."

228

"True," Martha replied. "But unless they find someone else, he'll hang for it."

Allie paled. "He won't. There's no evidence. Not enough, anyway."

"We were looking for you," Lily announced, hoping to engage their interest. "I've got a plan that you might be interested in."

"Oh?" Jennie replied, "What's of interest to us here is this Godforsaken place?"

"I was thinking about you not having any schooling; you were telling me about it," Lily began. She spoke in a carefree manner, as if their response mattered very little. "Perhaps if I were to come along to you, then the three of us could do a bit of reading and writing? Not much, just for fun. I'm helping some others along the point, but it's just for those who really want to."

"There didn't seem much need to go all the way over there to school." Jennie nodded in the direction of Dungeness.

"Of course," Lily agreed. "Hardly worth the bother. But if I were to come here..."

"We've still got no need for it," Martha added.

"No, I don't suppose you have." Lily shrugged her shoulders. "Not that it would be like school of course, not with all those children of all ages. This would be for adults, so maybe in a year or so..."

"But you'd come here, would you?" Jennie asked.

"Oh yes, perhaps twice a week," Lily replied. "If I had time, because there are a few people back at Dungeness who are very keen."

"We didn't say we weren't." Martha rose to the bait. "We were just wondering and asking."

"Say you wanted to read a recipe or write one down, or if one of you moved away and you wanted to write to each other..."

229

"Or even send a message," Jennie interrupted.

"And of an evening, it's nice to read a book. Not anything long, but a shilling romance or a mystery novel," Lily suggested.

"I'd like a romance," Martha giggled. "Nothing fancy."

"I buy them in Lydd," Allie told them. "I've got a whole shelf full at home."

"We know our letters," Jennie said. "We did do some learning."

"I know you did," Lily affirmed. "You're not children. This would be something quite different. So, I'll come along and see you both and we'll sit out on the shingle on a rug and have a look at some books."

"Not at a desk?" Jennie sniggered.

"I don't have desks," Lily pointed out. "But if it was raining or chilly, then perhaps in one of your homes?"

"Not mine, with the baby and all the little ones," Jennie replied. "But Martha, your ma wouldn't mind, would she?"

And so, an arrangement was made for Lily to return the next morning and again on the Friday, if they wanted to continue to learn. The girls showed them the cottage of tarred planks in which Martha lived and it was agreed Lily would meet them there. Allie and Lily left, feeling satisfied some progress had been made.

The next day, Lily watched as Emily left the cottage with her two grown-up children, one on either side. They were all dressed in their smartest clothes, boots polished and hair well brushed. Their faces gaunt and expressions strained, they still held themselves upright as if they bore no shame. The day where Ed was to stand before the magistrate had come and, despite the lack of evidence, it seemed unlikely he would be freed until someone else took his place for the crime. "And why bother looking further, when they have a man locked up already?" Emily said. It seemed as if she was to be proved right.

Good friends of the family, Tom Barton and Ben Webb, joined the diminished Brooks family, falling into step beside them. Looking on, Lily knew there was plenty of support for them and turned back to her pile of paper, notebooks and reading books. She needed to keep her mind busy and make a success of her first lesson at Galloways.

An hour later, Lily was making her own way to Galloways, picking her route across the ridges and using the lighthouse as her marker. The tower enabled her to judge distance; the day was bright, and it remained in her sight during the trek, which took an hour or more. Her basket was cumbersome, and Lily wondered about borrowing or making a backpack, for she was planning on making this journey twice a week.

The girls were sitting on a bench outside the front door of Martha's home. Lily had half-expected them to be off on some escapade or even that the agreement to meet had flitted out of their minds. But there was something wrong: they were bickering.

"I don't need them, but it was wrong of her to borrow and not return them," Martha's voice was high.

"It's summer, what does it matter? You have others." Jennie stood and it looked as if she was about to walk off.

"Good morning," Lily kept her voice bright.

"Hello," Jennie gave a wide smile. "We've been looking forward to our lesson. Wondering if you can make schooling a bit more fun than it was over there." She gave a slight nod in the direction of Dungeness.

"But someone shouldn't borrow and not return," Martha pouted, a contrast to her usual sunny disposition.

"They shouldn't," Lily agreed. "But it's something that happens all too often."

"It was only a pair of gloves." Jennie rolled her eyes.

"It was my good grey ones, and she took them without asking, because I wouldn't have let her. Not when there was only a bit of a chill. Mary didn't need them."

Why did Mary's name seem to crop up so much in the place where she no longer lived, Lily mused. She seemed drawn back to Galloways at every chance. What was she, perhaps twenty? Surely Lydd was more appealing to the young woman?

"I've got a reading book and some notebooks for you to write in, and cards for us to put words on," Lily began, "...and counting beads. Shall we sit around your table, Martha?"

With the squabble forgotten, the two of them rummaged in the basket, pulling out the contents onto the table. "*Alice's Adventures in Wonderland*," Martha muttered. "This is a bit childish."

"It's fun and a bit silly," Lily replied. "And we will not be reading an adult book until you can read this. I chose something that I thought would suit you. I have any number of schoolgirl stories at home, but I didn't see the two of you gaining any pleasure from tales of boarding school life. And as for the shilling romances, they will come later."

It seemed that the pair of them grudgingly admitted defeat. Perhaps, Lily wondered, they would grow to admire her if she showed a firm hand? They settled down to spend an hour discussing lessons remembered from their occasional times at school.

There was a healthy sense of competition between the two of them, along with an urgency to prove that they were able to learn if they chose to. Their handwriting was rushed, their reading laborious, but Lily was satisfied that both Jennie and Martha had a natural ability. They took a break after an hour and ended the session by sitting on the bench outside, heads close together, and poring over *Alice's Adventures in Wonderland,* with the illustrations reinforcing the story.

Lily left Galloways feeling uplifted by the experience. She could make a difference, really make a difference to these young people's lives. She was sure of it. Now to go home and plan for their next lesson. But before that, she wanted to visit one or two of the other people Hazel and Mrs Stubbs had suggested she try to help.

"He's being taken to Maidstone tomorrow," Emily said, as she entered the cottage.

"But there is so little evidence." Lily felt a chill settle over her body. It was what she expected, what they all expected, but the shock was no less for it.

"They have no one else." Emily slumped in the easy chair.

Allie, her face pale and gaunt, perched on the arm of the chair and her eyes met Lily's. No words were exchanged as Lily came and sat on the other side of Emily. She placed her hand on Emily's shoulder; it seemed as if there was no flesh between her thin clothes and shoulder-bones.

The three of them sat in silence for several minutes before Lily got up and pushed the kettle onto the hotplate on the range. Then she spread a thick layer of butter onto some fruit loaf, hoping to persuade Emily to eat a slice or two.

They ate, exchanging very few words. But after her second cup of tea, Emily pulled herself upright and spoke. "Well, we can't sit about feeling sorry for ourselves. There's no evidence apart from those men hearing him shouting. The police have been here, looking at every piece of Ed's clothing, and they can't match up the strands of grey wool found on the murder weapon. No one saw him go all that way to Galloways. It's miserable for us and it's even worse for Ed, but they'll not find him guilty and I know it."

"You're right, Ma," Allie replied. "But you need to start eating properly, and we'll all keep going, just like we always do. So when Pa comes home, everything is just as it should be."

On her second visit to Galloways, Lily was surprised to find a third young woman was waiting there for her.

"Mary wanted to come along," Jennie announced. "She's got some learning. More than us, but she wants to see what we're doing."

Mary nodded, her gaze fixed on Lily. "I can read some words and count up the money at the tearooms."

"But you'd like to learn more?" Lily prompted. "Come and sit with us today, but I would prefer to teach just one or two at a time."

"I want to write a story," Mary announced. "But I need better words and more of them. I need your learning to help me, Lily."

"A story?" Martha mocked. "What d'you want with a story?"

"We're here to learn to write a shopping list or a note to someone." Jennie rolled her eyes and continued, "Trust you to get fancy ideas!"

234

"It's not fancy. It's just something I want to do." Mary set her mouth in a stubborn line. "Just something for myself; nothing for you two to make a joke about."

"Why don't you and I talk about this afterwards?" Lily sighed inwardly. Jennie and Martha needed little temptation to be distracted from their learning. The last lesson had been such a success; she must be firm and make a promise to help Mary another time.

Mary smiled, apparently satisfied. There was something rather naive, childish even, about her manner. While her feelings were clear to read, Lily realised that Mary was vulnerable to the immature spite of the others. She may well have learned more words in her time at school, but this was probably only due to the fact she had attended regularly, rather than having any skills.

They sat around the table in Martha's home and looked through the words they had been learning last time. Not for the first time, Lily saw that both Jennie and Martha had the potential to be quick learners and hoped the competition between the two of them would push them to try harder.

Mary was different, more eager to gain Lily's approval. As they opened their handwriting books and began to practise firm strokes and neat loops, Mary sat with the tip of her tongue protruding slightly and laboriously produced line after line of nicely formed letters. In contrast, the other two rushed and so their letters became more of a spidery scribble. However, a glance at Mary's work encouraged them to slow down and Lily began to see an improvement.

They then started on the second chapter of *Alice's Adventures in Wonderland*, after thoroughly describing the first chapter to Mary. "It's a children's book of course," Jennie said dismissively, "but jolly good fun and so we'll read it as Lily promises us a shilling romance as the next book."

"I don't want a romance," Mary replied. "I'll read a detective novel."

"That won't help you catch a husband," Martha sniggered. "But perhaps you'll learn something and help that old inspector, him who's got Ed Brooks on trial for murder."

"I shan't be doing no helping," Mary scowled.

With the reading done, Lily set homework for the three of them. She wanted Jennie and Martha to go on a nature walk and to write a list of things they saw, both trying their best to think of how a word might be spelt. They would look through it next time and learn the correct spellings. For Mary, she suggested a similar walk around Lydd.

The lesson came to an end and Mary mentioned her plan to write a story. The other girls were quick to make fun of her.

"Who would want to read your story, Mary?" Jennie mocked. "You only know about that old tearoom and here at Galloways."

"It's not for anyone else; it's just for me," Mary replied. Her face took on a sullen look and Lily was disappointed that a good lesson had ended where it began, with friction between the three of them. Mary's wits were too slow for her to manage the banter from the other girls.

"So we won't be able to buy it with a fancy cover somewhere?" Martha asked. "What is it – a love story?"

"No."

"Well, she don't know about that, does she?" Jennie grinned and nudged Martha. "What is it then? About some poor girl from a tearoom who gets rich and wears fancy clothes like Lily here?"

"It's a murder story," Mary replied with bravado. "And I'll talk to Lily about helping me without you two making fun of it."

"That's just what I suggested earlier," Lily said, raising her voice a little and attempting to sound firm. "Let's sit out on the stones, it's lovely and warm now. You can tell me all about it. I'm very interested to hear your ideas."

Mary coloured slightly and a slight smile came to her lips. "I'd like that."

"Very well." Lily tried to retain a schoolmistress manner in order to show that she would stand for no nonsense. "Jennie and Martha, I will see you again next Wednesday. Mary, we'll have a talk about your story."

"I want to write about a man who got hurt and a woman who saved him," Mary began.

Lily, sensing Mary held romantic notions about the heroine of this tale, asked, "Did the man have an accident? Or are you remembering back to the war?"

"Oh, he had an accident." Mary looked down at the stones and pushed them about with the toe of her boot. "Definitely an accident. Here on the stones. But he didn't die because the woman – I want to call her... Gwendoline, yes, Gwendoline – she saved him."

"Gwendoline?"

"Oh, yes, it's a special name, don't you think? And this woman was very special. Very beautiful."

"He had an accident, here on the point?" Lily queried.

"He was walking somewhere and it happened."

"Is this in memory of Joe? To help you remember him?" Lily looked at the young woman who had clearly suffered since the death.

"Joe? Oh, no, it's not about him," Mary was quick to reply "It's about some other man I knew."

Uneasy about this story, Lily offered to help Mary make notes when they next met and suggested they plan a list of characters and choose some descriptive words. Then she gathered her basket and turned towards Dungeness. It had been a strange morning, with Mary's presence causing a disturbance, both within the lessons and in Lily's mind.

Chapter Twenty-Two

In many ways Lily was more contented than she had ever been in the whole of her adult life. As she tramped across the stones to Galloways twice a week to see Jenny and Martha or strolled along to the nearby homes of the other young women she taught, life suddenly felt more exhilarating. The days of carefully logging numbers in a ledger were gone; it seemed as if they belonged to another life. It was as if Lily from Ashford was a different person, and she almost was. Gone was the irritation and frustration with life; now she felt useful and was rewarded daily for her efforts with schooling the local women.

Yet in the evenings, while Lily jotted down ideas or pored over books, the people who were dear to her were suffering. Her mind was vexed, because she knew if she had never gone to Galloways then Ed would not be shut away in Maidstone Prison.

Suddenly, amidst the family's troubles, a new life began its journey into the world and Lily learned of a different use for the hagstones. Grace, wife of young Edward, began her labour pains one evening and the news of them came when he knocked at the door.

"She's started, Ma," The words came out in a gush. "Grace's pains have started, and she'll be needing you."

"You've put a pan of water on?" Emily rose from her chair, and it seemed as if a spark of life shot through her tired body. She was needed and so she would shake off the depression which threatened to cloak her at all times.

"Two pans, all simmering," Edward replied. "It's been hours now, but they're coming more often, every few minutes. It's time you were there, Ma."

Emily was at the door before her son had finished talking, and Allie was reaching for her boots. They looked back at Lily and Emily flashed a smile. "Come on, Lily, you're as good as family so you'd best be a part of this." Then she turned to Edward, "Have you got the ale, son?"

"Not yet, Ma. But it's time."

"Well, the girls can do that; fetch the jug, Allie."

Lily watched as Allie knelt and dragged a clay jug from the bottom of the dresser. "We'll walk with you to The Pilot, and then take the ale along for Grace," she told her brother. "You can come with me, Lily."

"Are you sure?" Lily faltered. "I'll go with you for the ale, but really I should..."

"No, Grace won't mind, and you can help with little Eva, stop her from getting in the way," Edward grinned. "It's time for the women to take over now; she doesn't want me fussing over her anymore."

Emily was gone, not prepared to wait while the younger ones talked it over. Allie was poised at the doorway, so Lily shoved her feet in her boots and pulled the laces tight. Then she was slamming the front door behind her and following Edward and Allie to the nearby Pilot.

The pub, said to be built from the upturned hull of a ship lured aground, was a low-lying structure, appearing to have various extensions added on over the years. Its plank walls were tarred and supported a roof of corrugated iron. Although it was June, and the sun had not yet set, a warm glow could be seen at the windows. Tobacco smoke and alcohol fumes wafted out through the pores of the building and the raucous laughter of the men could be heard. Lily hung back a little.

"Fill the jug, Edward, and we'll wait here," Allie handed the jug to her brother.

He opened the door; a blast of noise and the scents of the bar shot out into the evening air. It polluted the peace of the place, with its vast pale blue sky and the murmur of shingle being rolled about by the sea. The door closed and the noise from The Pilot subsided. It had been a warm day and now the air chilled rapidly as the sun lowered towards the west. Standing looking out to sea, Lily and Allie waited for Edward to return. Then the door was opening, and Allie was taking the jug.

"You'll let me know when it's over?" Edward asked.

"Of course. Have a few drinks and then wait at Brooks' Cottage," Allie replied. "You'll be a dad again in no time, and one of us will fetch you."

Lily couldn't help wondering about the importance of the ale. She'd never known Grace to drink the golden-brown liquid and, although knowing nothing about childbirth, wouldn't the new mother want a cup of tea, if anything? Or was this for Emily, who was to be at Grace's side until the baby was born? Yet Emily preferred a sweet sherry or a glass of wine.

Within minutes they were pressing on the latch of Edward and Grace's home, and again Lily felt inclined to hang back. But Grace was facing the discomfort of labour in her bedroom and the living area was empty. It was Allie who put her head around the doorway and asked if all was well.

"She'll settle when she's had the ale." Emily came to the door with the small child, Eva, at her skirts.

241

A glass, uneven and opaque, stood on the table. "It's the one Grace's own mother used," Emily informed the girls. Then she took a large brown hagstone from her pocket. Its hole, formed over centuries of friction in the sea, was large. With her thumb and forefinger, Emily held the stone over the glass. "You pour, Allie."

The clay jug was lifted, supported with both hands, and the ale flowed, gradually forming a steady trickle. Passing through the hagstone, it made a small pool at the bottom of the glass and rose until Emily gave a nod to indicate enough had passed.

Little Eva, not yet two years old, looked on; she held a blanket in her arms and looked weary. "It's past her bedtime," Allie said. "But no wonder she won't settle in her cot." Allie knelt down before the child, "I'll make you a nice bed here and you can sit with me and Lily. Would you like that?" Eva nodded. Her own bed was in the only bedroom, where Grace was due to give birth.

"The girls have brought the ale and every drop passed through the stone." Emily could be heard talking to Grace. "Let's sit you up and this will ease the baby's journey."

"Another use for hagstones?" Lily looked at Allie. She still kept Joe's stone on a lace with her own in a drawer in her bedroom.

"It's something we do here at Dungeness," Allie's smile was a little sheepish. Were the influences of the modern world having an effect on the young people of Dungeness? Did they, like the people of Lily's generation who lived in the towns, begin to question the traditions of centuries?

"Like magic?" Lily asked.

"I guess so," Allie frowned. "I hadn't thought of it like that."

242

"I've seen Jennie and Martha whirling the stones about." Lily tried to recall when, or for what reason they did it. "It must have been when I was staying there, at Galloways. Because I don't recall it clearly. I wish I did."

"That would be to wish the mists away," Allie told her.

"Of course, they wanted the sun to shine for the wedding." Lily felt relief; she wanted to remember, but those days remained dulled by the grey tea.

Allie fetched the bedding from the cot and they made a bed on the sofa for Eva. The little girl snuggled into it, and Allie stroked her soft brown hair while Lily read some nursery rhymes found in a tattered book. Eva's eyelids soon began to close and her breathing slowed as she fell asleep.

"They had them on strings," Lily whispered.

"That's right," Allie nodded. "They wanted the mists to pass so as to be sure when it was exactly midday."

"For the wedding?"

"Of course. They had to wait until there was no shadow cast by the pole." Allie placed a light kiss on Eva's forehead. "She'll sleep through it all now."

"Do you think it will be much longer?" Lily asked.

"No, the ale will do the trick," Allie smiled. "And she had no troubles with this one."

Not half an hour had passed, but the sun had dipped below the distant hills and the lamps had been lit when exclamations of triumph came from the bedroom. As the first unmistakable cries of a new-born reached them, Allie was pouring hot water into a jug and taking it through to the bedroom.

Looking on with awe at the button nose and perfect lips, the fine strands of dark hair and delicate fingers of the

243

baby, Lily couldn't help recalling her purpose as the Galloways Bride. This is what they wanted from her: a new life for the Galloways family.

It had worried her for a time; she had no recollection of any marital relations with Joe. But the nagging doubt had remained: what if she had been so drugged by the tea that he were able to take her as he wished, with no memory of the act remaining with her? What future would there be for her as the Galloways Widow with a child growing within her? To Lily's immense relief her monthly bleed had come, and then the next. She never spoke of her fears, but the sight of this new-born reminded her.

"Have you chosen a name?" Emily asked, bringing Lily's thoughts back to the present.

"Benjamin Edward. Ben," Grace said, easing her nipple towards the baby's lips.

Dear Mother and Father,

I write with good news, despite the sadness which haunts the family. Ed has been sent to Maidstone and there seems nothing we can do to stop him standing trial for murder. Nobody here believes he committed the crime and even Joe's family are sure of Ed's innocence. It seems that Inspector Morgan is satisfied; as long as someone is convicted, then his job is done. We can only hope and pray that the judge and jury give a fair and merciful trial.

The happiest of news is that the family has been blessed with the birth of a baby, to Edward's wife, Grace. Their new son is called Ben, and is a dear little thing, as placid as his big sister. He was born last week.

I know you worried about me leaving the bank, and I thank you for your letter supporting my new venture. It

244

has been three weeks now since I offered to teach some of the young women in the area. I walk to Galloways three times a week in the mornings and fill my afternoons with teaching people here at Dungeness. It brings me a feeling of being useful, which I am sure you will both understand.

I did tell you that I would visit often, and I am planning to come home for the weekend, travelling to Ashford on the Friday afternoon train, then returning on Monday morning.

Very much looking forward to seeing you both soon, With love from your daughter, Lily.

The morning came for Lily's planned trip to Ashford. Rather than go to Galloways in order to teach Jennie and Martha, she had already told them she would be going away for a few days. Their disappointment was clear and promises made to fit in an extra lesson within the near future. Just the evening before, Lily had decided to take the early train to Lydd and pay Mrs Stubbs a visit, then travel on to Ashford. She was eager to share her successes with the former headmistress.

For weeks, Dungeness had been basking in warm summer sunshine, a light breeze passing over the headland, and the sea rolling lazily to the shore. Tiny flowers had emerged amongst the patches of rough grass and seed heads had turned a coppery brown. The sea kale remained succulent and the viper's bugloss bore its blue flowers on hairy stems.

In the early mornings, the sea-mist had not yet evaporated and swirled over the Point. It left a veil of salty moisture over everything it touched, bringing a velvet softness to the landscape. In contrast to this

245

delicate beauty, the fog trumpet blasted a regular message to warn ships off the shingle peninsula.

Even as the steam train came to a halt at Dungeness station, the sun's rays were warming Lily and the mist was making its retreat. With her small case in her hand, she stepped into the coach and steadied herself before sitting. Several women joined her, some she recognised and knew to be from the railway carriage homes, another was a lighthouse keeper's wife. They gave polite smiles and curious glances towards the young woman who was still a newcomer to the area. The last person to step in gave a warm smile upon seeing Lily.

"Lovely to see you." Edith Browning seated herself opposite Lily. "I hear you've been doing some teaching."

"I have." Lily was pleased to see the woman who had cared so patiently for Charlie when he came to her home. "Have you seen Charlie? He seems to have suffered no ill effects since being so ill."

"We saw him just last Saturday. He invited my husband and myself for a dinner at The George Hotel; I thought it was kind of him. Very thoughtful."

"It was." Lily was pleased to know that Charlie had remembered to think of those kind people who had taken him, a stranger to them, into their home. "He seems very generous."

"He's certainly an interesting young man! Full of life, and he seems very taken with you."

"Oh, I don't think so… I'm sure he is just as friendly with everyone." Lily frowned. "But you have heard about my teaching; it's been rather successful! I'm travelling on to Ashford in a couple of hours' time but calling in to see Mrs Stubbs beforehand. She was the headmistress at Dungeness when my mother taught there. It's a little

246

early though. If only they ran a mid-morning train every day, and not just on a Saturday."

"Let me buy you breakfast in the tearooms then," Edith suggested. "I have time to spare before my appointment and would welcome your company."

An hour later, and Lily felt compelled to visit Joe's grave before walking across the Rype to Mrs Stubbs' home. She entered the churchyard, and paused to look up at the tall tower, before turning to the right. Picking her way past the gentle mounds, some topped with headstones and others with simple wooden markers, she noted that the morning dew had already passed. There was Joe's grave, still so new, with some bunches of withered wildflowers topping it.

It seemed so quiet there in the churchyard. The call of a delivery boy, the passing of a horse and cart, and the rumble of a motorcar were all muted. It was just Lily, standing there with the rustle of leaves and the birdsong. The old woman who had been seen in the distance had shuffled through the far gate and was out of sight. Lily appreciated the solitude; she just wanted a few minutes to reflect on the last couple of months. She was unaware of another young woman who had entered the churchyard.

Chapter Twenty-Three

"I don't know why I cried for him."

Lily hadn't heard the younger woman approach. Her footsteps had been soft on the damp grass and she made no sound to announce her presence, not until she spoke.

"He were going to leave us anyway." Mary stood beside Lily, her long black skirt and high-necked blouse making her look as if she had come from a different age.

"If he had left of his own choice, then he could have come back," Lily stated, taking a step away from Mary.

"He said he wouldn't. He said he were done with Galloways and the family." Mary's voice was low and, as Lily turned to look at her, she saw her eyes were misted. It seemed as if Mary looked into the distance, perhaps to the shingle lands of Galloways itself. "Evie cried. I never seen that before. She gave him ale and asked him to stop for a while. To think about it."

"You were there?" Lily asked.

"I were visiting. I like to go back," Mary replied. "I don't want to work in a tearoom. I want to live back there in my own cottage."

"Oh, would you?"

"I won't, though."

"Why not?"

"I'd need to be wed. They'd have to choose me, one of them would. But they won't."

"You're still young, Mary. Plenty of time." Lily struggled to find the words to comfort the girl.

"There's not many young men at Galloways." Mary's lips settled into a pout within her pasty face. "Why would they chose me over Jennie or Martha?"

"Well," Lily said, turning to look at Mary, "you have beautiful blue eyes, and a man wants a good housekeeper, and… and a sensible young woman."

Mary smiled, her eyes shining. "Yes, they do, and those other two are rather foolish."

Lily looked back at the grave; the soil was still soft and clear of grass. She was about to walk away when Mary spoke again. "He said his ale were bitter, but he were too busy arguing with Evie that he paid no attention to it."

"Bitter?"

But Mary continued, now seemingly unaware of Lily's presence, "And then he were packing, putting his good clothes in a cloth bag. He still wore his hagstone, of course. And I gave him another ale. 'Why are you fussing over him, Mary?' That's what Evie said. But she didn't know. She didn't know I made it bitter. And then he were off. He's a big man, Joe is. Tall and strong, but he were weak, thanks to my plan. He gave me the idea, Joe did. Then I used it on him.

"I'm clever, aren't I? Not like Jennie and Martha. I've got my letters and numbers and I'm making my book. That Lily, she's helping with my book. She doesn't know. No one knows. It's my joke; a joke that Joe gave me the idea."

"What idea?" Lily kept her voice soft.

"The Jury's Poppy, of course," Mary scoffed. "He gave it to Charlie. I like Charlie; he's funny and always nice to me. He makes me feel like I'm pretty. But Charlie came meddling, wanting Joe to say it weren't a proper

249

wedding. Joe wanted him to go away. He wanted to be married to Lily.

"I wanted Joe to go away. No, no, I wanted Joe to stay. I wanted him to be sorry. Why did he have to leave? It was my fault; I brought Lily to Galloways. They were happy with me. Happy I were clever, not like Jennie and Martha. He didn't notice it were bitter."

All awareness of Lily being there was lost as Mary sank on her knees upon the bare soil covering the grave, seemingly unaware that that her skirt would be badly stained. Tears now rolled slowly down her face as she knelt there, still talking to herself.

As Lily backed away, she heard Mary's words: "I loved Joe; I would have worn his stone. Any stone, even a brown one. But he were handsome so I brought him Lily, thinking he would be pleased with me. The wood was heavy."

Looking back as she left the churchyard, Lily saw the figure of Mary at the grave, but now her hands plucked at the loose soil. On reaching the High Street, she picked up her pace, crossing the road between the horse-bus and a motorcar. Her heart was racing, not from exertion, but from the urgency. What would she do if he was not there?

The door to the solicitors' office was ajar and, as Lily burst in, relief rushed through her body. Charlie was there, a sheaf of paperwork in his hands and talking to the receptionist. They turned and, for once, Charlie's expression was serious as he took a step towards her.

"I'm sorry for bursting in," Lily's words poured out. "I need to speak to you urgently." She glanced towards the receptionist. "In private."

But even as she spoke, Charlie was ushering Lily into his office and gesturing to a chair. Pulling another up, so he sat close to her, he leaned forward and said just one word: "Talk."

"I know who killed Joe," Lily blurted out and she told him about the story Mary wanted to write, the spoiled gloves, the wood which was so heavy and the Jury's Poppy." Charlie stopped her occasionally, firing a question, clarifying a point. The story was soon told and the pair of them were striding down the High Street towards the police station.

"Will they believe us?" Lily gasped for breath.

"They'll have to; it makes sense."

"Does it? Wouldn't they prefer to send a man with a temper to hang for this?"

"She'll be shut up in an asylum." Charlie replied as he placed a hand on her arm and guided Lily across the road. "I've wondered about her for a while."

While Lily digested this news, they stepped up the path to the police station.

"We need to see Inspector Morgan," Charlie's tone was brisk as he stood before the young constable at the desk in the reception area.

"He's gone back to Folkestone," the constable replied.

"Damn it, of course he has," Charlie scowled. "Your sergeant then and make it quick. This is important."

"He's gone over to Ness Road, some trouble with..."

But whatever the trouble was, Lily never knew, for Charlie was out of the door and pacing back down the path. She threw an apologetic look at the constable and scurried after the solicitor.

"She needs a doctor; we'll deal with that afterwards," Charlie said, as they raced along past terraces of cottages before turning into a side street.

251

Charlie had barely slowed his pace for Lily, and her heart pounded as they approached a small crowd in the street. The sergeant was there, standing over a man slumped in the gutter. Screeching her outrage, a portly woman in a vast apron stood with her hands on her hips and various onlookers appeared to be keen to watch as the scene progressed.

"What's going on, Betty?" Charlie asked. "Drunk again, is he?"

"Not only drunk but he didn't hand over me housekeeping." Betty leaned down and gave her husband a push. "Look at him, Charlie, I didn't expect all this when I got wed. He's bleeding lazy and now he's left me with no money for our food."

"Is this a case of trying to keep the peace, Sergeant?" Charlie asked. "Because I've news on Ed Brooks and the murder investigation."

"I'm afraid it is." The sergeant shook his head. "What with him singing half the night in the High Street, and her yelling at him, it's causing a bit of bother."

"Right." Charlie turned back to the irate housewife, "Look Betty, he's had a few too many and it's all getting out of hand. We can't see you and the kids getting hungry and you don't want him in the house like this, so take these..." He took a wallet from his pocket and peeled two pound notes from a thin sheaf and handed them to Betty, who looked astounded and was silenced by the action. "Now get your basket and head off to the shops and we'll have Wilf put in the shed with a blanket so he can sleep it off."

Betty muttered her thanks and flitted back into her house. Now Charlie turned his attention to the onlookers. "You, John, and you, Bert, take him around the back and make him comfy in the shed. Call at the back door and get a blanket from Betty. Make it swift

252

and I'll put a few shillings behind the bar in The Dolphin for you."

A couple of men turned to the man in the gutter and prepared to move him off the street.

"All dealt with, Sergeant?" Charlie asked.

"If only I could hand over some money and buy them a drink, life would be a bit easier," the bemused policeman replied.

"We need to talk, and this is important." Charlie turned back towards the main road. "Something has happened, and Lily here has the evidence we need to free Ed Brooks."

"It had better be good," the sergeant replied. "Inspector Morgan wants this wrapped up."

This time Lily faced the questioning with Charlie sitting beside her. She made a statement mentioning the story Mary's wanted to write, the conversation at the graveside and even Martha's distress about the grey glove Mary had borrowed and not returned. Notes were taken and questions asked. Charlie added very little, satisfied with Lily's recollection of events.

"If you could just sign here, Miss Stevens." Sergeant Banks pushed the statement across the table towards Lily. "I'll go along and bring Mary in."

"I suggest you have a doctor present." Charlie rose from his chair. "She is clearly disturbed and needs careful handling."

"I'll send the constable for him," the sergeant replied.

"But it's all taken so long," Lily blurted out. "She could be anywhere."

"She'll be in the town or heading back to Galloways," Charlie said, looking down at her and putting his hand on her shoulder. "Don't worry, Mary

253

won't go far; she's not worldly enough to think of it. She's not the type to imagine life beyond the tearoom and Galloways."

"And I'll have to get Inspector Morgan back from Folkestone." Sergeant Banks headed for the door. "I'll ask the constable to send a telegram to Inspector Morgan immediately... did you hear that, Stan? I'm bringing in a new suspect for the Joe Stoneman murder case. Please inform the inspector by telegram that he is needed back in Lydd immediately. Then we need the doctor over here for when I question the suspect; she'll have to wait in a cell until I am ready for her. This needs careful handling."

"She, sir?" The constable raised his eyebrows.

"Yes, she." Sergeant Banks was at the door with Lily and Charlie close behind him. "You've done well," he said to Lily. "I'll keep you informed. Call in whenever you like; I'll get word to you when I have news. Give Mrs Brooks my best wishes, please."

"I can't just go off to see Mrs Stubbs, as if nothing has happened." Lily looked up at Charlie, as they stood on the pavement outside the police station.

"Mrs Stubbs?" His expression was bemused. "What's Mrs Stubbs go to do with this?"

"I was going to see her, to tell her about the lessons I've been doing. But I've got to know, got to be sure Sergeant Banks finds Mary. I can't just go and have tea and talk about, well, you know..." Lily started walking back towards the church, with Charlie falling into step beside her. "Do you think she's still there?"

"I don't know. I'm here with you," Charlie replied.

Lily scowled. Had she begun to think he was less irritating? Perhaps a little. Of course, he didn't know where Mary was. *She* didn't know where Mary was. But she knew about Ed, trapped in a miserable cell, deprived of the open skies and salty winds. What if Mary had gone and they couldn't question her? How long would it take to find her, if she headed for the wastelands of Galloways or Denge?

"All we can do is go back to the church and see if Sergeant Banks has found Mary, and what his next plan is if she's gone," Charlie offered. "Getting upset isn't going to make any difference, you know that Lily."

Before the High Street veered to the right, Charlie took Lily's arm and guided her across the road and into a lane, fronted with pretty houses. The lane was short, ending in a gateway to the churchyard. The east end of the church loomed and, gathered about it, were its congregation of toppling headstones. Charlie and Lily followed a twisting path amongst the stones, moving towards the shadows of the chancel end, and stood beneath the huge decorative window. They didn't speak but moved slowly along the building before peeping around the buttressed corner.

"She's still there." Lily breathed a sigh of relief.

Sergeant Banks was guiding Mary away from the graveside; her head bowed and body slumped, she appeared to be allowing him to lead her without giving any resistance. Her hands and the sleeves of her blouse were caked in the soft soil that had topped the grave and her black skirt was streaked with muddy fingermarks. She was silent, no longer sobbing. The sergeant's voice could be heard as he offered gentle reassurances. Charlie and Lily stepped back into the shadows of the buttress, watching as the young woman and police sergeant left the churchyard.

"Let's go and have a cup of tea," Charlie said, leading the way through the churchyard and onto the High Street. "There's nothing else we can do. The doctor will need to see her and there are statements to be heard. There will be no more news today."

"I know, thank you." Realising that she felt a little shaky, Lily allowed herself to be ushered across the road and into the Beehive tearoom.

Sitting in a shadowed corner of the eighteenth-century building, Lily allowed Charlie to order tea and fruit cake. They spoke about minor matters until the teapot, cups and saucers were placed on the lace cloth, and the fruit cake was set down before them.

"Just ring the bell if you need anything." The waitress indicated a small brass bell on the table.

"It's a bit posh in here!" Charlie grinned.

"I can't believe it was Mary," Lily blurted out, keeping her voice low, for there were a few customers and the waitress hovered nearby.

"Poor girl, there's always been something a bit different about her." Charlie's expression was thoughtful. "It's good news for Ed, but I can't feel happy about it."

"And now Mary will hang." Lily felt her mouth go dry and her chest tightened a little. Mary must be a few years younger than herself.

"No, I'm sure she won't," Charlie poured their tea. Lily noted that he took charge, dispensing with the usual male role, and only interested in taking care of her. "She'll be sent to Chartham."

Lily knew what he meant; the village on the road from Ashford to Canterbury had a hospital for those with mental health problems. It was the type of place where those who were admitted rarely came out.

"But it is good news for Ed, and we mustn't forget it," Lily smiled and tried to sound positive. "Imagine the look on Emily's face when he comes home! Oh, but I won't see it, I've planned to go to Ashford, to see my family. It's too late to see Mrs Stubbs now; I'm going on the next train."

"He won't be home at the weekend, Lily. This could take weeks," Charlie reached across and took her hand. "No one can just rush in and release Ed; there are procedures to follow. But I'll get word to him that he's going to be all right, even if I have to go to Maidstone Prison myself."

"Oh, yes. I see."

"Actually, I will go to Maidstone," Charlie grinned. "It will only take an hour or so on the train. It's not eleven o'clock yet. Plenty of time."

"Then I must go back to tell Emily and Allie and Edward."

"But you won't make it to Ashford."

"I'll send a telegram and go the next weekend," Lily declared. She now ate the cake with renewed vigour and refilled their teacups.

Five minutes later and Lily was stepping out on to the pavement, with Charlie behind her, ducking as he walked through the Beehive's doorway. They parted, Charlie to walk back to his office and inform them of his unexpected journey to Maidstone, and Lily to cross the road to the post office.

Waiting in the queue, Lily formed the words of the telegram in her head. Needing to keep the message brief and convey her news, but without alerting the curious postmaster, would be awkward. It seemed as if the two women whose turn it was to be served first, would take an age, but finally it was time to step forward to the counter.

"I'd like to send a telegram," Lily announced and waited until the postmaster was poised to take her

257

words: "Visit delayed STOP Good news for Brooks family STOP Letter to follow STOP."

"Ah, the new baby," the postmaster nodded. He made it his business to know all the news.

"Wonderful news at this time," Lily smiled. Her family would know different, news of the baby had already been sent by letter some days beforehand.

Chapter Twenty-Four

Dear Mother and Father,

I am scribbling this note in Mrs Stubbs' front parlour. It comes with good news and apologies for my not visiting this weekend. I was in Lydd before catching the train on to Ashford, and came across a young woman, Mary, in the churchyard. She is from a Galloways family, and now lives in Lydd. I find her a little odd at times and today she was clearly distressed, rambling about Joe's death. It suddenly became clear, although it hardly seems credible, it was she who struck Joe with the wooden pole. She wanted to stop him from leaving Galloways.

I went to see the solicitor, then on to the police station. Inspector Morgan has returned to Folkestone, but it seems certain Mary will be charged and no doubt spend the rest of her days in an institution, such as Chartham.

Now I find myself unable to share the good news with Emily and the family, unless I return by train to Dungeness. I must do this and come to Ashford next weekend. I know you will be disappointed, as am I, that the visit is delayed. I promise that in another week, I will be once again travelling to see you.

With love to you both, Lily.

"It's so rude of me, Mrs Stubbs, but I couldn't think of

how to get the letter to Ashford and the telegram really isn't enough." Lily sealed the envelope on her first letter.

"I'm delighted to see you, Lily. Of course you must write to your parents and there will be plenty of time for you to tell me about your teaching venture. I've some soup on the range; perhaps you would like to stay for a little something to eat?"

"That would be marvellous, thank you. So much nicer than sitting alone somewhere."

"I'll slice some bread, and by the time it's ready, you'll have finished the note to your friend and I'm sure you'll be starving – young people usually are!"

Dear James,

I'm so sorry to have missed seeing you at the weekend. Thank you so much for your recent letters. It has been lovely to hear all the stories of Ashford and I was very much looking forward to seeing you.

There is such good news here: the true killer has been found and we hope Ed will be released as soon as all the tedious paperwork is in place. It means my visit home is to be postponed for a week and I will tell the whole story when I see you.

Let's hope for more glorious weather so we can enjoy our countryside picnic.

With my apologies and best wishes,
Lily

The rain hammered down on Dungeness all weekend. Those sunny days seemed like a distant memory after a few hours of being assaulted by wind and rain. Lying on her bed, Lily found it soothing as she concentrated only on the thunderous noise it made and cleared her head of all other thoughts. Racing to the privy was invigorating, rain slapping on her skin and threatening to soak her. By the range, steam rose from damp clothes and the air in the living area was moist. On the long walk to church, she was a sailing ship being pushed along, the wind on her back. Returning home, she held a shawl over her face in an effort to stop the wind from gagging her.

The Brooks family were in good spirits. Family meals were eaten with Edward, Grace and their young family, the baby asleep in his basket or cradled in someone's arms. Little Eva was entertained with books, nursery rhymes and played with her own baby doll. Lily saw Emily become less strained and noted the older woman was eating more. There was the occasional comment, or a hint, that the family wondered about the husband, father and grandfather who was due to return from those long weeks imprisoned. They knew Ed would have experienced horrors he might never speak of. Time would be a great healer, they hoped.

In Lily's mind, she saw Ed sitting repairing nets or crates with Tom Barton and Ben Webb. Or sitting on the long bench outside the Barton's Cottage, with a mug of ale in his hand, just passing the occasional word with his old friends. She prayed that the salt wind and undemanding company would heal his troubled mind.

Tuesday came and with it an easing of the rain, although the wind remained brisk. Lily chose to take a longer walk around the point, following the coastline until she reached the place where the bay from Dungeness to Fairlight stretched before her. The sea was rough and clouds raced across the sky. Shafts of sunlight lit the distant hills and the golden sands at Camber. She passed the ragged shells of the

261

abandoned homes at Denge and walked on to Galloways.

There was some activity on the beach at Galloways, and Lily slowed down to watch. A huge net had been firmly anchored to the shore and its position in the sea could be gauged by seeing the row of cork floats bobbing about. Not far out to sea, a small boat kept the far end of the net steady.

While the men kept watch on the net from both the sea and beach, a couple of women looked on and held the bridle of a waiting horse. There would be a catch coming in soon, Lily realised. The horse and cart would have it in Lydd as soon as possible. She recognised the bent figure of Evie standing beside the horse and saw the old woman had been watching her approach.

"So, it was Mary," Evie stated. "Her ma always blamed it on the stones."

"The stones?" Lily frowned.

"Aye, they went missing from her cot. All strung up they were and no one ever knew what happened to them." Evie reached up and patted the neck of the horse, then rubbed him gently on the nose, making soothing noises as she did so. "We made another string as soon as we noticed they were gone, but they must have got to the baby while the protection was gone."

"There were hagstones strung from Mary's cot?" Lily tried to make sense of the story. "When she was a baby?"

"Of course there were, all in a line to keep the witches away." Evie nodded, and continued, "You'd have known all about it, if you'd stayed and had a little one of your own. It's what we do here at Galloways. But that dear baby, her string was gone and no doubt a hag got to her in the night. Left her all mazed it did; she were a good girl most of the time, but not quite right in the

262

head."

"A hag?" Lily questioned. "The stones were protecting her from evil spirits, you mean?"

"I just said it, didn't I?" Evie shook her head. "Now what's to happen to her? There's none of us who can keep her safe now."

"She'll go somewhere secure," Lily said. "It's too late for Joe, but she'll be stopped from harming herself or anyone else."

"It's for the best," Evie replied. "We don't blame her; she was befuddled in the head, and we did our best for her. Got her that nice little job, but she weren't right." The old woman sighed and looked out to sea for a moment. "Look at that, Lil, they're closing the net in now."

The boat was circling towards the shore, pulling the net with it. Straining on the anchors fixed to the beach, the net was clearly heavy with fish. And, as the boat came aground on the beach, the catch could be seen, bellies shining and bodies writhing as hundreds of fish tumbled about.

"They never learn," Evie said. "Them mackerel, they never learn not to swim along the coast. They're after eating the whitebait but end up in our bellies instead."

Talking gently to the animal, Evie turned the horse and cart around, and began to back it down the shingle towards the water. The wide wheels on the cart moved over the stones with relative ease. They came to a stop at the water's edge and waited while the men hauled the net out of the sea and dragged the writhing bundle towards the cart. The back of the cart was pulled down and the fish heaved up into it. As Lily moved away, the horse took its first laborious steps up the shingle bank.

Jennie and Martha were waiting for Lily outside

Martha's home. They walked towards her as she approached, and barely greeted Lily before plunging into the conversation that was at the forefront of everyone's minds.

"She were writing about Joe in that story of hers, that's what we've been saying," Martha blurted out.

"She were befuddled, we always said it," Jennie continued. "They said be nice to her, not to tease her and we tried."

"We tried to be nice," Martha agreed. "But it weren't always easy when it were fun to tease."

"It's terribly sad," Lily said. "Joe has died, and we must all wonder if we could have done something to prevent it. But we couldn't; no one could have known what she was about to do. It wasn't planned, I'm sure of it. I feel sad for Mary too; she's done a terrible thing and it will leave her more confused than ever."

"They say she'll go somewhere for mad people," Jennie stated.

"Probably," Lily agreed. "Now we need to do some learning. To not let this stop us."

The girls rolled their eyes and sighed, which Lily tried to ignore as she led the way to Martha's cottage and placed her basket on the table in the centre of the room. What could be done today, with these two who were so easily distracted? Lily understood that it would be hard to get them to settle to anything.

"She won't come back here, will she?" Jennie asked and they both looked at Lily, who was not much older than them but knew so much more about life away from the shingle peninsular.

"No." Lily frowned, not wanting to mislead them in any way. "I'm sure she won't. It will be up to the court, and she'll go to prison or somewhere for people who are disturbed in the mind."

264

"But she murdered someone." Martha pulled the basket towards her and started flicking through the contents. "They might hang her."

"They might," Lily agreed. "But Charlie thinks she'll go to a place at Chartham."

"What's Chartham?" Martha asked, picking out *Alice's Adventures in Wonderland*.

"It's..." Lily considered her words, "It's a big red-brick place in a village outside Canterbury, somewhere for people who are ill in the head. People who can't be trusted to keep themselves or other people safe. They might not have done bad things, they might just not be sensible enough to care for themselves. But for Mary, it would be because she needs people keeping a close eye on her."

"Well, if Charlie thinks that's what will happen, then he's probably right. He knows all sorts of stuff, he does," Martha replied.

"Yes, I think you're right," Lily agreed. "He does seem to know things."

"It's hard to be nice about her, when she did that to Joe," Jennie muttered. "They say we should feel sorry for her, but I hate her. I can't help it."

Lily placed her hand on Jennie's arm. "I understand. She did a terrible thing." Then she recalled some advice she once heard her mother giving to a friend. It was during the Great War, someone had been injured and returned home, beaten by both the physical and mental terrors of war. "Let's write a letter to Mary, to tell her how we feel. You can say whatever you want and no one else will ever see it. We can write it together or write one each. Then we'll burn it on the range."

"We won't send them?" Jennie questioned.

"No, it's just for us." Lily confirmed. "Something private, but sometimes it's better that way. It's a chance

265

for you to say how you feel but without hurting anyone else."

"I'll try it." Jennie shrugged her shoulders.

"Me too," Martha agreed. "We'll do it together, take it in turns."

"That's fine." Lily pulled a piece of paper from the basket. "We'll just say whatever we want to say. One at a time. Whatever thoughts come into your head; there is no right and no wrong way of doing this."

"I'll start." Martha snatched at a pencil. "Dear Mary, you should not have sent Lily to Galloways. That was the start of the trouble."

"That's it." Lily took a piece of scrap paper and said, "Do you remember how to spell 'should'? It's like would and could, try it here first."

Walking home with the wind pressing at her back, Lily was satisfied that she had persevered with her teaching and settled the troubled minds of Jennie and Martha; her spirits were high. These long treks across the shingle gave her plenty of time to think. Life in Dungeness was good at the moment, with the prospect of Ed coming home soon and the lessons going well. Not once did she miss her days at the ledger in the bank or even, and it saddened her a little to think this, miss the friends she had known for so long. She looked forward to the coming weekend but was contented with her new life for the time being. But how long would she stay in Dungeness? Thoughts of James and another new chapter in her life flitted into her mind occasionally. But she knew her attraction to him was not yet strong enough to pull her back to Ashford and wondered if it ever would be.

When Lily set out for Ashford, a week later than

originally planned, there had been no news of Ed's release from prison. "It won't be long now," everyone said. There was no reason to think he would be detained any longer. Mary was still being held in Lydd Police Station and the news was that as well as the local doctor, another from Folkestone had visited her during the week. She was due to stand before the magistrate that very day. Lily, although tempted to stay and hear the verdict, felt she had no choice but to continue with her plans to visit her family.

"We'll send you a telegram," Emily told her as they parted at Lydd station. Lily was to travel on to Ashford while Emily and Allie were to go to court. They wanted to see for themselves.

"Thank you. It's all I'll be able to think about," Lily said, as she watched them open the carriage door and step onto the platform.

The engine eased its great bulk away from the platform. Lily looked back at Emily and Allie for as long as she could and then settled back in her seat to watch the flat lands of Romney Marsh pass by.

Chapter Twenty-Five

Lily was peeling potatoes for Sunday dinner when the noise of the knocker on the front door echoed through the hallway. It had been used with enthusiasm, with a short rhythm. Not expecting Helen and Polly to arrive for another hour, Lily assumed it must be someone for her father. She continued to manoeuvre the knife around the contours of the potato.

The sound of a male voice could be heard at the front door. But as the two voices, her father's and that of the newcomer, moved through the hallway, Lily paused and wondered. Her father would take a guest to the front parlour, but they were now walking the length of the hall. Could it be that James had come to see her before the others? Her heart lifted a little, as she let the potato drop in the water and reached for the towel.

"Charlie Scott to see you, Lily," her father announced. And there he was, Charlie, standing behind her father in the doorway, filling the space with his height.

"Oh," was all Lily managed to say in response.

"Hello, Lily. I hope I'm not interrupting, but I had some news, so… well, here I am!"

He was looking smart, wearing a single-breasted suit in a dark grey tweed. The material looked to be of a good quality with a muted check pattern, and it fitted him very well. The two-tone shoes were gone, to be replaced with plain brown, although still with the distinctive pointed toes. His brown hair was neatly trimmed. This was indeed a smarter Charlie, but still the Charlie she knew and... she knew and quite liked really.

It was rude just to stand there and say nothing, but the sight of the solicitor from Lydd in the kitchen of her Ashford home stunned Lily. And to make it worse, in the background, the *tippity-tap* of her mother's shoes could be heard on the stairs.

"Some news?" Lily repeated, and she could hear her voice, high and unnatural. Her mother's footsteps were coming closer and now she appeared in the doorway, in her calf-length skirt and cream blouse with the pearl buttons.

"Good morning," Alice said, extending her hand towards Charlie's. "You must be James. Lily has been telling us about you."

"No, no, Mother. This is Charlie, Charlie Scott," Lily felt a blush rising. "He's come from Lydd and has news for us."

"The young man whom Lily felt the need to rush through the night to check upon?" Alice asked, with a slight smile playing about her lips.

"The very same!" Charlie gave a big grin as he grasped Alice's slim hand.

"Let's not stand about." Alice lit the gas hob and lifted the kettle onto it. "Charlie, you must sit with Lily and her father in the parlour while I make tea, and then you'll have to tell the news again, for I don't expect Lily to wait a moment longer."

"You mustn't wait either, Mrs Stevens," Charlie replied. "Ed was released yesterday and returned to Dungeness in the afternoon. Lily will be back tomorrow, but I knew she would want to know as soon as possible."

"That's incredible news!" Lily felt her heart soar and she wanted to fling her arms around this man who brought the word, but instead she hugged her mother. "At last, Mother. How long has it been? Weeks and weeks, but at last he is home again."

"That is worth celebrating," Alice smiled. "Let's leave the tea and have a sweet sherry, and for the men… a brandy or whisky? Will you pour, George?"

As her mother led the way into the parlour, Lily followed, still bemused by Charlie's arrival and wondering how Ed was. Would he find it easy to adjust to life back at Dungeness? They were ushered into the pristine room with its square bay window facing towards Victoria Park. Charlie was directed towards the armchair by the fireplace, while Alice and Lily sat side by side on the upright sofa. Mr Stevens busied himself at the small mahogany table where three decanters stood alongside a cluster of glasses.

They spoke a little of Ed's release and the joy the family must be feeling. But although Charlie had been to Maidstone with Inspector Morgan, he knew nothing of the reunion with Emily, Edward and Allie. "I left him at Lydd, to make the last part of the journey alone," Charlie said. "It was time for him to meet his family and he needed to do that on his own."

"But how was he, on the journey back to Lydd?" Alice asked.

"Quiet," Charlie replied. "We were in Inspector Morgan's motorcar, so he wasn't going to say much, was he? Not with Morgan being the one who had him locked away. We spoke a little once the inspector left us at Ashford station. The first thing he wanted was a decent meal, so we went into the Kent Arms and bought a pie with lashings of gravy. Then we were on the train back to Lydd. It's going to be hard for him, getting used to being back there again, in Dungeness. He'd given up hope and you don't stay cheerful, not stuck behind those great walls of the prison."

"The new baby will cheer him up," Lily reminded them.

"Of course it will," Alice agreed. "Now Charlie, tell us a little more about yourself. Are you fully recovered from your dreadful accident?"

Lily listened while the danger of Jury's Poppy was explained to her father, to whom the peculiarities of life at Dungeness were unknown. She saw her mother nodding happily, as if it were perfectly acceptable to dull a man's senses with the crystallised juice from the poppy seeds. This was the Alice who had relived her own Dungeness times when she met again with Emily on her recent visit. These were glimpses of a mother not known to her own daughter.

As the glasses were drained, Charlie looked at Lily's father and said, "I borrowed my father's motorcar and was wondering if you would mind me taking Lily out for a picnic? I'll take good care of her."

"I'm sure you will," Mr Stevens agreed. "And I am happy for you to do so, but I believe Lily has other arrangements."

"With James?" Charlie enquired.

"Oh, Lily can go out with her friends any weekend she is here," Alice replied, before Lily had a chance to respond. "I'll pass the message on to Helen and Polly; you couldn't possibly refuse Charlie, not when he has so kindly driven here with the marvellous news."

"It seems that it is all arranged." To her surprise, Lily found that she didn't mind at all.

"I'd like to see your father's car, if you wouldn't mind," Lily's father was saying to Charlie. "I've decided to buy one for myself."

271

"Of course." Charlie rose from the chair. "It's parked outside."

"Do you need anything for the picnic?" Alice followed them into the hallway. "A rug, drinks, I've some fruit cake...?"

"No, but thank you. It's all under control," Charlie replied. "Just a companion, which you have so kindly provided!"

"Lily will just tidy her hair and be with you in a few minutes." Alice began to usher her daughter up the stairs. "And a cardigan, darling; there is a slight chill in the air."   It seemed that Alice was determined to offer her opinion as she followed her daughter. "What a charming young man. You can't possibly say this one is too dull for you, Lily! And a solicitor too..."

"Dull? No, I couldn't say that." Lily dabbed scent on her wrists and ran a brush through her hair. Had her own mother been sampling the grey tea, she wondered?

Looking on at the scene unfolding, Lily felt as if she were just a pawn to be moved through the next few hours of her life at the whim of her mother and Charlie. Where was the young woman who was so determined to make her own decisions? And how had Charlie managed to please her mother with such ease? But Lily was eager for adventures and so, with a cardigan tucked under her arm and auburn hair neatly in place, she joined her father and Charlie by the car.

"Where are we going then?" Charlie asked, as they drove away from the house.

"Going?" Lily was still bemused by the events of the last half hour. "I thought you had this all planned out?"

"I do. This is when I ask you where I can find a nice romantic spot for a picnic."

272

"Romantic?"

"Romantic," he confirmed.

Lily directed Charlie, as he drove towards the railway station and then up the hill towards the town. The streets were quiet as they passed the parish church and drove through the intersection of the High Street. Shops and offices were left behind as they took the Canterbury Road, passing the cemetery before turning off the main road. After a mile or so, they turned into a narrow country lane, with Charlie muttering about this being for horses not cars. But Lily insisted the final destination would be suitably romantic, as suggested, and so he grinned and slowed down, carefully avoiding overhanging branches and potholes in the rough road.

The lane narrowed further, and daylight filtered through the leaves of the trees lining it. Then oak and beech were exchanged for a line of ancient yews, and beyond, with its grey stones lit by the shafts of light, was an old church with its tower facing the road. Lily indicated for Charlie to park at the roadside and, as the engine died, they were able to appreciate the solitude of this magical place. The picnic was left in the car and they stood for a moment, looking up at the church still partly obscured by the trees.

"It looks in a bit of a state," Charlie observed. "I've never seen so much ivy." The tenacious creeper was covering one side of the tower, as well the whole of the end of the aisle.

"It's very sad, but beautiful too," Lily replied. "I don't know why they don't cut all this ivy away."

"What's that?" he asked, looking across the churchyard and through yet more trees. Something shimmered and sparkled as the sun's rays reached out across a cloudless sky.

"It's a lake." Lily began to move forward, stepping

273

between the yew trees and into the churchyard. "I thought we could sit over there, looking over it while we have the picnic, but I want to show you something else first."

Lily led the way towards the porch, and they pressed on a latch, allowing the old wooden door to swing open. On entering the main building, the effects of the ivy were significant, with only the smallest amount of daylight able to filter through the western window.

"It smells a bit rotten," Charlie muttered. "Maybe I'll choose the romantic place next time!"

"Come and see this sculpture in a side chapel," Lily persisted. "It's quite special."

She showed Charlie the monument of Emily Georgiana, Countess of Winchilsea, reclining on her chaise longue, with a book in her hand.

"What a strange place for her to be." He looked about the white painted chapel, kept in better order than the rest of the church, but still a place of faded glory. "What does this say?"

"It's the poem she wrote for her husband; she must have known she was going to die," Lily brushed a cobweb from the engraved words.

"*Come not to gaze at me weeping; I am at rest...*" Charlie murmured.

They looked at all the details carved in the marble, the words and the decoration, touching it with their fingertips, tracing the lines on the cool stone.

Charlie, who had crouched low in order to examine some carved text, straightened himself and took a step back from the monument. "This is beautiful, Lily, this Emily Georgiana, sitting about in all her... well it looks like she's draped in a sheet, if I'm honest." Charlie grinned and shrugged, "What is she wearing?"